Her heels sank into the dirt again, and she reached down and yanked them off

"I'm not going to rehash the past with you again. It's done. It's over. I was young and stupid. I'm not sure what your excuse was other than being a total asshole with a high-and-mighty attitude. I'm human. I made a mistake. Get over it."

She swung toward the door, heels in her hand, and just as quickly swung back. "Good luck with your marriage. I hope she never disappoints you, because you're one unforgiving bastard."

Levi drew a sharp breath and slung his hat across the barn. It landed softly on bales of alfalfa. The horse skittered away and he stroked it to calm her, but nothing was going to calm the churning in his gut. Myra made him madder than anyone. She knew how to push his buttons. Damn her!

Dear Reader,

A Texas Child is the third book in my Willow Creek, Texas series. In the first two books—*A Texas Hero* (July 2013) and *A Texas Family* (October 2013)—I shared how the ideas for the stories were born. *A Texas Child* was a little different, created by pure imagination and a little luck. Myra Delgado is a character from *The Texan's Bride* (Harlequin Superromance, October 2011), and Levi Coyote is a character from *Her Christmas Hero* (Harlequin American Romance, December 2010). Both have very strong personalities and I knew one day I would write their story.

First, I had to have a way to bring them together. Second, I needed a plot. Myra is an assistant district attorney and Levi is a private investigator. They both work in law enforcement, so I started by giving them a past. Voilà! That worked. I still needed a plot. One day on the news was a story about a woman who'd married a man from Mexico and he'd taken their child and disappeared. She couldn't get the law to help her, because the man was the boy's father. My imagination wheel began to spin and I thought I could work that in as part of the plot.

Believe me, it wasn't easy. My editor suffered through many emails and talks about how the story wasn't working. At times, I wanted to admit defeat. Miraculously, I finished it. Now you'll be the judge of whether it works or not. I have to say, though, that after all the frustrations and changes, I like this story. I hope you do, too.

Until the next book, with love and thanks,

Linda Warren

P.S.—You can email me at lw1508@aol.com, or send me a message on Facebook, www.facebook.com/lindawarrenauthor, or on Twitter, www.twitter.com/texauthor, or write me at P.O. Box 5182, Bryan, TX 77805, or visit my website at www.lindawarren.net. Your mail and thoughts are deeply appreciated.

LINDA
WARREN

—

A Texas Child

H HARLEQUIN® SUPER ROMANCE®

Recycling programs
for this product may
not exist in your area.

ISBN-13: 978-0-373-71891-7

A TEXAS CHILD

Printed in U.S.A.

www.Harlequin.com

ABOUT THE AUTHOR

Two time RITA® Award-nominated and award-winning author Linda Warren loves her job, writing happily-ever-after books for Harlequin. Drawing upon her years of growing up on a farm/ranch in Texas, she writes about sexy heroes, feisty heroines and broken families with an emotional punch, all set against the backdrop of Texas. Her favorite pastime is sitting on her patio with her husband watching the wildlife, especially the injured ones, which are coming in pairs these days: two Canada geese with broken wings, two does with broken legs, and a bobcat ready to pounce on anything tasty. Learn more about Linda and her books at her website, www.lindawarren.net, or on Facebook, www.facebook.com/authorlindawarren.

Books by Linda Warren

HARLEQUIN SUPERROMANCE

HARLEQUIN AMERICAN ROMANCE

*The Belles Of Texas
†The Hardin Boys
**Willow Creek, Texas

Other titles by this author available in ebook format.

To my dear editor, Kathleen. Thank you for patiently listening to me moan about this book for almost a year. And thank you for your continued support and faith in me and my stories.
I'm honored and blessed to have you as my editor. You're the best!

Acknowledgments

To the people on the internet who helped me sort through a lot of problems.

A big thanks to Tammy Medina for sharing her visits to Matamoras, Mexico.

And a special thanks to Crystal Siegert and Sarah Stanley for sharing all things baby.

All errors are strictly mine.

CHAPTER ONE

AN OLD LOVE slept on her conscience, gnawed at her heart and tortured her soul. Betraying Levi Coyote had scarred Myra Delgado for life. She'd spent the past seven years regretting, blaming and cursing herself, but it hadn't changed a thing.

As an assistant district attorney in Houston, Texas, she didn't quite understand what she was doing in Willow Creek, Texas, following the GPS in her Lexus to Levi's home. But then again, she did. Levi was the best private investigator in the state and she needed his help.

She'd called his office and left messages, but he never returned her calls. After all this time, she'd thought he might have mellowed enough to forgive her. Since she couldn't forgive herself, it was understandable that he couldn't, either. It just made her very aware Levi was not a forgiving man.

The GPS said to turn right, so she pulled over on the country blacktop road. Up ahead, bordered by ranch land, were a cattle guard and a mailbox. On the box was written Henry and Levi Coyote.

Had Levi moved here permanently?

He'd often talked about retiring to his grandfather's ranch, but Levi was too young to retire. They were both thirty-four; he was older by five months. But it might explain why he was never at his office. She'd waited there for an hour this morning and he'd never showed.

Driving over the cattle guard, she gripped the steering wheel as the pipe grids jarred her and the car. Barbed-wire fences flanked her on both sides. Cattle grazed on the left in the warm September sun. Horses frolicked on the right. The graveled road led to a small white-frame farmhouse with a wide porch across the front. A chain-link fence surrounded it. Barns, pens and sheds were in the distance. A typical ranch one would see all across Texas.

She stopped at the fence gate. Two trucks were parked in a carport, and a car was behind one of the trucks.

An elderly gray-haired gentleman sat in a rocker on the porch. Myra got out of the car, but loud barks had her scurrying back inside. A black-and-white dog barked ferociously at her and then darted through a hole beneath the fence and joined the old man.

Once again she stepped out, using the door as a shield. "I'm looking for Levi Coyote," she shouted to the man.

"What?" He evidently couldn't hear her, so she had no choice but to step away from the car. She left the door open, though. Seeing her, the dog made a dash for the hole.

"Come back, John Wayne," the man called, easing out of the rocker. "Pay him no mind, missy. He's harmless."

His dog's name was John Wayne. *Missy?* She didn't have time to react as the dog sniffed around her feet.

Please don't lick my shoes, she silently begged. *Not*

my Jimmy Choo heels. Deciding the shoes weren't that tasty, the dog dashed back to the man.

She heaved a sigh and collected her wits. She should be used to animals. Her friend Jessie had all kinds of friends of the four-legged variety, but Myra was more of an indoor person instead of the outdoor type. Now was no time to dissect her failings. There were just too many.

"I'm looking for Levi Coyote," she said to the man.

"He lives here occasionally," the man replied. "I'm his grandpa, Henry."

"Is he here now?"

"What's this about?"

"It's business."

"Ah." The man nodded as if he understood something she didn't. "You got a cheating husband you want him to follow?"

She ignored the remark. "Is he here?"

"Yeah, but he's out riding with his girlfriend."

Girlfriend? She hadn't counted on that. But why not? Levi was handsome, virile and available. He'd always wanted a family and a home of his own. One of the few things they'd argued about. He'd longed for children. She hadn't.

Why was she thinking of that now? It had nothing to do with the present.

"Do you know when he'll be back?"

"Nope. Levi's a grown man and he does as he pleases."

She hadn't driven all this way to turn around now. It was too important. "Do you mind if I wait?"

"Suit yourself, but it might be a while. With Valerie

around, Levi's not looking at his watch, if you know what I mean."

Sadly, yes, she knew. They used to spend Sundays alone together and never glanced at a clock.

Brushing back a stray strand of dark hair, she asked, "Is there a place I can get a bite to eat or something to drink?" She hadn't eaten a thing this morning. She'd been in too big of a hurry to leave Houston.

"Sure, about a mile up the highway is a convenience store and a café. Got good food there. But if you'd like something to drink, we got water, tea and beer."

"No, thank you. I'll just—"

The sound of hooves pounding against the hard ground caught her attention. Laughter floated on the wind as two figures on horseback came into view. A blonde with long flowing hair raced into the barn, followed by a man whose features were etched with broad, bold strokes on her memory: strong, hard-boned angles shaped his face, while a tall, lean body with unbelievable muscles, dark eyes and hair were indicative of his Indian ancestry. Levi Coyote personified strength and character and was a hard man to forget. Lord knows she'd tried.

"There he is," Henry said as if he needed to point out his grandson.

"Thank you. I'll drive to the barn."

"Suit yourself." Henry ambled to his rocker. John Wayne sat on his haunches beside him.

She drove to the weatherworn barn and got out, her heel sinking into the dirt. Damn it! She shouldn't have dressed in her business attire. Oh, well, all she needed was five minutes of Levi's time and then she could return to her comfort zone—the city.

The wind tugged at her hair and a pungent scent greeted her. Alfalfa, maybe. As she neared the big double doors, she didn't hear voices, which was strange. She stepped inside and saw why. They were kissing. The blonde had her arms clasped around Levi's neck and his enclosed her small waist, pulling her against him.

She should just walk away, but her feet wouldn't move. It was like watching a car accident. She couldn't tear her eyes away. She'd gotten over Levi a long time ago—only the regrets remained. She just didn't expect to feel this piercing pain in her chest at the sight of him kissing another woman.

This was invading his privacy and she needed to leave. Before Myra could move, the kiss ended and the blonde noticed her standing in the doorway like a voyeur.

"Oh," she said in a startled lilting voice.

Levi swung around and his dark eyes bore into her like a sharp arrow, intending to wound and to frighten her.

She dredged up every last ounce of courage she possessed, as she had so many times in the courtroom when faced with an egotistical alpha opponent determined to break her.

She pushed her sunglasses to the top of her head. "Hello, Levi."

AT THE SIGHT of her, Levi's heart crashed against his ribs in well-remembered pain. God, he hated the woman.

She'd hurt him more than anyone he'd ever known. Yet he couldn't deny her beauty. Long brownish-black hair was pinned behind her head. She looked like a model, with high cheekbones and black eyes that could flash with anger or smolder with desire.

He'd loved her more than anyone in his life and she'd broken his heart without a second thought. Myra was determined to succeed in a man's world and nothing stood in her way. Not even her love for him.

"What are you doing here, Myra?"

"It's business," she replied, walking farther into the barn in ridiculously high heels.

Valerie kissed his cheek. "I'll go, then. I'm running late, anyway."

Guilt zinged across his conscience. He'd forgotten Val was standing there. "Don't forget to say bye to Pop. He gets a little miffed when you don't."

"He's such a sweetheart." She hugged him and he returned it. "Don't forget I'm fixing dinner."

"I won't." They kissed briefly and Val walked out. Levi refused to introduce them. Myra wasn't going to be around that long.

He placed his hands on his hips. "What do you want, Myra?"

"She's nice," Myra said.

"What do you want?"

"It's about Stu. He'd like to hire you."

"No." The horses neighed and he turned to them, undoing a cinch on a saddle. "You wasted your time invading my privacy. I'm not working for anyone who has a connection to you. Not even Stu."

"If you had answered my messages, I wouldn't have had to come out here."

He threw the saddle onto a sawhorse. "I didn't answer for a reason. You and I have nothing to say to each other. Most people would have figured that out."

"Just give me five minutes. That's all I'm asking."

He undid the cinch on the other saddle. "You just don't give up, do you?"

"I try not to, especially when a friend is involved."

Swinging the saddle onto another sawhorse, he said, "If you were that committed to your love life, you would have been one hell of a woman."

"Why are you making this personal, Levi? I'm sorry I hurt you and I've apologized, but you couldn't seem to get past your anger. After all these years, I would have thought you'd have gotten over it."

His hat lay in the dirt where Val had thrown it. He reached down to pick it up and dusted it off, giving him time to gauge his next words. "I have. It's just the shock of seeing you again, so sudden like, brought back a lot of painful memories. I've moved on and I'm happy now. I don't need you complicating my life."

"I have, too." She tucked a flyaway strand behind her ear. "Yes, we have a past, but we're adult enough to not let it interfere with the present."

He leaned against the saddle and crossed his boots at the ankles. "That's true, but you see I don't want you in my present in any way. Not because I still have feelings for you. I don't. I'd just rather not clutter my life with a past I regret."

"It's not for me, Levi. It's for Stu, who needs a good P.I."

"Stu knows just about every private investigator in the state. Besides, if he wants to hire me, why doesn't he call himself?"

"His daughter's in a coma and he's very distraught."

That threw him. Stu was one of the best friends he'd ever had when he was a cop. But Myra had ties to Stu, too. "I'd rather not get involved."

"Five minutes, Levi. What harm can that do?"

He drew a long breath. "Okay."

"Stu's daughter, Natalie, works in my office in Houston."

"The D.A.'s office?"

"Yes. She's a secretary and has worked with us for about three years. After her mother died, she came to Houston to get closer to her father. Last year, she got involved with Marco Mortez and we all thought it was great she'd found someone. But he turned out to be a loser. On Monday, he beat her into a coma and took their nine-month-old son. The police haven't been able to locate him."

"Were they married?"

"No."

"Is he the boy's father?"

"Of course."

"How serious is Natalie's condition?"

She bit her lip, something she did when she was nervous. He was probably the only person who knew that, except for her friend Jessie. He'd heard that Jessie had gotten married but he wasn't in the mood to discuss any details about Myra's life.

"It's bad. The doctor said he must have banged her head repeatedly against the wall or a table. They op-

erated to stop the internal bleeding. Now they're dealing with the swelling of the brain. The doctor said she
will either wake up or she won't. She has a fifty-fifty
chance. The baby has to be there when she wakes up
or she will be devastated."

Levi felt himself being pulled into Natalie's plight,
but then, he was always a sucker where a baby was concerned. Still, he wasn't relenting.

"If the police are on the case, I don't see why you
need a private investigator. And like I said, Stu still has
a lot of pull in the police department." Stuart Stevens
had been the police chief in Houston, but he'd retired
after a bout with cancer.

She bit her lip again.

"You're not telling me everything, are you?"

"It's complicated, Levi."

He folded his arms across his chest. "Oh, really. I
don't do complicated anymore, Myra."

"Okay." She shoved her hands into the pockets of her
black slacks. "When the police couldn't locate Marco, I
did some checking on my own. His family might have
connections to a Mexican drug cartel."

"Might?"

"I don't have any evidence to back it up. Only what
people in the apartment complex told me about Marco
and the people who visited with him. I'm waiting on a
report from the FBI to confirm."

"Well, then, I'd say it's safe to say that baby is in
Mexico."

"Maybe not. Marco's parents have a home in Brownsville. The police there checked it out, but they said they

hadn't seen their son in weeks. They could be hiding him, though."

"If he's wanted in Houston, he's not hanging around in Texas."

"Levi, please," she begged, her eyes dark with emotions he remembered too well. "I know you can track Marco down and find him when no one else can."

"You have a lot of confidence in me." Confidence that came just a little too late.

"I always have."

He lifted a hand. "Let's not go there."

"Levi, just check into it. Stu is willing to pay your fee plus expenses and a five-thousand-dollar bonus if you bring his grandson back."

"You're asking me to get involved with the drug cartel in Mexico? That's like signing my own death warrant."

"All you have to do is locate him. The police will take it from there."

"In Mexico? I doubt it."

"I can see you're not eager to go into Mexico."

"No. Valerie and I are talking marriage and I'm not going to do anything to jeopardize that. I'm ready to settle down and have a family. Putting my life in danger is not going to happen."

She stepped forward and a heel sank into the ground, almost toppling her over. "Good grief, it's like quicksand in here."

"You're in a barn, Myra. It's called dirt. No one wears high heels in a barn."

She yanked the heel out and managed to stand upright. "I thought you would be in your office. I didn't plan on driving way out here to the middle of nowhere."

He pushed away from the saddle. "You wasted your time. I'll give you the names of some investigators in Houston. They can do just as good a job as I can."

"I work in the D.A.'s office. I know investigators all over Harris County, but it's going to take someone willing to go the extra mile to flush out Marco. I thought that man would be you. So did Stu."

"Sorry." He remained firm.

"You're one stubborn asshole. Do you think it was easy to come out here and face your wrath once again? It wasn't. A little boy's life is at stake. You may be able to ignore that, but I can't."

Myra was getting revved up, like he'd seen her do in a courtroom. When she was passionate about something, her Mexican lineage came out and she was unstoppable.

"And since you don't care one way or the other, there's another sad twist to this story. Did you know Stu had part of one lung removed?"

"Yes. I went to see him at the time."

"The cancer has spread. He's very ill. If I have to go to Mexico myself, I will. Stu and Natalie need a break and I won't turn my back on them."

Her heels sank into the dirt again and she reached down and yanked them off. "I'm not going to rehash the past with you again. It's done. It's over. I was young and stupid. I'm not sure what your excuse was other than being a total asshole with a high and mighty attitude. I'm human. I made a mistake. Get over it."

She swung toward the door, heels in her hand, and

just as quickly swung back. "Good luck with your marriage. I hope she never disappoints you, because you're one unforgiving bastard."

Levi drew a sharp breath and slung his hat across the barn. It landed softly on a bale of alfalfa. His horse skittered away and he stroked her to calm her, but nothing was going to calm the churning in his gut. Myra made him madder than anyone. She knew how to push his buttons. Damn her!

He removed the bridles and saddle blankets from the horses, and then opened the door to the corral so they could eat the sweet feed he'd put out earlier. They trotted through and he closed the gate. He always liked to rub them down after a hard ride, but today he feared he might rub through their hides. He was that angry at her.

Leaning on the gate, his thoughts turned inward. Seeing Myra again was like someone touching him in the middle of the night when he was alone. It was startling, jarring and frightening. And he'd responded badly. He was struggling to figure out why.

When they'd met seven years ago, he was a cop with the Austin police department and she'd just joined the D.A.'s office. They'd worked a murder case and theirs was an instant attraction. They'd slept together on their first date and, by the end of that week, he'd moved in with her. Their need for each other was insatiable.

At first, he'd thought it was just about the hot sex, but as the weeks passed, he realized it was much more. He admired her drive, her determination to succeed in a man's world. And her devotion to her friend Jessie was admirable, too. He liked everything about Myra. Her Latin looks were an added bonus.

He wasn't a dreaming man, but she'd had him dreaming about a future, babies and a home. And forever. He just hadn't counted on how much her career meant to her. More to her than he ever would. That's what hurt the most.

Things had blown up so fast they'd never had a proper goodbye. One wasn't required. Maybe that's what bothered him. Maybe he needed closure. *Closure?* Hell, that wasn't a word men used. He didn't. Men just moved on. And he planned to keep on moving. He'd found the woman for him and Myra Delgado was just a bad memory.

CHAPTER TWO

MYRA WAS FURIOUS and she had to let off some steam. The only way to do that was to talk to Jessie, who understood her better than anyone. Myra had never told her why she and Levi had broken up. There was a reason for that. She wasn't sure her friend would understand.

Jessie firmly believed in love and everything it encompassed, so how did Myra explain to her that she'd screwed up? Myra was angry enough to lay it all on the line this time and be honest. Mainly because Jessie would love her no matter what. She was that type of person.

Jessie was the motherless daughter of Roscoe Murdoch, the oil tycoon. When Roscoe's niece had been kidnapped and murdered, he became paranoid about Jessie's safety. He'd hired guards to watch over her, and Rosa and Felipe Delgado to care for her. Myra was two years older than Jessie and they'd grown up as best friends in the Murdoch household.

Since Jessie was guarded twenty-four hours a day, her life was a living hell. She rebelled numerous times, but Roscoe was always in control. Jessie gained her freedom the day Roscoe passed away. She fired the guards and went after what she wanted out of life—a man named Cadde Hardin. She was now happily married and living in High Cotton, Texas.

Myra set the GPS for the small town and sped down U.S. 290. When Jessie had lived in Houston, they saw each other all the time. But since she lived so far away now and had two babies, they had to make time for those special occasions.

As Myra drove, she thought of her next course of action. She wasn't giving up. She'd promised Stu she'd do everything she could to bring the baby home and she intended to do that with or without Levi. Like he'd said, there were other investigators and she just had to find a capable one.

The urge to pull the car over and have a pity cry was strong, but she was stronger. She didn't do the weak female crying bit. But, oh, God, she wanted to. However, she wouldn't waste one more tear on Levi Coyote.

She'd never dreamed it would be so hard to see him again and to reexperience all the anger he still carried from her betrayal. It was time to let it go—for good. There was no going back and there was no more apologizing. She had begged Levi for the last time.

Taking the cutoff to the county road that ran through High Cotton, she soon pulled into the driveway of the two-story colonial. Jessie's Suburban was in the garage, so Myra knew she was home. She glanced toward the house a short distance away. Cadde had built Myra's parents their own home as a way to repay their service over the years. They wanted to be close to Jessie because they loved her and had taken care of her for more than twenty years.

Myra didn't see her dad's truck. That meant they

were out. She was hoping to see them, but considering her state of mind, it probably was best if she didn't. Her mother had a knack for ferreting out her moods as if she were five years old.

The back door was open, so she went inside. Childish giggles and laughter echoed through the house. "Jessie," she called.

"We're in the den," her friend shouted back.

Jessie sat on the floor playing with four little kids, three boys and one girl. Jessie's hair was in a ponytail and her eyes were bright with happiness.

"Hey, friend, what are you doing out this way?"

Myra squeezed into the little group on the floor. "I was out this way and thought I'd drop in. You know, unannounced, like my mama told me never to do."

Jessie hugged her. "I'm glad you did."

Myra looked at the shining little faces. Jacob, who was two and a half, toddled over to her and plopped into her lap. She hugged him a little tighter than she should have because she needed to feel loved today. Cadde Thomas, twelve months younger than his brother, also fell into her lap and she held them close.

"I think they remember me."

"Of course they do." Jessie reached over and kissed her sons. "They know Auntie My."

Myra glanced at the other two children. "Are you running a kiddie day care now?"

"No." Jessie poked her in the ribs. "There's a problem with the oil well on the property. They're fracking it or something, and the Hardin boys of Shilah Oil are keeping a close eye on it. You know how Cadde and his brothers are about the oil business. They have to personally supervise everything."

Cadde had worked for Roscoe for years, and on his deathbed Roscoe had made a deal with Cadde: marry my daughter and keep her safe and I'll give you half of my oil company. It was a dream come true for Cadde and he gladly took the offer. He just didn't know that Jessie had put her father up to it because she'd been in love with Cadde since the first moment she'd met him. Luckily, it had all worked out, but not without a lot of heartache and pain. Myra wondered if real love had to be tested first, put through the bowels of hell before it could survive.

"That's Cody," Jessie was saying, "Chance and Shay's son, and the blonde cutie is Carly, Kid and Lucky's daughter."

"She's adorable." Blond curls covered her head and a pink bow was clipped to the side.

The back door opened and Myra heard a rumble of deep voices.

The three boys jumped to their feet. "Daddy! Daddy! Daddy!" they chorused, and took off running for the kitchen.

Carly stood up and Myra was surprised. She didn't think the little girl was old enough to walk. Cadde and Chance came into the den with their sons in their arms. Carly looked past them, her bottom lip trembling, and fat tears rolled from her eyes.

Jessie immediately gathered her into her arms. "Sweetie, Daddy's coming."

Kid burst through the door about that time. "Hey, what's wrong with my baby?"

Carly smiled, slipped from Jessie's arms and waddled to her father. Kid scooped her into his arms and everyone was happy.

Myra and Jessie got to their feet. Jessie hugged her husband and her boys and she seemed to melt right into them. It was clear how much love they shared, and it made Myra very aware that there was real love in the world. Jessie had been lucky enough to find it. For Myra, that would never happen, which made her a little sad. But only for a moment.

"Hello, Hardin boys," Myra said with her hands on her hips.

"The wicked lady's back," Kid quipped.

"You better believe it."

Kid grinned. "Always a pleasure, but I've got to run. We're meeting Lucky for lunch and that's a big part of our day."

"Me, too," Chance added. "Nice seeing you, Myra."

"I'll take the boys outside so you two can visit," Cadde offered.

"Thanks, honey."

Myra and Jessie sank onto the sofa. "What's wrong?" Jessie asked.

Myra made herself comfortable. "Why do you think something's wrong?"

Jessie sat cross-legged in shorts and a tank top. "Because you're here in the middle of the day when you should be at work. And you look a little stressed."

"Thanks."

"You're beautiful when you're stressed."

"I saw Levi today," Myra blurted out.

"Levi Coyote?"

"Yes. There's only one Levi."

"I always loved his name. He was just so big and strong and indestructible and I liked to see him smile. He reminds me a lot of Cadde. You know, tough and unbending. It takes a woman to soften them up."

"Levi's found someone to soften him up. He's getting married."

"That bothers you?"

"I… No."

"I think it does." Jessie touched her arm. "Tell me why you saw Levi today after all this time."

"You remember I told you about Natalie."

"Yes, how is she?"

"Still in a coma and the police haven't been able to locate the boyfriend or the baby."

"How sad."

"Stu, her father, and I had this insane idea that Levi would be able to find them."

"So you asked him?"

Myra took a breath. "Yes, and the response was a big *no* with capital letters and an exclamation point."

She could feel Jessie's eyes on her.

"You never told me why you and Levi broke up. At the time, you said you didn't want to talk about it. Do you want to talk about it now?"

Myra stood up. She couldn't remain still any longer. "I didn't tell you because I knew if I did you would look at me differently."

"What do you mean?"

"You'd think I was a horrible person."

"Not likely." Jessie lifted an eyebrow. "Nothing on this earth will ever change my opinion of you. You were the only bright spot in my dismal childhood and I know you as well as I know myself. If you did something you're not proud of, then it was just a bad choice."

Awkward silence followed and that was new for them. They could always talk about anything.

"Tell me what happened," Jessie said softly.

Myra resumed her seat on the sofa and gathered her thoughts and courage. "You remember when that serial rapist was released from prison and, a week later, he followed a mother and her sixteen-year-old daughter home from the mall?"

"Yes. Levi was involved. The story was everywhere, but I don't remember much of the details."

"A neighbor was looking out her window when the guy forced them inside the house with a gun. She called 9-1-1. Levi was in the area and the first to respond. He was ordered to stand down until the situation was assessed, but as soon as Levi heard who the truck in the driveway belonged to, he knew the man was dangerous. He'd arrested him before. He parked down the street, out of sight, and walked to the house. Hearing a scream coming from the upstairs, he acted quickly, disobeying a direct order.

"He got in through one of the downstairs windows. The father had been shot in the living room. The screams and sobbing continued as Levi made his way to one of the bedrooms. The mother was tied up and the guy was ripping clothes off the teenager. His gun lay on the carpet. Levi burst in and the guy immediately went for his gun. Levi shot him."

"I remember Levi received an accommodation for his bravery."

"Not at first. He was immediately suspended for disobeying a direct order. But the father survived, and when he heard what had happened, he was livid that Levi had been suspended for saving his wife and daughter. He had political connections, and once he got through making phone calls, the suspension was lifted immediately and the accommodation awarded."

"I don't understand what this has to do with you and Levi." Jessie's face scrunched into a frown.

Myra wrapped her arms around her waist as if to ward off what she had to say, but she had to tell Jessie. She had to tell someone.

"Before the father woke up, the cops and detectives were all behind Levi, especially Stu, who was assistant police chief, and they supported his choice to go into that house against a direct order. They got a petition going so everyone could sign to show their support, and it was to be given to the chief of police and higher-ups."

"Oh, Myra." Jessie placed her hands over her mouth. "You didn't sign it, did you?"

"No." It came out as a moan. She rested her head on the sofa and covered her face with her hands. "The D.A. hadn't signed it and I didn't know what my position was supposed to be. Can you believe that? I was afraid of losing my job and, in the end, I lost something much more important. When Levi saw my name wasn't on the petition, he came to my office and said, 'You didn't sign it,' and I had to say no. He walked out without another word. His things were gone from my apartment that afternoon and I never spoke to him again…until today."

"My—"

"Wait, that's not quite true. I met him in the hall a couple of times and told him how sorry I was. He walked away without a word." She drew a long breath. "Now you can tell me what a horrible self-centered bitch I am."

"I will do no such thing." Jessie scooted closer and hugged her. "I'm sorry, sweetie, but no one is perfect and—"

Myra sprang to her feet. "Don't do that, Jessie."

"What?"

"Be understanding and nice. I need you to be angry with me."

Jessie shrugged. "Sorry. Not gonna happen."

Myra paced. "When he walked into my office looking so hurt and disillusioned, I knew I'd screwed up so bad I could never make it right. I don't understand why I let him down so badly. I've never been afraid to speak up for what I believe in, and that day, it seemed like another person had taken over my body and my thoughts."

"It was your first big job and you had to go through several interviews before they hired you. Since you're a Mexican-American woman, you were afraid they wouldn't hire you. Which was totally ridiculous, I have to say. But they did and you worked hard to prove yourself, learning all you could to be part of the team. You were very young and that job was important to you."

"But it shouldn't have been as important as Levi."

"Maybe. But, in my opinion, you were trying to follow the rules for your department and you weren't sure what those were concerning a signed petition to support a cop whom you were dating. Why would you need to sign it?"

"What?"

"What weight would your signature carry? After all, your support should be understood and they shouldn't have asked you to sign in the first place. So, please, stop beating yourself up. If Levi was the man for you, you'd be together. Just let it go, My. And now how about some chocolate? I got chocolate. That cures everything."

Myra smiled. "I knew I needed to see you. You always make me feel better." Arm in arm, they walked into the kitchen. They sat at the large island eating Truman Chocolates and Myra felt as if the world had been lifted off her shoulders.

Almost. There was something Myra had left out, but she just might keep that secret forever. No need to bare her soul. In her heart, she knew Jessie would understand, as always.

"Where's Merry?" Merry was a dog Jessie had rescued. Someone had brutally abused her, stabbing her and cutting off her ears and tail. But Jessie had nursed her back to health, and she was usually under Jessie's feet, along with two little boys.

"She's under our bed, probably asleep by now. She's getting older and the kids sometimes tire her out."

Jessie had a loving heart and a goodness that went all the way to her soul. Myra could only hope that through the years a little bit of that goodness had rubbed off on her.

LEVI TOOK TIME to cool off before he went to the house. Pop could zero in on his moods like a rifle aimed at a target. Sometimes he hit the bull's-eye, and other times he veered so far off it wasn't worth the effort to endure the questions that would be fired at him.

Pop followed him into the house. "What did that fancy lady want?"

"She wanted to hire me." Levi washed his hands at the kitchen sink and dried them with a paper towel.

"I knew it." Pop slid into a chair at the kitchen table. "She wants you to find out if her husband is cheating?"

"What?" Levi threw the paper towel in the trash can. "No. I don't even know if she's married." And it didn't matter if she was. Myra meant nothing to him. But it might take a while to get her out of his head again.

"What did she want you to do, then?"

"Find a missing child."

"I guess you're packing. I did laundry this morning and your tighty-whities and socks are in your drawer."

"I'm not taking the case." He leaned against the cabinet.

"Why not? You just finished a case and you're always eager to help find a child."

"I'm busy." He walked into the dining room and sat down at his laptop.

Pop immediately followed. "That's a truckload of bullshit. What's wrong with you?"

Hurt feelings. Hurt pride. Hurt until he didn't want to feel it anymore. But, of course, Levi didn't say that to his grandfather.

"Nothing. Some cases I take. Some I don't. It's my choice."

"Mmm-hmm." Pop pulled out a chair and sat facing him. "Do you know how old you were when I could tell you were hiding something?"

Levi didn't reply, just kept checking his in-box.

"You were about seven, I think. I was called to the school about you, Ethan and Carson fighting with the Wilcott boys. Your dad was at a cattle auction and your mom worked in Austin, so I had to go. I asked you who started the fight and you stonewalled. You know what that is?"

"Pop, I'm not seven years old anymore, and if I don't want to talk about it, I'm not. And yes, I know what stonewalling is." He clamped his jaw tight and stared at his grandfather.

"Yep, that's it. When you do that, I know you're hiding something."

Levi leaned back in his chair. "Pop, don't you have something to do? Check on your cows? Or visit Walt?"

"Aw, I'm not going over to Walt's no more. He's keeping the baby and you can't make any noise. Hell, I'm old. I make noise. What's Ethan and Abby thinking, letting Walt keep that baby?"

Levi, Ethan and Carson had grown up like brothers in the small town. Walt, Ethan's dad, and Pop were best friends but sometimes it was hard to tell that by talking to them. Carson's dad had passed away last year, but not before wreaking havoc with Carson's life. Through it all, Carson had managed to find happiness with Jena. Both his friends were married with families. He was the lone bachelor.

"Do you know Abby milks herself?"

"What?" That grabbed Levi's attention.

"Yeah. Walt has it in his refrigerator. I almost drank it. He said Abby leaves it for the baby. Beats me why she'd want to do that. I don't understand young women."

"It's called a breast pump, Pop, and women have been using it for years. One of these days, you're going to have to start living in the twenty-first century."

"Like hell. I'm not using that cell phone you got me, either. If I want to talk to someone, I'll use the phone in the house."

"I bet Walt uses his."

"Hell, yeah. Abby calls ten times a day to check on the baby and so does Ethan. If the baby farts, they want to know about it."

Levi wanted to laugh and he wasn't in a laughing mood. "Did you take your blood pressure pill this morning? You're grouchier than usual."

"You're changing the subject."

"Well, you're rambling. I don't know what the subject is anymore."

His grandfather nailed him with one of those I-know-you-boy looks. "Who's the fancy lady?"

"Someone I knew a long time ago." He didn't bother to stonewall or lie.

"Thought so. Someone took her child?"

"No." He gave him a short version of the story Myra had told him because he knew Pop would keep jabbing until he drew blood.

"That bastard beat his girlfriend into a coma and took her baby? And it's Stuart Stevens's daughter?"

"That's about it."

Pop tapped the table with his arthritic knuckles. "You can be packed and on the road in ten minutes."

"I told you I'm not taking the case."

"Why not? It's Stu's grandson and his life is in danger."

"I'm not the only P.I. around."

"You're the only one who can find him in less than twenty-four hours and it looks like that little boy doesn't have much time."

"Pop..."

"Wait a minute. How do you know this woman?"

Levi tried hard not to grit his teeth. "I met her when I was a cop."

"Is she the woman you were holed up with for about six months?"

"We weren't holed up. I moved into her apartment."

"Same thing. It was like you were in heat or something. You couldn't come home. You had to be with her and then all of a sudden it just fizzled out."

"Yep." He wasn't talking about this with his grandfather.

"So what happened to all that heat?"

"Like you said, it fizzled out."

"Mmm. So what's the problem?"

"I'm not getting involved with her again."

Pop scratched his gray head. "Some of my brain cells nap, some of them have just plain dried up, but the ones that are working are confused as hell. The woman is just asking you to take the case. I don't see a problem. Oh, is this about Valerie? You sure as hell don't want to mess that up. She's making pork chops, mashed potatoes and gravy tonight. I'm not eating all day."

Levi closed his computer and got to his feet. While Pop was on another subject, he decided to make his escape. "I'm going into the office."

Pop frowned so deep his forehead looked like road ruts. "Wait a minute. We're not through talking."

"I am."

Pop pointed a gnarled finger at him. "If something happens to that boy, you'll never forgive yourself. I know you just as well as I know myself. You're a P.I. It's a job. Valerie will understand because she loves you, and if she don't trust you, well, then, son, you ain't got a thing." Pop pushed to his feet. "Now I'm gonna go drive my tractor and push some dirt around just for the hell of it, and if I feel like it, I might plant some winter coastal for my pain-in-the-ass cows."

It's not about Valerie. But explaining that to Pop would take more patience than he had right now.

Levi took a quick shower, pushing Myra to the back of his mind. She wouldn't stay there, though. Yanking on jeans, he tried to figure out what he was so angry about. She had some gall coming out here and destroying his peace. Grabbing a shirt out of the closet, he paused.

He was overreacting.

This wasn't about Valerie. This wasn't about Myra. It was about him and his damn pride. Myra had taken a strip of it and crushed his heart. It wasn't easy to trust again and let a woman back into his life. He loved Valerie and wanted to spend the rest of his life with her, so his anger was out of place.

Slipping his arms into a white shirt, he thought about his parents. They'd had a crappy marriage. His father had been a cowboy rancher and his mom was a city girl. They'd fought all the time. It had come to an end when his father was killed in a car/truck accident when Levi was nine. His mom had moved them from the ranch to Austin. Levi hated the city and had begged to live with his grandfather. That hadn't happened until his mom met someone else, a short six months later. They'd moved to Virginia and Levi refused to go, so his mother relented and allowed him to stay with his grandfather. After that, Levi had minimal contact with his mom and his sister. They visited every now and then, but they felt like strangers.

He was well aware he had a trust issue with women. He blew out a breath and admitted that maybe a part of him was never going to get over Myra. That was a long way from doing her a favor, though.

But what about Stu?

Opening his sock drawer, he pulled out a pair. Unable to stop himself, he reached into the back corner where he had a single sock stored. He sat on the bed with it in his hand and dumped out the object that was inside—a ring box. Flipping open the top, he stared at the solitary diamond he'd planned to give Myra that weekend long ago.

He wasn't sure why he'd kept the ring. Maybe as a reminder of the pain she'd caused him. Putting it back in the drawer, the anger left him. He'd learned from his affair with Myra. No one was perfect. Certainly not him. He didn't hate Myra. He'd hated what she'd done to his pride. It was a man thing. But he was tough and she'd made him tougher. It reinforced his decision not to get involved with her again—even if it was business.

As he headed for his truck, he couldn't help but think of what Pop had said. Could he live with himself if something happened to that little boy?

CHAPTER THREE

MYRA DROVE TO the Westwood Nursing Facility to visit with Stu and to let him know Levi wasn't taking the case. On the way, she called Mick Travers, another P.I., and left a message on his cell. She'd worked with him before and she knew he'd call her back.

Stu was lucky to have good health insurance that included extended care. He'd lived in a condo, but was so weak from the cancer treatments, Natalie had talked him into moving here, where he had constant care. The place was very nice and it brought Natalie peace of mind.

Stu and Myra went way back. Fresh out of law school, Myra had been searching for a job for weeks and had an interview with the D.A. of Travis County in Austin. She'd been sitting in the secretary's office when Stu walked in. She had no idea he was the assistant chief of police. He was dressed in ordinary street clothes. They struck up a conversation and she told him she had little hope of getting the job but she was a damn good attorney. He told her she had guts and that would see her through and he wished her luck.

After the interview, she was called back. The D.A. told her Stu Stevens had put in a recommendation for her and the job was hers. She was stunned, having no idea who Stu Stevens was. But it didn't take long to find out. Ever since then, they'd had a connection.

When he was offered the chief of police job in Houston, Stu moved on and she soon followed. He was the reason she had a job in the D.A.'s office in Houston. The relationship seemed to go on, too. She found him to be one of those trustworthy men she could count on…like Levi.

Stu had been one of the officers to start the petition to support Levi when he'd disobeyed the direct order. So she and Levi owed Stu a lot and she didn't understand Levi not helping the man who'd always been there for him. This wasn't about her and Levi. Couldn't he see that?

She stopped at the nurses' desk. "How's Stu?"

"Sad." Barbara, an R.N., shook her head. "We just called his daughter and the nurse held the phone to Natalie's ear so she could hear her father's voice. But she's still in a coma. I hope you have some good news for him."

Myra's heart sank. Too much heartache and there was nothing she could do about it, except curse Levi under her breath. That didn't help, either, though.

"Not really, but the police are still trying to find the baby," she replied, and walked off down the hall. At Stu's room, she knocked on the door.

At a faint "come in," she went inside. Stu had a private room and sat in his recliner with oxygen tubing in his nose. He was painfully thin. His dull, tired eyes lit up when he saw Myra.

"Is Levi coming?"

"No. I'm sorry, Stu. He's not taking the case. You

should have called him. Seeing me only made him more bullheaded to never work with me again."

"That surprises me."

At the thoughtful light in his eyes, she asked, "Why did you want me to see him in person? A phone call from you would have been more effective."

"Because, to get my grandson back, I need both of you on my team. I thought the two of you would have grown up enough to let the past go."

"If I didn't love you so much, I'd really be pissed."

A slight smile touched his face. "I've always liked your spirit. Don't worry, kid, Levi will come around." "Kid" was his nickname for her and she found it hard to stay mad at him.

"Just in case your instincts are off, I called another P.I. and I'll have him on it just as soon as he calls me back. The cops are still searching, too. I'm doing everything I can."

"I know. You've been a good friend to Natalie and to me, but as each hour passes we're losing time."

Myra didn't know what to say. Nothing was going to comfort Stu until Natalie woke up. Until Daniel was back with his mother.

"The nurse said you spoke to Natalie."

"I couldn't visit yesterday because I was so sick from the chemo. I had to do something. I was hoping my voice would trigger something and she would wake up."

Myra chewed on the inside of her lip, wanting to give him some hope. "Would you like to see Natalie today? I'll arrange it. Maybe in person your voice will be more effective."

"Let's do it." His voice sounded stronger.

"Well, then, I'll talk to the nurse and let you know what the other P.I. says."

"Thanks, kid."

"I'm making this my top priority."

It took Myra ten minutes to set everything up. The home had a wheelchair-accessible van and it was available for the afternoon. She drove over to the hospital to be there when Stu arrived in case he needed someone.

On the way, she got a call from the FBI agent and made an appointment to meet him in two hours in her office. Things were starting to happen now and Myra hoped Daniel could be found soon.

While she maneuvered through Houston traffic, her cell buzzed again. It was her mother. Myra groaned. She knew a lecture was coming.

She clicked on. "Hi, Mama."

"You come to High Cotton and you don't take time to visit your parents." No hello. Just go right for the juggler.

"You weren't home and I had to get back to Houston."

"You always have to get back to Houston. You never have time for your family."

One. Two. Three.

"There's a girl who works in the office and her boyfriend beat her into a coma and took their little boy. We're working very hard to locate him."

"I know. Jessie told me. I have to hear everything from Jessie."

One. Two. Three.

"As soon as everything settles down, I'll come and spend a weekend."

"We do have phones, Myra. If you had just called, we could have been home today to see our only child."

One. Two. Three.

"I'll call soon, Mama. Tell Papa hi. I've got to go."

And that was the weekly sermon for the ungrateful, disrespectful daughter. Her parents had never understood her desire to be a career woman. They wanted her to be a wife, a mother and a homemaker, and they never failed to remind her that a woman's place was in the home.

Myra never went gaga over babies like Jessie had. Nor did she ever have the urge to bake cookies. Her mother was domesticated enough for both of them. She wasn't sure why she was so different.

Until she was about nine, they'd had a normal life. Her dad had worked as a welder at a trailer manufacturing company and her mom was a housekeeper for Roscoe Murdoch. Then two things happened that changed their lives forever. Her father was laid off from his job and Roscoe's niece was kidnapped and murdered.

Since her father had been in Vietnam and knew how to use a gun, Roscoe had hired him to guard Jessie, and the Delgado family moved in with the Murdochs. The house had been a little cramped, so Roscoe had built a fortress and they had plenty of room. Her parents poured all their energy into watching over Jessie, and sometimes Myra felt invisible.

She loved Jessie dearly and she didn't begrudge her one second of her parents' time. But sometimes she wished her parents had recognized that she needed them, too. Myra had become tough and independent and determined to make it on her own.

Roscoe had paid for her college education. He made

it very clear, though, if her grades slipped or she got in trouble, her educational funding would stop. She'd graduated in the top 10 percent of her class and gone on to law school. She'd had boyfriends along the way, but not once did any of them instill in her the urge to settle down and have babies.

Until Levi.

She'd often wondered if they could make a marriage work. He wanted kids and she didn't want to be forced into that situation. Both partners should want a baby with all their hearts and she hadn't been there yet. She'd kept stalling and, in the end, it hadn't mattered. She'd lost him, anyway.

She found a spot in the parking garage at Memorial Hermann Hospital and made her way to the critical care unit. She stopped at the nurses' station. Since she'd been here so many times, most of the nurses knew her.

"Any change?" she asked one of the nurses.

"No, and the doctor just checked Ms. Stevens."

"They're bringing Mr. Stevens from the home," Myra said.

"I know. The nurse called. The doctor's going to allow it for a few minutes."

"That's about all he can handle. I'll wait for him." She walked to the waiting area and sank into a chair, feeling hopeless. She needed a miracle, but they seemed to be in short supply these days. Pulling out her cell, she called Detective Tom Hadley, who was handling the baby's disappearance.

"Hi there, Myra. How are you today?" Tom was divorced and considered himself a ladies' man. Being unattached made her a target for his unwanted flirting.

"Any news?"

"No. Nothing is popping up. It's as if he's disappeared into thin air."

"Have the Brownsville police made another visit to Marco's parents' house?"

"Now, sweet cheeks, they've got as big of a caseload as we do and they're not going to keep tabs on that house. They don't have the manpower."

She took a deep breath. "A little boy is missing."

"I know that and we're doing everything we can. If I hear anything, I'll call you."

"I'm hiring outside help."

"Well, sweet cheeks, that's your prerogative. But I didn't know the D.A.'s office was into funding preferred cases."

"This has nothing to do with the D.A.'s office. This is personal and we're not using public resources, so you can take your snotty-nosed comments and stick 'em."

"C'mon, Myra, I—"

She clicked off and took several deep breaths. "Idiot." She wasn't going to let that chauvinist ass upset her. As a lawyer, she'd met numerous Tom Hadleys and their egos were the biggest part about them.

She checked her messages. Why hadn't Mick returned her call? He was usually very prompt. Movement by the nurses' station caught her attention and she saw Stu and an orderly had arrived. Myra hurried over.

"You okay?"

"Yes. Just a little tired." Stu was in a wheelchair with a portable oxygen tank attached if he needed it, which he did. His face was flushed from the drive over.

"I'll take him in," she said to the orderly.

"Have you seen her?" Stu asked.

"I was waiting for you, but the doctor says there's no change."

She pushed Stu into one of the small rooms that faced the nurses' station. Natalie lay completely motionless with tubes in her arms and a ventilator tube in her throat. A tube was also attached to her head where they had drilled holes in her skull to release the pressure on her brain. They'd shaved her head, too. The left side of Natalie's face was badly bruised, as was her neck. She was very pale and the only color on her face was the dark eyelashes lying softly against her skin. The only sound in the room was the beeping of the monitors.

"Oh, my poor baby girl." Stu reached out a hand to touch his daughter. "Baby, it's Daddy. Can you hear me? Please wake up. Daniel needs you. I need you. Baby, please wake up."

As Myra watched her lifeless friend, she blamed herself. She'd seen all the signs, the bruises and heard the lame excuses Natalie made for them. They were roughhousing or making love and Marco didn't mean to hurt her. Then her vibrant energetic friend had turned into someone Myra didn't know. Natalie was continually late for work, broke their lunch dates and, most of the time, looked stressed. When Myra questioned her, Natalie would become defensive, so she'd backed off and let her live her life her way. Looking back, Myra should've had the bastard arrested the first time she saw a bruise. Why hadn't she? She respected Natalie's privacy. But that counted for very little now.

"Ms. Delgado," a nurse spoke from behind her.

She turned. "Yes."

"There's a man asking for you."

"Here?"

"He's in the waiting area."

"Did he give a name?"

"No."

"Give me a minute."

The nurse walked out.

It had to be Mick. He must have tracked her down, but that was odd for him. "I'll be right outside," she said to Stu.

"Take your time. I just want to look at my baby girl."

Myra patted Stu's shaky hands and went to the nurses' station. The nurse pointed to the waiting area and whispered, "If he's single, I want his phone number."

Myra was taken aback. Mick was portly and bald. She couldn't imagine him generating that kind of response. She stopped short in the entrance to the room. The place was empty except for the man standing at the window looking out: tall, broad shoulders, in jeans, boots and a Stetson. Only one person stood that straight with a proud lift of his head.

Levi.

She swayed as the blood rushed from her head to her now-wildly beating heart. Had he changed his mind?

"Levi, what are you doing here?"

LEVI SWUNG AROUND, wondering the same thing. He did what he'd been taught his whole life. He told the truth and didn't stonewall. "You wanted to hire me. I'm here."

"But you said—"

"I know. I let my anger get the best of me, but I realized I don't have to work with you. You're just the middle person. I'll do my best to find Stu's grandson and then we'll part ways again. This time for good."

"I see."

The hurt look in her dark eyes got to him for a second and then he quickly pushed it away. He wasn't making this personal.

"What about Valerie?"

"She understands my job takes me away from time to time and she trusts me."

"Must be nice."

"Mutual trust always is."

She opened her mouth to say something and snapped it shut. Myra wasn't known for holding back. Maybe she had matured.

"If the trail leads to Mexico and the drug cartel, Stu will have to admit it's a lost cause. There's no way to guarantee anyone's safety in that situation."

"I've already contacted another P.I.," she said more to herself than to him, it seemed.

"Good. I just didn't want to not take this case because of something that happened between us."

"He hasn't agreed to it yet."

"Make up your mind, Myra. We're wasting time."

She tucked a loose strand of hair behind her ear and he watched her graceful movements even though he didn't want to. "Okay. I know you're the best and, as you said, we're losing time. Stu is here visiting his daughter."

"I know. I'm waiting to see him."

She walked away and he blew out a breath. He didn't quite understand what he was doing here, but he couldn't discard his code of ethics to help people just because Myra was involved. And it was for Stu. Levi owed the man. His emotions were all over the place and that was odd. He'd been told by more than one woman that he didn't have any. It seemed one dark-eyed dark-haired woman brought out the worst in him.

Myra pushed Stu in a wheelchair into the room. His ashen skin and gauntness seemed to have worsened since Levi had last seen him. His heart went out to his friend.

"Hey, Levi." Stu held out his weak hand and Levi shook it. "I knew you'd come."

"You kind of know me inside and out."

"You bet."

"But, as I was telling Myra, I have some limitations. I will not get involved with the Mexican drug cartel."

"You locate my grandson and I'll take it from there."

"Deal." They shook hands again. "I'll need a photo of the baby."

"Sure. Myra will get you one." Stu's voice was hoarse and now it was more of a wheeze, and Levi could see his old friend was exhausted.

"My daughter doesn't know that monster took him. At least, I don't think she does. Myra and I haven't mentioned it in case she doesn't. No one knows what happened in that apartment."

"When did the father take the child?"

Stu had to stop and take a breath, so Myra answered. "It happened on Monday. Natalie has an hour for lunch, and when she wasn't back in two hours, I got worried. At three, I drove to the apartment and found her in a pool of blood. I immediately called 9-1-1, and an ambulance had her at the hospital in minutes. The E.R.

team worked with her and then they took her into surgery. I realized it was time to pick up Daniel from day care, so I called another girl in the office to see if she could get the baby and keep him for a while. In fifteen minutes, she called me back to say Natalie had gotten him at noon."

"My grandson probably saw his mother being beaten," Stu choked out.

Myra patted Stu's shoulder to comfort him and Levi stared for a moment. This was a different side of Myra, one he'd never seen. And it was a little jolting.

He swallowed. "The police have confirmed that Marco Mortez is the assailant?"

"Yes," Myra replied. "Nat told me Marco was in town and she was meeting him for lunch."

"But she didn't mention picking up the baby?"

"No. Marco must have told her to bring him."

He caught her eye. "When did you start accepting assumptions for facts?"

She gave him a heated glance that could melt chocolate in a refrigerator. "There was a call on her cell from him at 12:05 p.m. The last call she took. That's fact. Jerry Black, who lives in the apartment complex, said he saw her go into her apartment with him and the baby. That's fact."

"Just checking." He stopped her before she got all fired up.

"I do my job, Levi. Thoroughly."

He let that pass. "You said Marco was in town. Did Natalie live with him?"

"No. He stays with her when he's in town. He's away a lot on family business."

"Which is?"

"As far as I can tell, they restore vintage cars and ship them all over the world. Marco drives a Jaguar. Natalie said some of the cars are worth millions."

"What's his father's name?"

"César."

"He lives in Brownsville?"

"Yes."

"Anything else you can tell me?"

"Marco was very secretive and he never let anything slip."

"Levi, find my grandson. He has to be here when my daughter wakes up."

"I'll do my best, Stu, but as I told you, if—"

"Let's stay positive," Myra said.

"It's difficult, Myra." Stu coughed into a handkerchief.

Myra squatted by the chair. "You're getting tired. Levi and I will take it from here."

An orderly walked up. "Ready to go, Stu?"

Stu looked at Levi. "You're the only investigator who can bring my grandson home. I trust you, Levi."

"I'll do my best."

"If you'll come back to the home, I'll write you a check."

"Don't worry about it, Stu. Just take care of yourself and I'll catch you later."

"Thanks, Levi. I'm indebted to you."

The orderly pushed Stu down the hall, and Levi and Myra stared until they were out of sight.

"Why did you interrupt me?" he demanded, not letting her off so easily.

She faced him. "Haven't you heard of finesse, Levi? You've already told him you weren't getting involved with the drug cartel. You didn't need to jam it down his throat again."

"He's a cop. He knows the truth just like you and I do."

"Leave him with some hope."

"When did you get to be so damned considerate?"

"When did you get so hardhearted?"

"Myra—" He slammed his hat onto his head. "This isn't going to work. Maybe it would be best if you hired the other guy."

"You gave your word to Stu."

"Then stay out of it. You don't need to control everything."

"I'm only trying to help a man I admire who's been blindsided by grief and tragedy."

"I know that, but Stu needs to be aware there is a very good chance that baby is in Mexico and there is no way to get him back."

She lifted a dark eyebrow. "Is that a fact you can back up? You're big on facts."

"Damn it, Myra."

"You can't," she said with a touch of glee in her voice. "Until you can tell him with certainty, you're not mentioning it again."

He stepped closer to her, so close he got a faint whiff of her fragrance. The gardenia-scented lotion she wore. It used to weaken his concentration. Now it only infuriated him. "Let's get one thing straight. You will not tell me what to do. I get it, you're concerned about Stu and Natalie. I am, too, but my patience is not as good as it used to be. So back off."

"Fine. Do you need the detective of record on the case?"

He sighed and walked past her. He knew his job and he didn't need her to explain it to him.

"Levi."

He told himself to keep walking, but against every sane thought in his head he turned back.

"Thank you."

He nodded, trying not to look into her dark eyes, trying not to get caught in the allure that was Myra Delgado.

CHAPTER FOUR

MYRA WASN'T UPSET at Levi's high-handedness. He was on the case and that's what she'd wanted. But she did wonder what had changed his mind. He probably couldn't ignore his code of ethics and honor, and he had a soft spot for kids. Of course, Stu was a big pull, too. She was glad her old friend hadn't been proven wrong. Now Levi just had to find Daniel.

Levi had a rocky relationship with his mother. She'd remarried within six months of his dad's death, which was something Levi just couldn't understand. At nine years of age, he'd refused to move with her and her new husband to Virginia. It was one of the few personal things Levi had shared with her. In his childish mind, he'd been hoping his mother wouldn't go, but she did, leaving Levi with his grandfather. He'd felt deserted by a mother he loved and he'd never quite got over that. It made him tough, independent and, without a doubt, bullheaded. When Levi made up his mind, very little could change it. That's why she was so surprised to see him today. But the thought of a child being separated from his mother had hit Levi in the heart.

The buzz of her phone interrupted Myra's thoughts. Looking at the caller ID, she saw it was Tom. She quickly clicked on.

"Hey, sweet cheeks, we finally got a break. You might want to come down to the station."

She gritted her teeth at the words *sweet cheeks* but didn't respond. Tom wasn't getting to her. He just annoyed her. "What have you got?"

"Brownsville police spotted the Jag on International Boulevard going into Brownsville." She whipped into another lane, her heart pounding. This was the break they needed. "Have they stopped the car?"

"No. We're keeping a tail on it to see where he goes and we want to be careful in case the baby's in the car."

"I'll be at the station in a few minutes."

Clicking off, she took the next exit and pulled into a restaurant's parking lot. She poked in the FBI agent's number.

"Steve, could you meet me at the central police station? They've spotted Mortez's Jaguar near Brownsville."

He quickly agreed. It was all coming together and Daniel might be back with his mother by nightfall. Maybe they didn't need Levi, after all.

She sped toward the station, found a parking spot and hurried inside. Before she could reach Tom's desk, she got a call from the D.A.

"Myra, I heard they've located Mortez's car."

"Yes, Mr. Chambers, I'm at the station now."

"Good. Stay on it and keep me posted. If something happens to that baby, the D.A.'s office and the police are going to look bad in the eyes of the public and I don't like looking bad."

"I'm on it, sir."

"Have you checked on Natalie?"

"Yes. She's still the same."

"I want that son of a bitch caught."

"I'm on my way to talk to Detective Hadley. I'll call as soon as I'm finished."

She knew Clarence Chambers was more concerned about reelection than he was about Natalie, but that was the nature of politics.

Tom wasn't at his desk. She looked around and a detective sitting at a desk pointed down the hall. "Tom's in there."

"Thank you." Walking down the hall, her heels made a clickety-clack noise. She tapped on the door and went in.

Lieutenant Moyer met her. "Mr. Coyote says he's been hired by Stu to help find the child."

"Yes. Considering our investigators are overloaded, I thought we could use a little outside help. Daniel Stevens needs to be found as soon as possible."

"I'll allow him to sit in, then. Tom's in charge."

She nodded and he walked out.

Levi, Steve and Tom sat at a table strewn with laptops, iPads and phones. She eased into a chair next to Steve, across from Levi and Tom, who was talking on his cell. She wasn't surprised at seeing Levi here. She knew he would make contact with the lead detective, which was protocol. She was just surprised he'd done it so quickly.

Tom laid down his phone. "Okay, counselor, are you ready for the police to stop the car?"

"The D.A. wants to wrap up this case, but he wants to be very careful the baby is unharmed. As do I."

Tom snorted. "Like we go around hurting babies."

He made the call. "Stop the car, but make sure the baby is safe."

They waited in silence. Myra hoped the stop went well and that Marco would soon be in custody. The time dragged. She glanced at Levi and he was doing something on his iPad. With today's technology, he was probably keeping tabs on the car. One of the cool things about Levi was that he was a whiz with a computer.

The buzz of Tom's phone startled her. He immediately clicked on. "Son of a bitch." He slammed a fist onto the table. "Are you sure?…Yeah….Yeah….Let me know what he says."

Tom ran a hand through his hair. "The driver was Juan Reyes. He works for the Mortez family and was ordered to pick up the car at the Brownsville International Airport. Juan says that's all he knows. They're taking him in for questioning."

"Was there a car seat in the vehicle?" Levi asked, still on his computer.

"Damn it." Tom reached for his phone again and asked the Brownsville police that question. Laying his cell on the table, he said, "Yeah, there was a car seat."

Levi leaned back in his chair. "That baby is well hidden in Mexico by now and the law will never find him."

Myra's stomach churned. All she'd eaten today had been chocolate, and she had a niggling sense she was about to throw it up. She took a couple of deep breaths. What she'd feared most had just happened. Daniel was lost to them and to Natalie. How did she accept that?

Steve opened his computer and turned it so they could see the screen. He touched the keys. "This is the Mortez home in Brownsville. It sits on about ten acres with several metal buildings that are cooled and heated for those expensive cars. As far as we can tell, César Mortez, his wife and Marco live there. An agent checked the house yesterday and just the servants were there. One said the Mortez family had gone to the Matamoras home for a few days." Steve clicked another key. "This is their home in Matamoras."

Myra saw a three-story beige concrete structure with a red tiled roof. What caught her eye was the stone fence around it. It looked like a fortress and Steve echoed her thoughts.

"If Mortez has taken the baby to the Matamoras house, there's no way in without Mortez's permission and there's certainly no way out without it, either. It would take a small army to infiltrate it, and the Mexican police will not help. There are not many Americans who are willing to go in, either. So I say we have a dilemma here."

Levi studied the house on the screen. He pointed to several spots. "High-tech digital cameras are everywhere. They know you're coming before you even get there."

"So we just let him keep the baby?" Myra tried to keep her anger in check at this turn of events. It was hard for her to simply give up as the men were suggesting.

"There's not much we can do, Myra," Tom replied. "Not without getting a lot of people killed. After all, Marco is the boy's father and he's not in imminent danger."

Myra jumped to her feet. "Don't tell me that shit, Tom. Marco brutally beat a woman into a coma in this country and took her child. Natalie Stevens has full custody of that child. Marco broke the law here and he needs to be punished."

"Marco is a Mexican citizen and I'm not sure what we can do to him in this country except deport him. I'll contact the Mexican authorities, but I can guarantee you they will do nothing."

Myra knew he was right, but it didn't keep her from seething.

Tom looked at Levi. "Now, if Mr. Coyote wants to go in there and tackle Mortez and the drug cartel, he's welcome to go, but no one from this department will volunteer. Sorry, that's just the way it is."

Levi's eyes were on Steve. "What's the Mortez family into?"

"We know it's either guns or drugs, but we haven't been able to catch them with anything. We've raided the house in Brownsville, stopped those vans carrying the expensive cars and found nothing. They seem to know when we're coming."

"How do you know they're involved with the drug cartel?" Levi kept on.

Steve tapped another key and photos popped up. "That's César, the father, with one of the kingpins of the cartel. Here are more of meetings in Brownsville. The Mortez family is involved with moving guns or drugs for them, we're sure. We just can't prove it, but one day they'll slip up and we'll get them."

There was silence for a moment.

"Concerning the baby..." Steve closed his laptop. "Ava Mortez seems like a nice enough woman and I'm sure she's taking care of the child. The conditions in

Matamoras are not as good as they are in Brownsville and Mrs. Mortez spends most of her time in Texas. Once this cools down, she'll probably bring the baby back to Brownsville. We keep close tabs on that house and we'll let you know when that happens."

"Sorry, Steve." Myra reached for her purse. "I have a friend who is fighting for her life and I just can't wait that long. If she wakes up and Daniel's not here, I don't know if she'll survive. The only choice for me is to go to Matamoras on my own."

"Are you insane?" Tom was the first to speak. "Stu wouldn't want you to do that."

"Probably not. But I'm going."

"Myra, it's not safe for a woman to go there alone. You've worked in the D.A.'s office long enough to know that."

"Yes, I have, Tom. It still doesn't change my mind." She turned and walked out of the room.

Steve followed her. "Myra, please think about this. Just give this some time and we'll flush him out."

"Natalie doesn't have time and Stu doesn't, either." She looked over Steve's shoulder and saw Levi watching her. She could read his thoughts in his eyes: *You're crazy.*

"Thanks, Steve. I appreciate your concern, but I have a feeling I'm on my own on this." She continued her journey for the door and her legs were a little shaky once she reached her car. It was crazy. It was insane. But she couldn't seem to do anything else. Wherever Daniel was, she knew he was afraid and wanted his mommy. She would take things slowly and feel her way. There was no need to talk to Levi. He'd already made his position clear. Under no circumstances was he going into Mexico. She made her way to her office in the criminal justice building to tell her boss her plans.

Sitting at her desk, she gathered her thoughts. Could she do this? She thought of her parents and Jessie. And then there was Stu and Natalie. Who would help them if something happened to her?

Before she made any concrete decisions, she needed food. Opening her bottom drawer, she pulled out a protein bar and then went down the hall to the kitchen for bottled water. Munching on the bar, she resolved she couldn't leave little Daniel in Mexico.

She hurried to the D.A.'s office and spoke to his secretary. "Is he available?"

"Depends."

Myra knew this drill. She wasn't getting inside unless it was important. "It's about the Stevens baby."

"Did they find him?"

Myra lifted an eyebrow. "You know I can't tell you that." Oh, turnaround was fun.

"Go in," the girl said with a frown.

Myra tapped on the door and poked her head around. "Do you have a minute?"

Clarence waved her in. He was on the phone. Laying his cell on his desk, he asked, "Any news?"

She took a seat and told him what they'd learned.

"That pretty much takes it out of our hands."

Myra smoothed an imaginary speck off her slacks. "I'd like to ask for some time off."

Clarence nodded. "Sure, sure. I know this has been stressful for you. It has for the whole department. Natalie was very likable and easy to work with."

Myra shifted uneasily in the chair, not sure how to say what she had to without him blowing a gasket. It was at that moment she realized she could lose her job over this. In the old days, that would've stopped her immediately, but she wasn't young and naive anymore. She had the battle scars to prove it.

"I'm planning to go to Matamoras."

Clarence pushed his glasses up the bridge of his nose and leaned back in his big leather chair with a shocked expression on his face. She waited with bated breath for his next words.

"You're going to try to find Natalie's baby?" He quickly held up a hand. "No, don't answer. I don't need to know that. You do what you feel you have to and leave the department out of it. I'll let everyone know you're on vacation and what you do on vacation is your business."

Myra was positive disbelief was written all over her face. She expected him to try to talk her out of it and, for the first time since she'd worked for him, she admired that he was willing to take a risk because this could surely come back to bite him in the butt. Only if she didn't succeed.

She got to her feet. "Thank you."

"Don't worry about Natalie. I'll get Michelle to look in on her daily."

"I'd appreciate that."

"Myra, just realize you can't save everybody from the bad guys."

She frowned. "Do I do that?"

"You're one of my best prosecutors because it somehow eats at you when a person gets away with bad behavior. But sometimes you have to let go. Sometimes the bad guys win."

He was right. The thought of that monster keeping that little boy was eating away at her like an acid in her stomach. Now she had to really look at her motive and understand what she was doing.

"My advice is to take someone with you. Preferably someone big and strong and not afraid of the devil."

Levi blasted across her consciousness. He fit the bill, but he wasn't willing to take a risk and ruin the life he had planned. But there were other men. Surely.

"I'll think about it."

Back at her desk, she made notes of what she'd need to carry and checked airline reservations. No way was she driving across the border. Her cell went off and she reached for it in her purse. Mick. Just the man she needed to talk to.

"Hey, Mick, you took your time calling back."

"Sorry. I got caught up on a case. What do you need?"

"I need a bodyguard."

"Hell, Myra, I'd guard your body any day of the week."

Mick was like any other man. He had to get that sexual innuendo in there. But he wasn't as sleazy as Tom. "I guess you read in the paper about the girl in our office who was beaten into a coma by her boyfriend."

"Yeah, it was in the paper and on the news."

"The boyfriend has taken their son into Mexico and we believe he's hiding out in Matamoras."

"If you're suggesting what I think you are, the answer is no. I work in Texas. I have a wife and two kids and I'm not going into Mexico."

"Do you want to think about it?"

"No, sorry, Myra. But if you need a job done here, I'm your man."

"Thanks, Mick."

Fiddling with the phone, indecision gripped her. Everyone was telling her this was insane, so why wasn't she listening? Maybe, like Levi, the thought of that little boy being taken from his mother had gotten to her. Something needed to be done.

She found herself headed back to the hospital. She needed to see Natalie to resolve all the doubts in her head. It was getting late and the hospital seemed very quiet, or maybe that was just the uneasiness in her. The nurse allowed her to see Natalie for a moment.

Myra stared at her friend, who was only a shadow of the vibrant young woman she used to be. The bruises stood out against her pale skin. When she woke up, how was Myra going to tell her that Daniel wasn't here?

Dr. March walked in with a chart in his hand. "Good evening, Ms. Delgado."

"Good evening," she replied. "Is there any change?"

He scribbled something in the chart. "No. Sorry."

"If her son was here with his baby chatter, would it be a stimulus for her?"

He closed the chart. "Yes, that's why we allow her father to visit. A familiar voice can be a trigger to bring her out of this deep sleep. Have they found her son?"

"No. I was just wondering."

"Keep positive thoughts," he suggested. "Her body and mind have been traumatized. It takes time to heal."

"I'll try to remember that."

She reached out and touched the limp hand on the bed. "Get better, Nat. I'm doing all I can, but you have to help me. You have to get better."

There was no response and Myra knew there wouldn't be. As she stood there in the quiet room, with only the hum of the machines, a calm came over her. Doing nothing wasn't in her nature. If she let Marco have Daniel, she would never be able to face Natalie again. Natalie looked up to her, but it was more than that. Natalie trusted her, and now Myra had to trust her own instincts. She had to tackle the most dangerous job she'd ever attempted.

But first she had to tell Jessie and her parents.

LEVI DROVE STEADILY toward Willow Creek and home. His services weren't needed and there was nothing else he could do. Thinking about Myra and her ridiculous plan only pissed him off. She'd been told the risk repeatedly and, as always, Myra did as she pleased. His conscience was clear.

He wasn't sure why he kept glancing in his rearview mirror. He had no reason to feel guilty. Going to Houston in the first place was a crazy thing to do. He'd sworn he wouldn't help Myra, but both Stu and the thought of a kidnapped baby who needed his mother had swayed him. And then there was that little matter of living with a conscience that continually mocked his decisions.

The more miles he left behind him, the more his conscience chimed in. Myra's body would probably be found on the banks of the Rio Grande within days. If there was one thing the drug cartel didn't like, it was

Americans asking questions, and Myra was good at asking questions. It was her forte and it would be her downfall.

He pulled over to the side of the road. Cars whizzed by on the warm September day, the heat intensified by revving motors and blacktop. He told himself he wasn't responsible for Myra's actions. Her number was on his phone and he quickly found it. What could he say to her that hadn't already been said? Could he go back to his safe life and leave her to face an untimely death? Tapping his fingers on the steering wheel, he knew there was only one answer. He finagled his way back into traffic and headed for Willow Creek.

MYRA SPENT AN hour with Stu explaining the situation and, though he was upset, he didn't try to stop her. He left that decision up to her, but strongly suggested she hire guards to go with her. Stu wanted Daniel home with Natalie and he offered to pay for a bodyguard.

Nothing much was said about Levi. Stu only commented that Levi wouldn't let them down. Telling him Levi already had seemed cruel, so she didn't.

On the way home, she stopped at a sporting goods store and got appropriate apparel, plus hiking boots. Then she went home to figure out her next move.

After eating yogurt and an apple, she called Jessie and told her the situation and quickly added, "I just wanted you to know in case you don't hear from me for a while."

"My, are you sure about this? Let the authorities handle it."

"It's a delicate situation, but I'll try to stay in touch so don't worry."

"Oh, please. This sounds a little insane even for you."

"Thank you very much."

"You know what I mean."

"Yes. I'll admit I'm a little scared, and if I feel the situation is too dangerous once I get to Matamoras, I'll call everything off. I haven't lost my mind completely."

"That's good to hear."

"I was going to call Mama and Papa, but they wouldn't understand and we'd just get into an argument. If they mention they can't get in touch with me, make an excuse or something."

"I'm not lying to them, My."

Myra sighed. She knew Jessie wouldn't lie. That was one of the things she loved most about her. She was very honest and up-front.

"Okay. I should be back in a few days. Say a prayer for me, and I love you, kiddo."

"Myra, please ask Levi to go with you."

"He made it very clear he won't go into Mexico, but I'll hire someone, so don't worry. I'll call as soon as I get there."

"Take care of yourself."

Myra sat for a long time with the phone in her hand. She should call her parents, but it would turn into a big argument she wasn't in the mood to deal with. Since her parents had moved so far away, she didn't talk to them as much. If she was lucky, she'd be home before they realized she'd been gone, and by then she'd be prepared for the lecture.

Even she couldn't make *that* argument sound convincing. She touched the number to call home. Her mother answered.

"Hi, Mama. I'm sorry I was short today. I just have a lot on my mind."

"I know you're worried about your friend."

Myra didn't expect so much understanding and she was speechless for a brief second. "Yes, it's been very stressful."

"Well, then, come home for a few days and relax."

Myra chewed on her lip. "I can't right now. I'll probably be leaving for Matamoras tomorrow. We have a lead on the baby."

"Matamoras?" She could almost see the worry gathering in her mother's eyes like clouds before a thunderstorm.

"I'll be careful."

"Why do you have to go? Aren't the police supposed to do that?"

Myra didn't feel she needed to go into a long explanation. "I just wanted you to know in case you were trying to reach me. I'll call as soon as I get back."

Her mother wasn't having any of it. She called to Myra's father, "Felipe, talk to your daughter. She's doing something crazy."

She explained the situation all over again to her father. "Papa, I have to go. I just wanted to touch base before I left.

"Take care of yourself, *bebé*. We love you."

That's all she wanted to hear, just in case she didn't make it back.

For the next thirty minutes, she contacted retired

police officers who might want to make some extra money, but none of them wanted money that badly. The realization of just how serious the situation was finally began to sink in. She hung up from the last one feeling frustrated. She took a long breath and paced in her living room. What did she do now?

She didn't have an answer, so went to take a shower. Slipping into shorty pj bottoms and a tank top, new energy surged through her. She emailed Steve, requesting all the info he had on the Mortez family. He replied within minutes and she sat in the living room reviewing the Mortez compound in Matamoras. An outsider had no way in. That left no options, except one. She had Marco's cell number. She'd tried it a couple of times and he hadn't answered and she didn't leave a message. But if she left a message saying she was in Matamoras, he might meet with her. And how stupid would that be, meeting him alone on his turf where *justice* was a foreign word? What did she do?

Her doorbell chimed and she jerked her head up in surprise. Who could that be? Due to her work and prosecuting hardened criminals, she lived in a gated community. She had to buzz people in and no one had rung the buzzer. It might be a neighbor, but then, they usually called.

She went to the door and stood on tiptoe to look through the peephole. She blinked and looked again. Could it be...? No. She took another glance to make sure.

Levi.

CHAPTER FIVE

"MYRA, LET ME in."

She released the dead bolt and unlocked the door. Levi strolled in wearing worn jeans, a black T-shirt and a backpack. Mystified, she could only stare at him.

"What?" he asked, as if it was natural for him to drop by her home unannounced.

"What are you doing here?"

He shrugged out of the backpack and dropped it to the floor. "Hell, I don't know. I have a perfectly good life in Willow Creek, and yet I can't get the picture of you lying dead on the banks of the Rio Grande out of my head."

A shiver ran through her at the image. "Are you trying to scare me?"

"Is it working? You ready to change your mind?"

She heaved a sigh. "No."

"God, you're stubborn."

"What are you doing here, Levi?"

He dragged the backpack into the living room and plopped onto the sofa. Unzipping the pack, he pulled out his iPad. "I found I couldn't live with your death on my conscience, so I'm taking you to Mexico to search for the boy, but you will follow my orders and be as docile as possible."

"Oh" was all she could say. Her heavy heart suddenly felt lighter and she sat cross-legged in a chair facing him. "Thank you." She felt she needed to say that.

"Yeah" was his short reply. He was already engrossed in the iPad.

"Do you have a plan?"

He glanced up briefly. "Plans are usually shot to hell in these types of situations. We'll play it by ear. In the morning, we'll head out for Brownsville and cross the border and see how it goes."

"I thought it would be easier to fly."

That drew a dark scowl. "Tourists are easy targets and that's what you'll be getting off the plane in Matamoras."

"Okay. I'm flexible."

"Yeah. Since when?"

She took a deep breath. "If we're going to do this, we'll have to call a truce with the snide comments. To work together, we at least have to be civil to each other."

His brown eyes held hers and she resisted the urge to squirm. "You're right. For us to have any success, we have to work closely together. I'll have to be able to trust you."

"Is that a problem?"

He didn't answer for second. "Yesterday, yes. Today, I have to go on faith. I'm here, so that's about all I can say."

She swallowed. "I'll take it." She pointed to her laptop on the coffee table. "Steve sent over everything he has on the Mortez family. Or at least what he could share."

"I already have it."

That surprised her. An agent didn't share information with outsiders, or maybe Steve didn't consider Levi an outsider. But she was still curious. "How?"

"I snatched it from his computer when we were at the station."

Now she was more curious. "How?"

"I have a thingamajig on my phone…."

"Thingamajig?"

"That's all you need to know."

"But how did you do it? Steve was in the room with you the whole time."

"While Steve and Tom were talking to the lieutenant, I laid my phone against his laptop and, in a few seconds, I had everything on the Mortez family."

"Sometimes you're scary, Levi."

"Remember that and this trip will go smoothly."

"You know what you did was illegal." Why she was pointing that out, she wasn't sure. Maybe just to annoy him, like he was trying so hard to annoy her.

He lifted a dark eyebrow. "In the next few days, we'll be doing a lot of illegal stuff. Are you prepared for that, counselor?"

"Whatever it takes."

"Mmm."

Nothing was said for a few minutes as he worked on the iPad. She watched as he was totally focused on the computer. In the old days, he'd grasped things quickly and his memory was phenomenal. She was sure that hadn't changed. He paid great attention to detail. It drove her crazy sometimes when he could tell her exactly what she wore on a certain day and with what earrings or high heels. And yet the same man had trouble matching up his socks. She would bet that the socks he had on now were mismatched. It was a Levi trademark.

She remembered so many things about him. His gentle touch when she was down about something. His kind heart and concern for everyone. When he loved, there was no holding back. He gave all of himself and there was never any doubt that he loved her. She had failed their relationship.

Her eyes were drawn to the black T-shirt molded to the muscles in his arms and across his chest. As he worked the keypad, his forearms rippled, reminding her of everything she'd lost. And of everything she could never get back—mainly his trust.

"We'll leave early in the morning." His words broke through her thoughts. "And try to make it to Brownsville by noon. Do you have a passport?"

"Yes."

"I have Daniel's so we're set to go."

She frowned. "How did you get Daniel's?"

"On my way back, I called Stu and he sent someone to Natalie's apartment for the boy's birth certificate and a photo. When I arrived at the home, I faxed the items to a name Stu gave me and I picked up the passport on the way here."

"You've thought of everything."

"For us to succeed, I have to."

He reached into the backpack and pulled out a laptop and a phone. "This is a cheap phone you can use while we're in Mexico. Put all the numbers on it you'll need. Leave your expensive one here."

"Okay." She took the phone, very impressed with his thoroughness.

"I have to take mine, but I have all my information stored in case I lose it. I'll leave my laptop under your sofa."

"Sure."

"Do you have some old clothes?"

She jumped up. "I just bought some clothes to wear." She ran upstairs to her bedroom and came back with what she'd purchased.

He stared at the clothes in her hands. "Camouflage? This is not a military mission. We want to appear incognito and that means we have to blend in. We'll stop at a thrift store and get you something."

"Thrift store?"

"Yeah, Myra. Preferably something old and grungy."

She wasn't going to argue because he knew what he was doing. She held up the boots. "How about these?"

"They'll do, but we'll have to make them look worn and old."

"If you say so," she replied, trying to keep the annoyance out of her voice.

"Try to get some rest. I'll wake you about four-thirty."

"You say that as if you're staying here tonight."

"I am," he replied without even looking up.

"I just have one bedroom. The other bedroom I converted into an office."

He looked up at that. "Believe me, Myra, I can restrain myself. I lost those feelings for you a long time ago." He patted the sofa he was on. "I'll sleep here. Good God, is this white?"

"Yes, white leather." Levi's concentration was phenomenal, too. He could totally shut out the world when he was focused on something.

He glanced around and she knew he'd cataloged the entire room in that one glance. His eyes settled on the white area rug covering part of the hardwood floor.

"Everything in here is white."

"And silver and black," she quipped.

"I noticed."

She laid the clothes and boots in a chair. "That reminds me. How did you get in here? This is a secure complex."

He went back to the iPad. "No building is secure. If someone wants in, they'll find a way to get in."

"How did you do it?"

"I waited until someone was allowed in and then zipped my truck right in behind them. Easy as eating pie with both hands."

"No one noticed?"

"It's dark and I'm very fast. C'mon, Myra, stop grilling me. I have more important things on my mind."

"What are you doing on the computer?"

"Don't ask questions, either."

She threw up her hands. "If I have to get up at four-thirty, I'm going to bed."

"Do you have a sheet or a blanket I can put on the couch? I'd hate to drool on this white thing."

"You don't drool." That came out of her mouth without thinking. She didn't know how he slept these days. But in the old days, he'd slept sound, quiet and beautifully.

"That was seven years ago. I've changed."

She lifted an eyebrow, but decided not to voice her

thoughts. She needed his help and she wasn't going to complicate things. Or at least she was trying not to. She went to a hall closet and pulled out a blanket and a sheet and carried them back to him.

He stared at them. "White? What is it with you and white now?"

"I like white. What's wrong with that?"

"Nothing if you're superhuman. A child could have a field day messing up this place."

"I don't have a child."

"Yeah."

Suddenly the room was full of palpable tension. She felt it. He felt it. They both chose to ignore it.

"I'm going to bed." She stopped at the bottom of the stairs. "Thank you. I'm glad you changed your mind."

"Do you have anything to eat?" he asked, completely ignoring her thanks.

Another thing about Levi—he had a killer appetite. "Um, I have some yogurt and fruit. There's ice cream and frozen dinners in the freezer."

"That's it?"

"I'm not here that much."

"Oh, yeah, I forgot about your long hours." He stood and marched into the kitchen, opening her refrigerator. With yogurt and an apple in his hand, he opened the freezer and pulled out a TV dinner. Looking around, he said, "I'm not sure where to eat in here."

"There are bar stools on the island," she said, pointing to the white-and-chrome stools. "And there's also a table. Are you unfamiliar with these things?"

"I don't want to get anything dirty."

"I'm going to bed. You figure it out." She left him

with his dilemma. One would think he'd never been in a nice place before, but she knew that wasn't true. The apartment they'd shared wasn't as upscale as this, but it was still pretty nice. Actually, she couldn't recall him ever commenting on their decor. He was just being cantankerous now because he didn't want to be here.

As she made her way up the stairs, he hollered, "Where's the bathroom?"

"You're an investigator so it shouldn't be that hard to find."

"Funny. Okay. I found it. I just didn't know if there was one downstairs."

Memories, like photos from a favorite album, floated around her. *Myra, have you seen my shoes? Myra, are my keys in the kitchen? Myra, where are my socks?* For a man who could locate murderers, robbers, cheating husbands and missing children, he was hopeless at keeping track of his own stuff. Levi was a conundrum.

She didn't bother to close her door. There was no need, because she knew he wouldn't set foot in her bedroom. She crawled beneath her white sheets and relaxed even though she didn't know what tomorrow was going to bring. That was okay. Levi would be with her and he would protect her and keep her safe. He might not admit it, but it was the reason he was here. She went to sleep with that thought on her mind.

LEVI ATE TWO TV dinners, two yogurts, an apple and a couple of protein bars he found in a drawer before he finished off the ice cream. Then he went back to the sofa and spread the sheet over it. He laid the blanket at the end in case he needed it. Sitting down, he reached for his phone.

It was almost eleven and he was sure Valerie was asleep. She had to be at the hospital at five, so she always went to bed early. Since she was upset at his sudden decision to take this case, he wanted to talk to her. Not wanting to wake her, he sent a text.

I'm sorry you're upset. I do take a lot of dangerous cases. I just never realized that bothered you. We'll talk when I get back. Love, L.

He went back to his iPad and worked until after twelve. By then, he had an idea of what to do. He removed his clothes, flipped off the light and stretched out on the sheet, staring at the ceiling. Thoughts bounced like Ping-Pong balls across his mind. For a man who was never indecisive, he felt more vulnerable than he ever had in his life. He would've sworn when Myra left his barn this morning he'd never take this case.

He'd made it all the way to Willow Creek before he'd known he had to go back. He'd talked to Pop, which was like an exercise in practicing patience. As usual, Pop didn't see a problem. Stu's grandson had been taken and Levi needed to rescue him. It was so simple in his mind, but Pop tended to believe that Levi was ten feet tall and bulletproof.

Usually Valerie was very understanding about his work. But today, her understanding didn't stretch to him spending time with an old love. He flipped onto his side, knowing he could control the situation, but that was hard to explain to Valerie. This was just a case and he would treat it like all the rest. There was no need for his emotions to get involved.

He closed his eyes and let the world drift away. He needed rest to cope with tomorrow. As sleep tugged at him, he saw Valerie's beautiful face and his body relaxed. The image was quickly replaced by Myra's darker features, and blood pounded through his veins in remembered passion. He hated that he couldn't control his reaction. He hated that he couldn't completely erase her from his mind.

LEVI AWOKE AT four and headed to the kitchen to make coffee and soon realized there was no coffee or a coffee-maker. He'd forgotten. Myra always drank Starbucks. Damn it! He needed coffee.

He grabbed his clothes and headed upstairs to take a shower. The bath downstairs was only a half bath. The house was dark but he could find his way. A small night-light lit the hall. The tougher-than-rawhide prosecutor needed a night-light? Go figure.

After locating the bath, he took a quick shower and slipped into his clothes. He didn't shave because he wanted to be as scruffy as possible. Leaving the bath, he walked down the hall to her bedroom and flipped on the light. The only color in the big white bed was her dark brown hair splayed across the pillows.

"Wake up. We need to be on the road. You have five minutes. No makeup and old clothes."

A moan came from the bed.

"If you're not downstairs in five minutes, I'm leaving without you."

Taking the stairs two at a time, he thought he should

go alone. She was only going to slow him down, but if he left without her, he knew her well enough to know she would follow. And he didn't need any sudden surprises in a dangerous situation.

He folded the sheet and the blanket and left them neatly on the sofa. As he put his iPad in the backpack, she came downstairs in jeans and a multicolored blouse. He'd forgotten how good she looked in jeans, all curvy, all woman.

She sat in a chair to put on her hiking boots. Her hair was all over the place, hiding her expression. He placed his hands on his hips and watched, not sure she was even awake. After lacing up the boots, she whipped her hair into a ponytail without even brushing it. Her olive complexion, dark eyes and eyebrows showed she had no need for makeup. She looked beautiful without it. Maybe too beautiful for his peace of mind.

"I'm ready."

"Do you by any chance have coffee hidden somewhere in this place?"

"I always go to Starbucks before work. There's one just around the corner."

"It's 4:20 a.m. We'll have to stop at a convenience store. Let's go."

"Wait." She darted for the stairs. "I have to get my bag." She came back down with a bag and a pillow.

"Do you have your passport and driver's license?"

"Yes."

He didn't say anything else, just held the door open. The warm September morning embraced them. The landscaping lights lit their way. He walked to his truck and they crawled inside.

She clicked her seat belt, stuffed the pillow against the window and laid her head against it. "Wake me when it's daylight. Oh, turn right at the corner and, once you run over the sensor, the gate will open."

"Thanks." He drove out of the apartment complex and found a convenience store as fast as he could. While she slept, he went inside and ordered a large coffee and two tacos. Back in his truck, he slipped in a Zac Brown Band CD and headed for Brownsville. Sipping coffee and listening to the music, he was at peace with the world for a brief moment.

Myra woke up before they reached Victoria and was immediately on the phone checking on Natalie and Stu.

"How is she?" he asked when she put her phone down.

"The same."

"How did she get mixed up with someone like Marco Mortez?"

"She and some girls from the office went to a car show at the George R. Brown Convention Center. Marco was there and they hit it off. They went out and then he started coming back to see her. She was so in love she couldn't see the real Marco. The next thing I knew, he was staying at her apartment when he was in town. It was all downhill from there. He was very controlling, especially after the baby was born."

"Why didn't they get married?"

"She kept waiting for him to take her to meet his family, but he always made excuses."

"Maybe he's already married."

"Yeah. I thought of that, but I couldn't find any record of a marriage."

"He probably has a Mexican wife."

"Mmm. Could we please stop at a Starbucks? I really need coffee."

"We're about twenty miles from Victoria. We'll stop then, but only for a few minutes. Why don't you have coffee in your apartment?"

"I get a latte on the way to work."

"What about when you have a man over? Every man I know wants coffee first thing in the morning."

"Not all," she said with a teasing note in her voice. "I'm all the stimulation they need."

He kept his eyes on the road and refused to react to the taunt. It brought back too many memories of waking up in her arms and needing nothing but her kisses.

His cell beeped, indicating he had a message. He opened it to read: I'm just worried about you. That's all. I love you. V.

He relaxed. Everything he wanted waited for him in Willow Creek. Now he had to get Myra out of his life forever.

Pulling into Victoria, he stopped at a red light and searched on his cell for a Starbucks. "Not many Starbuckses in Victoria. The only one I can find is on Navarro and out of our way."

"Please."

He tried to ignore that pleading note in her voice and failed. He turned off the highway and zoomed toward Navarro. Myra went inside for coffee and then they were on the road again.

"I heard that Jessie got married." He thought it best if they kept the conversation on neutral ground.

"To Cadde Hardin. They have two boys a year apart. She's happy."

"And doesn't need you to mother her anymore."

"I didn't mother her," she snapped.

"You called her at least twice a day."

"Jessie had a very sad life. I just wanted…"

"To mother her," he finished, and glanced at her to see those dark eyes boring into him like hot coals. But it didn't stop him. "Just like you're doing with Natalie now. You say you don't want children, but you sure have a lot of motherly instincts."

So much for neutral. Everything came back to the two of them and their relationship.

She twisted the coffee cup in her hand. "Could we talk about what happened between us?"

He froze for a moment, not expecting her to take the conversation further. "No. The past is done. We can't go back and change a thing, so it's useless to talk about it."

"Sorry, I can't accept that. I need to talk about it. Since we've both moved on, I don't see the problem."

He wasn't having this conversation. He'd put it behind him and he wasn't dredging up those old feelings of pain and disillusionment.

"All I have to do is concentrate on the job ahead of me. That's it. I don't need you doing a number on my head."

"Levi…"

He swung into a parking lot. "This is what we need. A resale shop." He looked at the sign on the door. "It's open. Maybe we can find you some grungy clothes."

"This isn't over, Levi."

"It is. You get one favor from me and going into

Mexico is it." He turned off the engine and got out of the truck. She trudged after him.

The place smelled old and mothy. A big sign hung from the ceiling. All Clothes Have Been Washed. Clothes were stuffed onto racks and were stacked on top of them, too. Two women at the counter were tagging more for sale.

"We're looking for women's jeans and shirts," he said to one of the women.

She pointed to a rack and he and Myra went to look. He pulled out a couple of pairs that looked worn.

Myra frowned when he held them up. "What?"

"A size fourteen. Do I look like a size fourteen?"

"Oh, I didn't check. Pick a size."

She said something under her breath he didn't catch, and reached for a pair. They were worn with holes in both knees and frayed at the cuffs. "Will these work?"

"Perfect," he replied, and pulled a faded blue chambray shirt off a rack. "And this."

While she tried them on, he found an old hat for himself and a pair of sneakers for her.

Myra came out and twirled around. "How's this?"

He could only stare. How did she manage to look so attractive in old rags? The blue of the shirt brought out the smoothness of her skin and the brightness of her eyes. The jeans emphasized her curves just as the other jeans had.

"Maybe we should have gone with the size fourteen and a belt."

She lifted an eyebrow and he knew she knew he hadn't forgotten a single curve on her body. That threw him. He loved Valerie and was planning a life with her.

How could he remember Myra so vividly? For the first time, he wondered how deep his feelings were for Val.

Just as quickly as the thought shot through him, it disappeared. He wouldn't let Myra get to him.

CHAPTER SIX

THE REST OF the way to Brownsville was made mostly in silence. Myra was on her phone and Levi stared broodingly ahead. The land wasn't much to look at, mostly flat, but the nearer they drew to the big city, the more the landscape was dotted with lush palms.

Myra insisted on washing the clothes and Levi didn't object. They found a Laundromat and then had lunch at a hamburger place next door.

Even though she was hungry, Myra picked at her food.

"Eat. You'll need your strength for later," he said in that I-couldn't-care-less voice.

She took a sip of her tea. "I'm just nervous about what lies ahead."

He looked up. "Are you changing your mind?"

"No, but I would like to know what to expect. You have a plan, so what is it?"

He wolfed down the rest of his burger, took a swallow of tea and wiped his mouth. His movements were sure, confident. He did everything that way. She could watch him all day, which she should avoid doing for her own peace of mind.

"I've been in contact with a used car dealer and I'll be picking up an old truck. I'd rather not take mine, which is too new. I'll leave it in his lot. When we cross the border, our story will be that we're husband and wife."

Her heart gave a little jolt at that.

"We're hiding out in Matamoras because I'm running from the law."

"What did you do?" She knew he had it planned out to the last detail.

"Stabbed a man in Corpus Christi."

"Why am I with you?"

"You're my wife. Why would I leave you behind?"

"Usually people running from the law don't take family members with them."

"You do if you're afraid the police might arrest them since they were at the scene and might have information about the crime."

She nodded. "Okay. That should work, but who'll be that interested?"

"Once we're there, I'll have to buy a gun and we'll need a place to stay. They'll ask questions."

"Oh."

"But *we* won't ask questions."

"How will we find out anything?"

"I'll handle the conversations. You just stay close to me. Mortez is well-known in the town and we don't want to throw up any red flags."

She glanced at her watch. "I better put the clothes in the dryer. I'll be right back."

It didn't take her long and soon she slid back into her side of the booth. Levi was on the phone. She could hear his side of the conversation.

"Do you have my location?…Okay. We'll be crossing the border about two. I'll let you know if we run into any trouble....Today should go fine. It's tomorrow I'm worried about. I'll stay in touch....No." Levi chuckled. "I'm not interested in a trip to Monterey. I got all I can handle right here. Thanks, friend."

"Who was that?" she asked.

Levi slipped his phone into his pocket. "Turner Pettibone. His family has a charter service and flies people everywhere. He flies into Mexican resorts and I thought he might come in handy if we run into trouble and can't get back to the truck. It's just a backup plan."

"You mean he'll fly in with a helicopter or something to pick us up?"

"Yes."

"Is that legal?"

"I'm not worried about legal. I'm worried about surviving, but I do have to have my phone for that plan to work. That reminds me, I need to buy a map of Mexico. I have a GPS on my phone, but I want to back it up with something analog."

He really had thought of everything. She felt better, but this was only the beginning.

She changed into the old clothes in the bathroom at the Laundromat. The sneakers were much more comfortable than the boots. She didn't argue about wearing them. She had faith in Levi's instincts.

They spent time at the car lot while they changed trucks and filled out paperwork. Levi wanted to take make sure the 1990 Chevy truck would get them there. After that, they found a coffee shop that allowed computer usage. Levi filled out the forms online to cross the border and paid a fee to use the printer to make copies. They were set to go.

Levi went over again how careful they had to be and soon they were on U.S. 77 and headed for the Veteran's Bridge. Her nerves were jiggy, but that was understandable.

Cars and trucks waited in line to pay the toll to cross the bridge into Mexico and they followed them through, paying when it was their turn. Once they drove over the bridge, the Immigration and Custom checkpoints were easy to spot.

Levi pulled into a parking area and walked to a small bank branch to get pesos if they needed them. He said American cash was welcome, even preferred, by many Mexicans, but he wanted to be prepared. Finally, they left Immigration for Matamoras.

The highway was much the same as in Brownsville. Almost immediately the landscape changed to narrow streets and conjested traffic. In a market area vendors were selling Mexican crafts, trinkets, clay pots and everything imaginable. Tourists milled around. Levi drove slow so as not to hit anyone.

Houses were jammed together in the brightest colors she'd ever seen—pink to blue to yellow to purple and red and everything in between. With the small streets and so many people out and about, she had a claustrophobic feeling.

Most of the buildings were run-down and some were boarded up. People were dressed much as they were, and small children ran around in nothing but shorts. Stray dogs were everywhere. Levi pulled into a store parking area, looking at his phone.

"Mortez's home is north of here."

"We're going there now?"

He glanced at her. "I just want to get a feel for the place."

They drove through a residential area of more small, colorful concrete houses. As they turned a corner, the Mortez house rose up out of nowhere. It looked exactly like the picture, except much scarier. It was set on more land than the other houses and the stone fence really made it stand out. A guard stood sentry at the gate.

"What are they hiding in there?"

"Drugs," he replied. "Drugs people kill for. Some of those boarded-up buildings we saw are drug houses. Mortez probably supplies them."

"I wonder if Daniel is there?"

"Tomorrow we'll cautiously watch the house, but we don't want anyone catching us at it. Before I came to your apartment yesterday, I blew up a photo of the security cameras and was able to identify the manufacturer. If I can get close enough, I might be able to turn them off with my phone."

"Really? Do you ever get arrested for this kind of stuff?"

"Nah." His lips curved into a smile and her heart knocked against her ribs. "I'm sneaky. Now—" he looked over his shoulder "—we better find a place to spend the night."

"I saw a hotel when we crossed the border, and there's a Holiday Inn here, too. I was planning to stay there."

He turned the truck around. "We're not staying at a Holiday Inn. That will blow our down-on-our-luck story. It has to be someplace seedy."

"Oh, God. Did I ever tell you I hate cockroaches?"

"Just think of them as pets that need love, too."

She made a face at him and thought how handsome he was when he let down his guard. The five-o'clock-shadow thingy gave him a Blake Shelton look. His brown hair had a slight curl to it and it was longer than she'd ever seen it. It curled against his neck, giving him a roguish appeal.

He drove into an older, busy part of the city. Mexicans were everywhere trying to sell goods to anyone who would stop. A few bars or cafés had open patios where customers drank and talked loudly. Some of the patrons were a little frightening with their unkempt appearances and somber expressions. On every corner something was happening.

Levi parked the truck. "I'm going to do a little listening. Keep the doors locked." He reached for the old hat he'd bought and settled it on his head. "What do you think?"

"You'll fit right in. Do you speak any Spanish?"

"What I learned from you."

"I didn't teach you any Spanish."

"Sure you did. Remember all the times you cursed at me in Spanish?"

"I did not curse at you."

"How about the times when I was in a hurry to get to work and left the towel on the bathroom floor? The little vein on your forehead would almost burst and a few choice words would fly out of your mouth."

"How hard is it to pick up a towel?"

He pointed to her forehead. "That vein is starting to work."

"Shut up. I did not curse that much."

"If you say so." He opened his door. "I know enough Spanish to get by." He got out and waited for her to lock the door before walking down the street.

Bastardo was on the tip of her tongue, but she wouldn't say it. Maybe because she remembered those little scenes always ended with them making love on the bathroom floor. Then he would rush off and she'd put the towel in the hamper. At that point it didn't matter anymore. Until the next time.

Down the street she saw Levi talking to a group of men. The Mexicans gestured with their hands. Levi seemed to be listening, but soon walked off. A guy lounging in a doorway shouted to him and Levi stopped to converse with him.

Out of the corner of her eyes she saw two men come out of a bar. The sign read El Cantina. They had tats and wore bandannas and reminded her of gangbangers she'd prosecuted many times. One chattered on his cell and the other puffed on a dark-looking cigarette. They walked by the truck and the one with the cigarette paused and glanced at her. Goose bumps popped up on her arms and she was glad when he moved on.

Levi strolled to the truck and got in. She let out a long breath. She hadn't even realized she was holding it.

"What's wrong?"

She glanced out the back window. "Those guys give me the creeps. One of them was staring at me."

"We don't need to draw attention to ourselves."

"*He* was staring at *me*," she reminded him.

He lifted an eyebrow. "And you were going to come here alone."

"I know. It was crazy. I just want to locate Daniel and get out of here. Did you find out anything?"

"The guy in the doorway was helpful. I told him my made-up story and that I needed a gun. He said he could get me one." He pointed down the street. "We'll check into that fleabag hotel and he'll bring it there."

"Are you sure that's a hotel?" The dirty yellow two-story building had rusty bars over the windows. Two other buildings were crammed up next to it.

"Yep. He said there's parking in the back and it's cheap." Levi drove around to the rear. A strange odor greeted her when they entered. She could swear it was marijuana mixed with dust, sweat and mildew.

A portly man in a sweaty T-shirt, chewing on a cigar, signed them in, or if one could call it that. Levi gave him some money and he pointed to a door down the hall.

The room was small with a concrete floor and barely big enough to hold a full bed. The one window had a broken pull-down shade hanging lopsided over it. Nothing else was in the room, except maybe a family of cockroaches.

"Where's the bath?" she asked.

"It's down the hall. It's communal."

"Are you kidding me?"

He gave her a dark look. "Just remember the reason you're here."

She made a face and sat on the bed to test it. "Firm and springy." Pulling back the thin bedspread, she added, "The sheets look clean, but the color is questionable."

"It'll have to do." He set his backpack on the floor.

She still had her bag over her shoulder and eased it to the bed. "What do we do now?"

"Wait for the guy to deliver the gun."

She removed her sneakers and scooted up against the headboard. "I guess we wait, then."

He retrieved his iPad from his backpack and immediately went to work.

"What are you doing?"

"Reading more about the Mortez security cameras. They're digital and hooked up to a TV screen. I just wanted to jumble it up to confuse it long enough to get into the place."

"So you're planning on going in?"

"I'll see what tomorrow brings, but I don't plan on staying in this place very long."

"I'm in agreement with that."

A light knock sounded on the door and Levi got up to answer it. He stepped out into the hall and she quickly put her shoes on just in case. Levi came back in with a small handgun. He stowed it in the backpack.

"Let's get something to eat and then we'll turn in early."

They ate at one of the outdoor patios, a mariachi band playing in the background. Large Christmas lights hung from the rafters and were the only lights. The place was cozy and could even be romantic if…

It was best not to go there. She placed her bag at her feet because Levi said it wasn't safe to leave their things in the room. He ordered an El Grande plate, which had a little bit of everything and was actually a lot of food. She ordered enchiladas and guacamole and he had a beer and she had a glass of sangria. The food was delicious. Since she hadn't eaten much lunch, she was hungry and even ate a tostada off Levi's plate, which drew a scowl from him.

They walked back to the room in darkness. People milled everywhere, laughing, talking and drinking. Levi seemed to have an eye on everyone, watching for anything out of place.

In the room, she asked, "Where's the bathroom?"

"Down the hall. It'll have *Señoritas* on it. I'll leave the door cracked in case you run into problems."

She took her bag and went down the hall and found the door. No one was around, but she tapped, anyway. When no one responded, she went inside and caught her breath. The smell of urine hit her in the face like a baby's diaper. She held her sleeve over her nose, trying to block the smell. Cockroaches swarmed around the drain in the shower. She'd intended to take a quick one but immediately changed her mind and hurried back to the room.

Levi looked up from his iPad. "That was fast."

"Don't ask. I'm not bathing until I get back to Texas and I'm sleeping in my clothes."

"That bad, huh?"

"You wouldn't believe it. I used the toilet and that's it." She removed her sneakers and pulled the sheet back. "I probably won't sleep but I'll give it a try."

Levi laid his iPad on the bed. "I'll be right back."

Myra stared at the shade. People could look right in. She got up and used the string to tie it a little higher so it covered the window. The thing was literally covered with roach droppings. She did her best to put that out of her mind and went back to the bed.

As she crawled into bed, she thought how odd it was that neither she nor Levi objected to them sleeping together in the small bed. For her, it would be difficult sharing a bed with him again. Old memories would play the devil with her mind. For Levi, it didn't seem to matter. He was truly over her. She should be happy about that, so why wasn't she?

As LEVI WENT back to the room, he heard voices in the lobby. He was sure he heard the word *gringo*. He listened closely but the voices were too low for him to understand. He'd have to be on guard.

Myra frowned when he entered the room.

"Now what's wrong?"

"It's hot in here. There's no air-conditioning."

"Maybe we can open the window."

"It has no screen on it."

"Well, then, we'll have to tough it out." He retrieved the gun from the backpack and checked it to make sure the firing pin hadn't been removed, then slid it beneath his pillow.

"Why'd you do that?"

He sat down on the bed to take off his shoes. "There are some shady characters in the lobby and I want to be ready in case they think we have money and plan to rob us."

"Oh."

Levi reached to pull the string to turn off the light. There was fear in her voice and he wanted to reassure her, but there was no reassurance in this situation. They'd just handle what came at them. He lay back on the bedspread and closed his eyes.

Myra kept tossing and turning. "I can't sleep in this shirt and socks. It's too hot."

"Take them off, then."

She climbed out of bed and was doing something. The room was in total darkness and he couldn't see a thing, except for a sliver of light that shone through from the sides of the shades. He'd noticed when he entered the room that she'd tied up the shade. He'd meant to do that earlier, but of course Myra had taken care of it. She was the most self-sufficient woman he knew.

She climbed back in the bed. "I feel a little better."

"Get some rest."

"I don't think I can sleep in here."

"Just relax."

They were quiet, but noises from outside could be heard clearly. He wasn't going to sleep, either. He never slept much on a job. So maybe it was time to talk. "Can I ask you a question?"

"I suppose."

"Why are you willing to risk your life for Natalie?"

"I don't know. She just seems so sad at times. She's an only child and I can identify with that. We talked a lot about her relationship with Stu. After her mother's death, she came to Houston to be near him, to spend time with him. But things were tense because of all the years Stu hadn't been there for her. Since Stu has been so good to me, I tried to show her he really wasn't a bad person—he was just committed to his job."

He clamped his jaw shut to keep from responding.

"They grew much closer and then Marco came into her life. Stu disliked him on sight and Nat was determined to see him. A typical I'll-show-you relationship.

And yes, I guess you're right. She's a lot like Jessie. She's just a very good friend and I know if she wakes up and Daniel's not there, she won't make it."

"Have you prepared yourself for the fact she might not make it, anyway?"

The answer was a long time coming. "I'd rather not think about that."

"C'mon, counselor, you deal in facts."

"Nat was so excited when she found out she was pregnant. Marco was furious, said she tricked him and he didn't come around for a while. Natalie was upset, but she said she would have someone to love who would never leave her."

And there the past was between them once again. He refused to give in to those feelings.

"Of course, Marco came back and they made plans for a future together. He wasn't there when Daniel was born. I was the first one to hold him. I was used to holding Jessie's boys and it was very natural. Daniel and I made a connection. I guess that's another reason. A baby should be with his mother."

Loud noises erupted in the hall and Levi jumped out of bed with the gun in his hand. There was singing and laughing, and then the voices went into the room next door.

He shoved the gun back under the pillow and lay down. "Just some hotel guests."

"Do you think I'm crazy?" she asked.

"No. You're just very passionate about your friends."

The music next door grew louder. A headboard bumped against their wall and moans and groans followed.

Myra sat up. "You've got to be kidding me. Are you sure this isn't a whorehouse?"

"I'm not sure of anything."

The loud lovemaking continued and Levi started to laugh.

"It's not funny, Levi."

"Oh, I think it is. If someone had told me a week ago that I would be in a roach-infested motel in Mexico with Myra Delgado and listening to someone else making love, I would have laughed my head off."

She flipped onto her side. "I'm going to sleep, and do not touch me."

"I don't plan to."

The raucous noises died down about midnight and Levi drifted into a light sleep. He awoke when Myra curled into him like she had so many times when they were together. A delicate scent reached him. That damn lotion again. He loved to lie in bed and watch her rub it on her legs and arms. But that was in the past and had nothing to do with now. Today, they weren't even friends.

He eased away from her and got up, but his eyes strayed back to her smooth skin and dark hair. Memories spun like a loom weaving together vivid, colorful pictures of their passionate relationship. He drew a deep breath, shoving them away.

A drizzle of daylight peeped around the edge of the shade. He slipped on his boots and laced them. As he stood, he stared at Myra's dark hair spread across the pillow. She was now on his side of the bed.

Maybe some people were unforgettable. He should have listened when she wanted to talk about the past.

The only way to forget her was to get rid of the load of anger he carried around his heart. He had to forgive to really move on.

Before they parted for good this time, he had to do that. He had to forgive Myra for breaking his heart.

CHAPTER SEVEN

WHEN MYRA AWOKE, she was alone in the bed and panic gripped her. But she soon relaxed. Levi wouldn't leave her here. She quickly slipped on her shirt and sneakers. Two roaches scurried up the wall and she picked up her bag, watching them the whole time. There was a slight crack in the wall and they disappeared inside. She shivered.

After brushing her hair, she whipped it into a ponytail. Levi came back in and her heart fluttered at the sight of him. That wasn't good. Her heart was getting involved again. But he looked so sexy with his growing beard.

"You're up," he said. "I brought you a towel and a washcloth in case you want to brave the bathroom."

She took the towel, which may have been white at one time but looked as if it had been washed many times. At least it looked clean. "I'll brush my teeth and wash my face and probably hold my breath the whole time."

He chuckled.

When she returned, he was zipping his backpack. "Ready for breakfast?"

"Yes." She grabbed her bag and they walked out the door to the lobby. "It seems very quiet this morning. The amorous couple must be sleeping."

He held the door for her. "One can only hope."

They found a café serving breakfast and they ordered huevos rancheros and coffee. She doctored hers with milk and sugar and it was still bitter. But it was coffee.

"I paid for another night," he said before sipping his. "It'll be a good place to leave the truck if we have to."

"What's the plan?"

"Check out the Mortez house and see who goes in and when."

After breakfast, they drove toward the house. The streets were so narrow Levi half parked in a driveway behind another car. The road to the house was empty and there didn't seem to be any activity. They couldn't even see the guard.

For three days, they repeated the ritual and nothing out of the ordinary happened at the house, except big trucks went into the compound a couple of times. And a Mexican woman drove to a grocery store and returned quickly.

Myra grew frustrated with the situation. Not to mention she hadn't had a shower in days. Levi's beard had filled out and he was an imposing figure, even to her. They continued to rent the hotel room and maintained an amicable truce, but she was more aware of Levi than she'd ever been.

After breakfast on the fourth day, Levi drove to the house once again.

"Do you think we're wasting our time?" She glanced at him.

"Probably," he admitted. "If nothing happens by the end of the week, I'll have to rethink my plan. There has to be a way to find out if the baby is in there."

Suddenly, the gate opened and a black van came out. Levi followed slowly behind it. The van went into town and parked. Two men got out and spoke to the people filling the streets.

"What do you think is going on?" she asked.

Levi parked some distance away. "I'll check it out."

"I'm going with you."

On the way, Levi stopped in front of a lady who was selling handmade scarves. "Put this on your head so you'll look like everyone else." He bought a dark blue bandanna from another lady and tied it around his head.

Myra fitted the scarf over her head and they walked closer to the little crowd that was gathering. One man spoke rapidly in Spanish and gestured with his hands.

"Can you make out what he's saying?" Levi asked.

"Something about the big hacienda needing maids. If anyone wants to apply, they're to meet back here in an hour and he'll pick two to take to the house. He said to bring a bag and be prepared to stay. This is good, Levi. An easy way in."

"I'm not too sure about this. If Marco is there, he'll recognize you."

"I'm sure he's not doing the hiring. I can scope out the place."

He took her arm and led her away from the crowd and back to the truck. "We have to talk about this," he said as they got in.

"What's to talk about? We've been waiting for this."

"It seems too easy. Once you're in the house, how can you leave with the baby? Marco isn't going to let you just walk out the door. And we don't even know if the baby is in there."

"So what do we do?"

"It's certainly an easy way in. But it may be hours before I can find a way into the compound, too. This whole scenario bothers me."

"Do you have a better plan?"

"No." He turned to face her. "I'll likely have to wait until night so there's less chance of being spotted. Can you stall that long?"

"I hope so. I'm sure someone besides Marco will interview the new maids. There's no reason they'd take my phone from me and I can call or text you once I figure out the layout."

He gave a derisive laugh. "If only it was that simple. Listen to me. This is dangerous. This is not Texas where you can dial 9-1-1. You can call the Mexican police but good luck with that. Mortez has a lot of power in this town."

"What are you saying?"

"I'm saying we have to be very, very careful."

She took a long breath and knew this was the most dangerous thing she'd ever attempted in her life. She could turn around now and go home to Texas and leave Daniel with his father. Clarence had said she couldn't stand it when the bad guys won. He was right. She couldn't. Marco deserved to be in jail. A sane person would go home. She looked at Levi, whose eyes were boring into her.

"It's your call, counselor."

"Do you think you can get in undetected?"

He shrugged. "I'm almost certain, but getting out is another question."

She stared into his eyes. "So we have to trust each other."

"Now that's a hell of a mouthful."

Myra wiped her hands down her jeans. After coming here, she couldn't make herself leave. She kept seeing Natalie's bruised face. She'd put men in prison for lesser crimes.

"Okay." She blew out a breath. "Let's do it. I trust you to get us out."

He looked at her as if he was seeing her for the first time since they'd met again. "I could say something scathing here, but I'm not."

"Thank you." She swallowed at the heat in his eyes. "Uh, this may be a moot point since they may not choose me."

"Oh, Myra, you really need to look in a mirror."

"This isn't about looks, Levi. And I think I'm beginning to smell."

He shook his head with a glint in his eyes. "Have you noticed that most of the women here look tired and beaten down? They'll definitely pick someone young and fresh, even if she smells a little."

"Do I?" She raised her arm and sniffed.

"Oh, God. Focus, Myra." He started the truck. "It was your choice not to shower. You do know once you turn on the water, the roaches scurry down the drain?"

"Eww!" She made a face.

"Get a grip. You don't smell. Let's go back to the hotel and discuss the details, and I don't mean your fear of roaches."

Easy for him, she thought, but if they were still there tonight she might brave it. She wondered what he would say if she asked him to go to the bathroom with her. The urge to laugh out loud was strong. She wouldn't put him in that position.

In the room, they went over and over their options. "You'll have to have another identity other than Myra Delgado. Marco will recognize the name."

"Okay. I'll be Maria Gamez."

"People have already seen us together so we'll have to stick to my story. Hopefully, they won't ask questions, but you have to be prepared."

"So I should go by your last name?"

"I don't think that'll be necessary. You can just say we're not legally married, just living together, but we don't want to alert anyone by telling different lies." He reached into his backpack and pulled out a cell phone. "This is small enough that you can slip it in your sock or your bra just in case they take yours. Or you can tape it to your ankle. It's a way to stay in touch. Which would you prefer?"

"Ankle."

When he pulled tape out of his backpack, she knew he was prepared for anything. It took a moment to get the small phone situated on the back of her calf above her ankle, but she was ready.

"Let me have your ID and passport. We don't want them to have a way to identify you. Once you get in, I can track you at all times. Be sure to turn off your phone so it won't buzz. If you're feeling uncomfortable, turn it on so I can hear what's being said. As soon as it gets dark, I'll make my way to the house and do my best to turn off the security system. Once I'm in, I can locate you and, with a little luck, we can find Daniel and get out. If we can leave without being detected, we can make it to the border. But if they're on our tail, we're going to have a big problem. I'd better talk to Turner."

While he was on the phone, she took everything out of her bag that could identify her and placed it on the bed. Her hands shook and she realized this was the beginning of a harrowing day.

"One more thing," Levi added as he ended his call to Turner. "If you find out Daniel isn't there, make an excuse like you're ill or don't want the job and get out of there."

Within minutes, they were ready to go. Levi still had the bandanna tied around his head and looked dark and dangerous. Thank God he was on her side.

"Let's go," he said, but she hesitated.

"What's wrong?"

She shrugged. "I'm very grateful for what you're doing."

"I don't want your gratitude, Myra. And we have a long way to go before this is over."

"I know, but—" She stepped forward and wrapped her arms around his neck and pressed into his hard frame. She expected him to push her away, but he didn't. His arms held her tight. His body was strong and muscled and hers reacted to that. It always had. They had this powerful sexual connection. She kissed the warmth of his neck, breathing in the masculine scent of him. Still, he didn't push her away.

His beard was rough against her skin and it only egged her on. She touched his lips gently, but the fire was lit and she knew there was never a stopping point for them. He groaned, deepening the kiss with a wild, uncontrollable desire. She floated with the moment, giving, taking, enjoying the taste and feel of him again.

Finally, he tore his lips away and took a deep breath. "I…"

"It's okay, Levi." Her voice was hoarse with raw emotions churning inside her. "I just had to do that. Sorry if it upsets you."

He seemed at a loss for words, but quickly regained his composure. Picking up his backpack, he said, "We better go. The hour is almost up."

They drove in silence to where the van was parked. Several Mexican women stood waiting. The men were already talking to them.

"I better go. I don't want to be left out."

Before she could get out of the truck, he grabbed her arm. "Be careful and—"

"What?"

His eyes were dark and it was obvious he was troubled about the kiss. She shouldn't have done that, but she had to reexperience his touch to sustain her through the dangerous ordeal ahead.

"I'm…I'm not angry with you anymore."

Her body sagged with relief. It was exactly what she needed to hear and he knew that. She climbed out and ran to the women. She glanced back to see Levi leaning against the truck, watching, making sure she was safe. But how long could he do that? Soon she would be on her own. Now she had to put Levi out of her mind and concentrate on the job ahead of her.

The man was asking questions in rapid-fire Spanish. He pulled a woman aside and waved others away. Myra waited patiently in line.

When it was her turn, the Mexican looked her up and down. "What's your name?" he asked in Spanish.

She stood straight and looked him in the eye. "Maria Gamez."

"Can you take care of a baby?"

A baby? Daniel? Were they looking for someone to care for him? Myra almost cried out in relief, but she couldn't give herself away. She swallowed and shrugged.

"Sure, of course. What woman doesn't know how to care for a kid?"

"Do you have children?"

"No."

He pointed to the side and she joined the other woman standing there. Actually, she looked more like a girl not more than sixteen. And she seemed frightened to death. Maybe that expression was on her own face, too.

With two women left to question, the men stepped aside to talk. Myra listened closely and it was hard because they talked so fast.

"He said someone young and pretty. He doesn't want an old hag."

"Take the one in the shirt. She'll do. Anyone can take care of a baby."

"I like the young one."

Myra frowned. Was she the old one? Okay, not the time to take offense.

"We'll take both. Gloria needs help in the kitchen and she'll be around for our entertainment, too." The man laughed and Myra shivered.

One of the men held the door open and gestured for

them to get inside. Before she crawled in, she glanced at Levi. He took a step toward her and then stopped. In that moment, she wanted to run to him, but she was in too far and she had to see it through.

"I'm José and this is Lupe. We'll be seeing a lot of each other." They laughed again as if it was a private joke. *Jerks*.

The van rolled toward the big house. When they reached the gate, it opened and Lupe drove around to the back. There were several buildings, and Myra noticed men in combat boots and cargo pants. They carried guns. She didn't have time to look too closely, as they were ushered inside a large kitchen with Mexican tile on the floor.

A short, plump Mexican woman met them. The same woman she and Levi had noticed going to the grocery store. A large apron covered her dress. "What took so long?" she demanded in Spanish, and Myra had the feeling she was head of the household.

"We had to talk to the women," José said, and grinned. "Everyone wants a job."

Gloria eyed Myra and then the young girl. "Why you bring someone so young?"

Lupe snorted. "Maybe I bring her for me."

"You sick bastard. Señora Ava will hear about this. She will not like it. Señor César will hear about it then, and you may not have a job tomorrow."

"Shut up, Gloria. You're just a lot of hot air and you better not get us fired."

Gloria pointed to the door. "Out, bastards.

"Come with me," Gloria said to Myra and the girl, and they followed her to some stairs off the kitchen.

The wood in the house was dark and tile covered the stairs, as well.

As they went up, the young girl whispered to her, "What are they going to do to me?" She spoke in Spanish.

"Stay close to Gloria and everything will be fine. She's our ally. What's your name?"

"Calida. I just want a job."

They entered a long hall. "These are the servants' quarters," Gloria told them.

As they turned a corner, they heard a baby crying. "Bitch," Gloria said under her breath. She opened a door into a nursery and there sat Daniel in the corner of a baby bed, wailing loudly.

Myra's heart lifted with happiness. He was alive and unhurt, except he was missing his mommy. She had to force herself not to run to him.

"Lupita!" Gloria shouted.

A woman maybe in her thirties ran into the room. "What?"

"Why is baby crying? Señor Marco will be much upset."

Lupita waved a hand. "Baby cries all the time. I can't make him be quiet." They started speaking so rapidly in Spanish Myra struggled to keep up.

She couldn't stand the pitiful wails any longer. "I'll try to comfort him," she said in Spanish, and walked to the bed. Daniel quickly crawled to the rail and pulled himself up, holding his arms out for her. Tears welled in her eyes, but she didn't react. She only lifted him from the bed and patted his back. "There, there, little one." He rested his head on her shoulder and the cries stopped.

Gloria pointed to them. "See, that's how to take care of a baby. You're an idiot. Go back to the kitchen."

Lupita hurried away.

"You will take care of the baby," Gloria announced. "What's your name?"

"Maria."

Gloria nodded. "Good. Easy to remember. Everything you need is in here and you will sleep on the cot. You are not allowed in the main part of the house. If you need anything, you come to the kitchen. Señor Marco will call when he wants to see his son and I will take the baby to him. Do you understand?"

"Sí." That was a load off her mind. Marco would not be bursting into the nursery, but she had to wonder why the nursery was in the servants' quarters and not the main house. It could work to her advantage, though. It would be much easier to slip out with the baby than having to go through the main house.

Gloria turned to Calida. "You will work with me in the kitchen and I will keep those bastards away from you."

"Thank you." Calida's relief was evident. Myra felt better, too.

"Gloria." Someone was calling the housekeeper, and from the nervous look on the woman's face, she knew it was someone important. Gloria hurried to the door, but it opened before she reached it and a blonde middle-aged woman stood there. Her hair was cut in a bob and diamonds hung from her ears and around her neck. A slim-fitting dress showed off her figure. Myra couldn't imagine who she was.

"Señora Ava, there's no need for you to come up here."

Marco's mother. Myra stared at the woman and the thing that struck her the most was that his mother was white. Marco had black hair and eyes and she would have never suspected that. She was sure Natalie hadn't, either.

"I heard the baby crying from my quarters. You know how this upsets Bonita. This has to stop."

"Sí, señora. I just hired this woman and the baby has taken to her. She will make sure he does not disturb Señora Bonita anymore."

The woman stepped close to Myra. "Take care of my grandson."

"Sí." Myra nodded her head, averting her eyes and bouncing Daniel in her arms.

"I will take care of everything, *señora.* Do not worry," Gloria tried to reassure her.

"See that you do. Bonita's mental state is very delicate." The woman walked out of the room. Myra wondered why she didn't hold her grandson or even attempt to touch him. A lot of questions raged in her head, but she had to focus on getting Daniel out of the house.

"Who is Bonita?"

Gloria turned on her. "Do not ask questions!"

From the woman's tone of voice, she knew she'd made a big mistake. She should have kept her mouth shut and just observed.

"Sí."

As soon as Gloria and Calida left, she sat on the

floor and reached for her phone in her bag while juggling Daniel on her lap. He smiled at her and her heart melted. "Don't worry, little one. I'm taking you home to your mommy."

She had to let Levi know she'd made it inside the house and that she'd found Daniel.

LEVI PACED IN the hotel room, waiting for a message from Myra. His nerves were wound tight and he tried to relax. It would take time for her to get settled in, so he just had to be patient. Under the circumstances, though, it was difficult.

He sat on the bed and studied the Mortez security system on his iPad. This he could work on and maybe not think so much about what was happening at the big house. But his thoughts were troubled. Not only because Myra was in a dangerous situation, but because of what had happened earlier. He'd kissed her back without one thought of Valerie. That bothered him. He wasn't the cheating kind. He believed in love and forever. He wasn't sure why, since his parents had had such an awful marriage. Maybe it had to do with his grandparents. They taught him about life, love, honor, respect and about never giving up and being true to oneself.

Kissing Myra felt right and he couldn't explain that feeling to himself. She had a wildness about her that he craved and he could never seem to get enough. He wanted to kiss her. It was that simple, yet so complicated. There was no future for them because he couldn't trust her. Once they were out of this place, his priorities would resurface and those old feelings would disappear.

But at this moment, she was his number-one priority.

If anything happened to her, he wouldn't be able to get over it. That was like a slap of reality in the face. He'd told her he wasn't angry at her anymore and he meant it. For someone who knew what he wanted out of life, he was feeling as wishy-washy as a fourteen-year-old.

He put the computer back in his backpack and headed down to a small cantina. Listening to the locals might prove beneficial. He sat at the table and ordered bottled water. There were very few patrons this time of the day. The lunch crowd was over. The waiter looked to be a man in his fifties and Levi thought he'd try his luck at getting some answers.

The waiter set the bottled water on the table. "Do you know of any work around here?"

"No, *señor*."

"Earlier there was a black van down the street and the men were looking for maids. They were from the big house. Do they hire men, too?"

"I don't know, *señor*." The man spoke English and was visibly nervous now, wringing his hands.

"They hired my wife as a maid and it would be good if I could get a job there, too."

The man's brown skin paled.

"What is it?"

"The women who go there, they don't come back." The man looked around to make sure no one was listening. "I got to go."

"What do you mean?"

The man shook his head.

Levi took some bills out of his pocket and laid them by the water bottle. The waiter wiped the table and scooped up the money into the cloth.

"Bad *hombres* live there."

"What do you mean, the women don't come back?"

The man leaned close and whispered, "A girl from a nearby village went to work there and a month later her body was dumped on a dirt road. She'd been beaten and raped. About two months ago, it happened again. The young girl was only sixteen. Another one, her family is still looking for her. Women don't come back alive from that place. Please be very careful."

Son of a bitch. Levi was on his feet. "Thank you."

"*Señor,* evil lives there. Stay away."

Levi slipped on the backpack and hurried down the street. Staying away wasn't an option. He had to get Myra out of there and he had to do it in daylight. He wasn't leaving her in danger one more minute.

As he rushed into the hotel, his phone beeped and he yanked it out of his pocket. He had a message from Myra. Thank God! His hand touched the screen. The moment he did that he knew he wasn't over Myra. He still loved her. He could deny it all he wanted, but he'd only be fooling himself.

CHAPTER EIGHT

LEVI READ THE message while walking into the room.
I'm in. Daniel is here. They hired me to take care of him.
He seems to remember me. I'll text later.

He let out a long breath. She was okay. For now. And
the boy was there. Now Levi just had to figure out a
way to get them out.

He texted her back. Call as soon as you can.

While he waited, he downloaded her location onto
his iPad. She was on the south side of the house at
the back, and nowhere near the gate. That could be a
problem.

His cell buzzed and he picked it up. "Levi, I can't
talk long." She was whispering.

"Are you okay?"

"Yes. It's a little scary, but I'm fine."

"I learned some information I want you to be aware
of. A waiter in the cantina said there are bad men there.
They beat and rape the women. Please be very careful."

"I've gotten that same feeling. There's a young girl
here in her teens and they have their eye on her. I'm
worried about her."

"Worry about yourself."

"I am."

"Have you learned anything?"

"I'm in the servants' quarters, in a nursery, which seems odd."

"I already have your location."

"I should've known that. I have orders to stay in my room and take care of the baby. His crying is upsetting someone named Bonita, who is obviously someone important here."

"I'll do some checking."

"Marco's mother came into the nursery and I was surprised to see she's white. Marco never mentioned that. I'm sure it doesn't make a difference. I'm just surprised."

"I'll check into that, too."

"Daniel is getting fussy. I better get off the phone."

"Myra, let me know if anything happens out of place. Stay away from the men."

"I plan to. Since I have orders not to leave this room, I won't have contact with anyone else."

"Don't let your guard down. As soon as it gets dark, I'll make my way to the house. Just stay alert."

"I will. I'm just worried about the young girl."

He sighed. "Myra, you can't help everybody. Your life is at stake here. These men are bad people. Just remember that."

"Okay."

"Stay in contact and…"

"What?"

"I'm glad the baby's okay."

That wasn't what he wanted to say. The words rose in his throat. Words he needed to say. Words that surprised him. Words he couldn't even voice in his head. He just wanted her safe and he had to make that happen.

As long as he had contact with her, everything would be okay. He had to keep telling himself that.

After an extensive search, he found information on Bonita Guzman. Her father was a well-known drug lord. She'd married Marco five years ago, rumor had it to solidify a drug empire. That was the reason Marco never introduced Natalie to his parents. And the reason the baby was in the servants' quarters. He had a wife—an important wife. The baby was upsetting to Bonita. He had to wonder what Marco's plans were concerning his son.

Ava Gilman Mortez hailed from Galveston and her family was in the yachting business. She was known for her charitable works in Mexico and Texas. She didn't quite fit in with the Mortez drug scene, but he didn't have time to dig further. It was getting late and he had to focus.

CALIDA BROUGHT A bottle and baby food for Daniel, and beans, rice and tortillas for Myra. Daniel bounced in her lap with glee at the sight of the bottle. She sat with him in a rocker to feed him.

"I don't like it here," Calida said.

"Just stay close to Gloria." The girl was very nervous and Myra didn't know what else to tell her. Myra's Spanish was rusty and she was trying to keep up.

"Can I sleep in here with you?" Calida asked.

Myra was taken aback by the request. She wanted to help her, but she didn't want to jeopardize them getting Daniel out. "There's only a cot in here and your room is right across the hall. If you need me, just holler and I'll come."

Calida wrung her hands. "Okay. I gotta get back."

Daniel was asleep in her arms after finishing his bottle, and she hadn't even fed him the baby food. He probably wouldn't have eaten it, anyway. Natalie bought a special brand for him.

She gently laid him in the baby bed and covered him with a blanket. At least the house was air-conditioned. Before she could take the bottle to the bathroom to rinse it out, the door burst open and a woman in a flowing silky black negligee stood there. Her long black hair hung down her back and all around her face. She had a wild-eyed expression that Myra had seen in drug addicts.

"Shut that baby up!" she screamed.

At the loud sound, Daniel raised his head with a wail. Myra ran to him and rubbed his back, as she'd seen Natalie do, and Daniel went back to sleep.

"I'm sorry if he disturbed you. He's sleeping now."

The woman grabbed her head as if she was in pain. "Why does he cry so much? He's taunting me." She pointed a finger at Myra. "That's what he's doing. He's taunting me. I will be pregnant soon. He doesn't have to taunt me. He's evil. He has to go."

Myra backed toward the crib, not sure what the woman would do.

Gloria came up behind the woman. "Señora Bonita, what are you doing here? Come, I take you back to your quarters."

"Why is he here, Gloria? I am Marco's wife. His *puta*'s baby should not be in my home."

"Sí, señora."

Ava joined the group. "Bonita, darling. You need your rest."

"I can't take it, Ava. Marco is flaunting his *puta*'s baby in my face. It makes me angry. I want to kill it. I want to kill Marco."

"Shh." Ava put an arm around Bonita. "In a few days we will go to the home in Florida. You'll love it there. We'll spend long hours on the beach sipping margaritas. We'll have a good time."

"I want that baby out of here," she snarled, and then in a pitiful voice, she asked, "Why can't I get pregnant?"

"Marco loves you. You have to be patient."

"Why does he need all these women? Why am I not enough?"

"That's just men and, Bonita, you really need to understand that. You're his wife and those other women don't mean a thing. No one will be able to take your place."

"Why did he have to bring the baby here? And why do you support him?"

"It's a delicate situation, but I promise you the child will not touch your life. We will send him away soon."

"I want to tell Papa, but he will kill Marco. I love Marco. I don't know why he has to hurt me so much."

"Shh. Everything will be fine." They walked off down the hall.

Gloria stared at Myra. "Stop gawking and get back to work. And make sure you keep that baby quiet."

"Sí."

Gloria snapped the door shut.

Myra carried the bottle, which was still clutched in

her hand, and went into the bathroom. Marco had a wife who was close to the edge and Myra knew who had driven her there. She was just surprised Marco hadn't gotten rid of her by now. There had to be a reason he hadn't. Bonita had said something about her papa. The two families were probably connected and probably by drugs and marriage.

She placed the bottle back on the tray Calida had brought in. What had Ava meant by sending Daniel away? Where would they send him? The obvious conclusion would be to his mother, but Myra knew that was not the answer.

Myra wasn't too concerned with what was going on in the house. In a few hours, she and Daniel would be out of here and the only place she wanted to see Marco Mortez was in the courtroom. She glanced at her watch. It was almost six. At least another two-hour wait.

Daniel sucked on his thumb while he slept. Natalie had broken him of the habit but now he was doing it again. The little guy was upset, too.

Hearing a noise, she went to the window and saw a big covered truck backed up to one of the buildings. Men were unloading something, but she couldn't make out what from her position.

Restless, she walked around and the time seemed to drag. She opened the door and heard male voices. She stepped out into the hallway to listen. The voices were close and she took a couple of steps to get nearer. They had to be in the big dining room she'd glimpsed off the kitchen.

"I'm tired of cleaning up your messes, Marco."

It had to be Marco and his father talking.

"What else was I supposed to do? That bitch demanded I marry her or I'd never see my son again. No woman tells me what to do."

"If Bonita's father finds out you have a child by another woman, he will bring holy hell down on the Mortez family. Do you understand that?"

There was no response.

"Your mother has arranged for her cousin in Galveston to take the boy. He will have a new name and have no connection to you and you will not see him. Is that clear?"

"No, it is not clear, Papa. He is my son and I will make arrangements for him. You cannot run my personal life."

A loud sound of skin slapping skin echoed. "You will not talk to me that way. I am your father and I demand your respect. You are the one who is jeopardizing everything we have worked for. Do you think you are my only son?"

A powerful silence followed.

"But you are the only son of my wife. There is a difference, Marco, and it is time you learn what that difference is. You do not bring your women friends' children into the family. Is that understood or would you like to be taken back to Texas? I can make that happen in a heartbeat."

"You would turn me in to the cops?"

"You are my flesh and blood and I love you, but I will not tolerate disrespect and disobedience."

"I'm sorry, Papa."

"We had a shipment come in today. Take care of it."

Myra hurried back to the nursery, grateful Daniel

was still sleeping. Poor baby was going to be shuffled off to someone else. How pitiful was that? Especially when he had a mother who loved him.

Natalie had demanded that Marco marry her. That's probably what had sent him into a rage. Myra wondered why she'd taken the baby into that situation. What a mess. And what a lovely family. She trembled. The sooner she got Daniel out of here, the better it would be for everyone.

She toyed with the idea of talking to Marco and offering to take Daniel back to his mother, no strings attached, no questions asked. But Marco didn't deserve any type of leniency. With Marco's short fuse, she might find herself in a shallow grave.

Daniel awoke and she played with him. He was so adorable with his big eyes and dark hair that curled slightly. Natalie was waiting for him to turn one before cutting it. The baby pointed to the door.

"No, sweetie. We can't go outside today."

When Natalie visited her apartment, Myra used to take Daniel out on the patio and let him look at the swimming pool and the people lounging around it. He liked the outdoors.

There weren't any toys in the room except for a ball and a small truck. What did they think he was going to play with? Children needed stimulation and it was probably the reason he was crying. That and he missed his mother.

The door flew open and Calida ran in. She was crying and shaking and her blouse was torn at the shoulder.

Myra put Daniel in his bed. "What's wrong?"

"Gloria sent me to take food to the men in the quarters," Calida fired off in rapid Spanish. "One of them grabbed me and pushed me to another one and he pushed me to another and they started touching me. I was so scared."

"What happened next?"

"Gloria showed up with a broom and started swatting them with it. She told me to run to the house. I want to go home. I don't like it here. Please let me stay in your room. I don't want to be by myself."

It was getting dark outside and she knew Levi would be contacting her soon. She had to be ready to go. What did she do about Calida? She just couldn't leave her here to be raped and possibly worse.

"Is Gloria looking for you?"

"I don't know and I don't care."

"Rest on my cot. I have some things to do." Calida curled up on the bed and Myra packed Daniel's diaper bag. She put the empty bottle in, but they would need a full bottle, if not more, to make the trip. "Calida, could you watch Daniel while I go downstairs to get him a bottle?"

Calida sat up. *"Sí."*

"Just play with him so he won't cry."

"I have eight younger brothers and sisters. I know about babies."

"Good." She turned toward the door. "I'll be back in a minute."

As she neared the bottom of the stairs, she could hear people in the kitchen. She crept closer to ensure Marco wasn't one of them. It was Gloria and Lupita.

"Señora Gloria, the baby needs more milk."

Gloria shot off words to Lupita. "She will bring it. Go back to the baby."

Myra started to say something about Calida, but realized that would only be stirring up another problem. In the little while she'd been here, she sensed that Gloria was in charge and she didn't like anyone contesting that. She went back up the stairs, intending to get Calida out of here, as well.

Lupita came up almost immediately and handed Myra a bottle. She eyed Calida on the bed, but didn't say anything. It didn't take Gloria long to come charging up to the bedroom.

"What are you doing in here? There's work to be done in the kitchen."

"I…don't like it here. The men are cruel."

"Then why did you volunteer to come? This isn't Disneyland. Now get downstairs before I lose my patience with you."

Before Calida could move, Ava entered the room again. The frown on her face did not bode well for Gloria. "What is that young girl doing here?" She motioned to Calida.

"Lupe and José brought her to work," Gloria replied.

"I saw from my window what was going on and I will not have it. I will not have a repeat of what happened two months ago. Get Roberto to take her back into town. Now!"

"Sí, señora."

The relief on Calida's face said it all as she followed Gloria from the room. She glanced back at Myra in farewell.

Ava stared at Myra. "Do your job and stay away from the men."

"Sí, señora."

Myra let out a long breath as Ava left. The woman was not a trophy wife. She wielded a little power of her own. Myra was grateful the young girl would not be brutalized.

She brought her focus back to Daniel. Everything was packed; she just had to wait for Levi. Her cell buzzed and she quickly clicked on. She had a message. On my way. Be ready.

She texted back. Ready.

She opened the door to look out. Everything was quiet. Evidently, everyone was in their quarters or having dinner away from the servants' area. There wasn't even any noise coming from the kitchen.

Since the weather was more warm than cool, she dressed Daniel accordingly with jeans and a T-shirt. She put socks and shoes on him and waited.

This was the worst part, but she knew she could depend on Levi. If anything went wrong, it would be on her end. She thought about Calida and hoped she was on her way home.

She paced. *Come on, Levi.*

LEVI PARKED THE truck as close to the Mortez house as he could without being detected. Slipping on his backpack, he started the trek to the entrance. Everything he had on, from the bandanna to his shoes, was dark so he wouldn't be noticed or picked up easily by cameras.

A spotlight shone at the gates and he stayed out of the light that illuminated the road. About twenty yards from the concrete wall, he dropped to his knees and crawled the rest of the way. Hugging the wall, he pulled out his phone and prayed that he could jumble up the security cameras.

He heard voices behind the wall. Men were still moving around the compound, so he sank to the ground and waited. As the darkness thickened, the noises ebbed. He got to his feet. It was time.

First he texted Myra. I'm here.

Poking in numbers, he held his breath, and nothing happened. The cameras were still running. Damn it! He tried again, hoping for some sort of miracle. Typing in a code, he said a silent prayer and clicked Enter. And the lights went out. Damn! He hadn't expected that. Somehow he'd tripped the breaker, but he'd take it. The light on the camera was out, too, so that meant the system was down. He inched along the wall until he reached the gate. Shouts could be heard inside. Taking a quick peek in the darkness, he couldn't see anybody at the gate. He scaled it in two seconds and was on the inside.

Men were running everywhere and shouting in Spanish. No one noticed him. He ran around to the back of the house. Women came out the back door and stood some distance away. He inched along the side of the house and slipped in the door before they saw him.

He texted Myra. Kitchen. Hurry.

In less than a minute, she was there holding a baby. He had the urge to hug her, but he didn't have time. They had to get out. Now! "Let's go."

As they turned toward the door, the lights came on and Mexicans with assault rifles stood there with the guns pointed at them. Levi had a gun in his hand, but he knew he was outnumbered. They were caught. Son of a bitch!

His gun was quickly jerked out of his hand. "Señor Marco," one of the men shouted, and a dark-haired man came in with a weapon in his hand. "We caught intruders."

Marco stared at Myra in disbelief. "You stupid bitch. You think you can come into my house and take my son?"

"Let me have him, Marco. Natalie needs him."

Myra had guts. Levi thought she'd be shaking in her sneakers, but she was confronting the bastard instead. He wasn't sure what was going to happen next and he had to be prepared. But it was the first time he wasn't prepared for the next move.

"That bitch will never have him."

"You won't, either, Marco. Your wife hates him, so why deprive him of a life with his mother?"

Marco pointed the gun at Myra's face, inches from his son's. Daniel's bottom lip trembled and Levi knew tears weren't far away. "You do not tell me what to do. No woman does."

Daniel let out a loud wail.

"Take him," Marco ordered one of the men.

"No." Myra backed away with the boy and there was nothing Levi could do.

"You defy me," Marco shouted. "I will kill you."

Levi stepped in front of him as he moved toward Myra and the gun was pointed in his face. "Who are you? Are you a cop?"

Levi shook his head. "Come on, man. Do the right thing for your son."

Marco jammed the butt of the rifle into Levi's gut and pain shot through him, but he refused to bend to this man.

Marco motioned to one of his lackeys, who then jerked the baby from Myra. She held on for dear life and Daniel's cries grew louder, but to no avail. The baby was whisked away.

"Now, fiery Myra, you and I will have some fun. You've always had the hots for me."

Myra burst out laughing, which wasn't the wisest thing she could have done.

Marco backhanded her. She flew backward into the cabinet and fell to the floor. Levi immediately jumped Marco and three men were on him in an instant, holding him down on the cold tile floor.

"Search them," Marco ordered.

"Get your hands off me," Myra screeched, kicking the heavyset man, who had his hands on her, in the shin.

Oh, God. She was going to get them killed sooner rather than later. A man with bad breath had a knee in Levi's back and another had the barrel of a gun pointed at his head. They took everything he had on him. He'd never felt so helpless in his life.

"Señor Marco." Another man entered the room. "Your father wants to see you immediately."

"Take them to the basement. I will deal with them later."

The man holding Levi let him up and he helped Myra to her feet. A red splotch the size of a man's hand marred Myra's face. He wanted to hurt Marco in the worst way. The Mexicans pushed them toward a door and they went down a set of long winding stairs.

They were shoved inside a dimly lit room. One of the men leered at Myra. "When Señor Marco is through with you, he will give you to us and we will enjoy your pleasure." His sickening cackle echoed long after the slam of the steel door.

"Are you okay?" Levi wrapped his arms around her and felt her tremble.

"I'm fine." She rubbed his chest and, even though sex was the last thing on his mind, her touch evoked a weakness in him. "How about you?"

He drew a deep breath. "Other than my stomach being slammed up against my back, I'm fine, too."

"I'd really be afraid if I didn't know you had a backup plan."

He stilled, and wasn't sure how to tell her.

"What?" She looked up at him.

"I don't have a backup plan. This basement or whatever this is wasn't on Steve's computer. I'm not prepared for this."

Her eyes grew big. "So…this is it?"

He looked around at the inky darkness, the only illumination coming from the single bulb at the head of the stairs. It was hard for him to admit defeat, but if this was a basement, the only way out was up the stairs and through the steel doors and past high-powered weapons. He'd failed to protect her and his stomach roiled at the reality of their situation. All he could do now was be honest and not sugarcoat their situation.

"We knew the risks when we started. There's a saying about fools rushing in where angels fear to tread. Well, that's us. Now we wait for our fate."

CHAPTER NINE

MYRA SANK TO the floor and buried her face in her hands. "I'm sorry I got you involved in this, Levi." A sense of doom settled over her and she wanted to cry, but she'd save all her tears for later—and later weighed heavily on her mind.

"Well, we can second-guess this to death, but instead of waiting for them to put a bullet in us, let's see what the hell is in this place."

She shivered. He disappeared into the shadowy darkness. "It looks like a lot of boxes and they're stacked to the ceiling. I haven't found the end yet. This place is huge."

To ease the horrible thoughts in her mind, she stood to join him and that's when she felt it.

"Levi," she shouted, and sat on the floor again to pull up her jeans.

"What?" He came running.

She ripped the phone off her ankle and winced. "Damn. I did that too fast."

"You still have the phone?" he asked, his voice excited. "I thought they took it."

"I kicked him when his hand went down my leg and he didn't try again. Oh, this is good, right?"

Levi sat beside her and yanked the tape from the phone. "Yes, if we can get a signal." He fiddled with it for a moment and then stood up and walked into the darkness. "Damn. Nothing. We're too far underground."

Myra sagged with disappointment. "That's it, then?"

"Looks like it." He slipped the phone into his pocket. "I'll keep checking from different areas." He tapped one of the boxes with his knuckles. "These boxes aren't cardboard. They're wood. That means something valuable like weapons are inside, and there are a hell of a lot of boxes in here."

"Marco and his father probably sell them to drug lords."

"My guess is they sell these weapons all over the world, including the Middle East." Levi looked up the stairs. "It doesn't make sense they'd haul these crates down those stairs and then up again. There has to be an easier way in here. I'll look around."

"I'm coming with you." She wasn't leaving Levi's side.

As Levi had said, the place was huge. They finally reached the end of the crates and went around them to find the other side. That's when they saw another set of stairs. A tiny bulb glowed at the top, revealing a pair of double doors.

Levi bounded up the stairs and tried the doors. "They're steel and locked tight. Damn!" He pulled out the phone. "I might get reception here, though.

"No. Nothing." Slowly, he came down and they sat on the bottom step.

"What do we do now?" she asked.

"There's not much we can do but wait." He took a deep breath in a defeated sort of way and she just wanted to reach out and touch him, but she'd gotten them into this mess and touching him wasn't going to make it right. She felt defeated, too.

"Did you learn anything while you were in the house?" he asked.

"I overheard a few snippets of conversation," she replied, willing to help any way she could. "Marco's father is upset with him for bringing Daniel into the family. If Bonita's father finds out, César is afraid of what he might do. At least, that's what César was telling Marco. He added if Marco didn't get his act together, he'd take him back to Texas and he'd have to sort out his dirty mess with the cops himself."

She tried to think of everything she'd heard. "The young girl who came with me was attacked when she took food to the men in the barracks. Evidently, Ava saw this from her window and became upset. She ordered Gloria to send the girl back to town because she didn't want a repeat of what happened two months ago. I'm guessing someone was raped or murdered and she didn't want to bring that attention to the compound again. The young girl couldn't be more than sixteen."

"It seems to be a pattern here. If we get out, we'll have to let Steve know, but I'm not sure what he can do about it."

"I'm just glad she's safe."

"Still trying to take care of everyone, Myra?" There was a note of censure in his voice.

"Maybe," she answered, trying not to get her feelings hurt. Because it really wasn't a time for hurt feelings. "Anyway, César and Ava are concerned about Bonita, Marco's wife. She came into the nursery and was rant-ing and raving about the baby being in the house and I could tell Ava was walking on eggshells around her. It seems Bonita is trying to get pregnant and can't, and she feels like the baby is taunting her. She seems a little unhinged. I got the impression Ava and César are trying to please Bonita's father more than Bonita. I'm sure it's drug-related or something. César did mention that a big shipment had come in and he needed Marco to take care of it."

"So Marco might be busy soothing his wife and his family and it might give us time to figure a way out of here. But this place looks secure."

"It's going to be a long night."

"Yeah." He stood up. "Let's find a place to get comfortable."

There weren't many places to get comfortable. They wound up sitting on the floor, leaning against the crates. Nothing was said for some time.

"Try to get some sleep," he suggested.

"That's not going to happen. My eyes are wide open and my nerves feel like Brillo pads, rough and caustic." She was restless and got to her feet, needing to move, needing to do something to bridge this emotional gap between them. "You must really hate me now."

He raised his knees and rested his forearms on them. "I've tried hating you for years and thought I had accomplished that, but seeing you again, I realize it had nothing to do with hate and everything to do with hurt pride."

She sank down by him again, the darkness enclosing them in their own private cocoon. "I'm sorry I hurt you and I've tried so many times to explain my feelings, but…"

"I'm listening now."

Her heart raced. She hadn't expected this. She struggled to find the right words and realized there weren't any. Only the complete truth would suffice. He deserved that.

"Remember the night of the shooting?" He started the conversation and she relaxed.

"Of course." He'd been very upset because it was the first time he'd killed a man. She'd held him all night and assured him over and over he'd done what he had to do to save lives.

"I couldn't have gotten through that without you."

"It was a very difficult time."

"I knew you were on my side. Others would point fingers in judgment, but you understood I did what I had to. Whatever I had to face in the days ahead, I knew you would be with me all the way. So when I read the petition and your name wasn't on it, I wondered if I'd ever known you at all."

She swallowed with difficulty. "Did you ever think I might have had a reason for not signing it?"

"No. It all seemed clear to me. You were afraid you might lose your job if you signed it."

"You would never listen to my side of the story."

"As I said, I'm listening."

She'd waited years to tell him this and she wondered if it would even make a difference now. It would to her—and he needed to know. "Do you remember how sick I was before the shooting?"

She felt his eyes on her in the darkness. "Yes. We thought you had the flu."

"I didn't have the flu. That morning I bought a pregnancy test."

"What?" He sat up straight and she could almost see his mind whirling.

She started this and she had to finish. "Right before the shooting, I took the test and it was positive."

"And?" His body went rigid.

"I didn't have time to think about it. I was worried about you and just wanted to get to you to make sure you were okay. You were so distraught I couldn't tell you then. I thought I'd wait until everything cooled down."

"But you didn't."

"After you were suspended, I thought about the baby and how we were going to make it with only me working. The petition came out of nowhere and I couldn't sign it because it might jeopardize my job. I needed that job for us, our future. But above all that, I needed to be there for you. I never dreamed you wouldn't give me a chance to explain. I never dreamed..." The tears she'd been denying herself suddenly filled her eyes and she couldn't go on.

He gathered her into his arms. "Oh, God, I'm sorry, Myra."

She wiped her face on his shirt. "When you moved your things out of the apartment, I lost it and cried like a baby."

"Tough as nails, the cops called you."

"Yeah, but you knew differently."

He brushed strands of hair from her face. "What happened to our baby?"

She took a deep breath. "I lost it two weeks later in the doctor's office. I went to have the pregnancy confirmed and started having cramps while I was there. It was over very quickly and at times I've wondered even if I was pregnant."

"Were…were you happy about the baby?"

"With everything that was going on I never really had time to think about it. All I could think about was you."

"You always said you never wanted children."

"I don't know anymore. All I know is this is a hell of a time for a confession."

"I…I don't know what to say. I've been a total jackass."

"Yeah, but we're both to blame."

"All these years I thought you let me down, but in truth I'm the one who let you down."

"We're two very stubborn people."

"Mmm. I can't go back and change a thing, but now I'm at peace about what happened. Whatever happens here, I know your love at the time was as strong as I thought it was."

She bit her lip and had to say the words. "But that time has passed."

"Yes. We can't go back and recapture what we had."

She forced herself to keep talking, despite the thickness of her throat. "No. A part of me is always going to love you, though."

They sat in silence as they said goodbye to a past that had haunted both of them. Now they were free— free to…die.

MYRA SLEPT RESTLESSLY against him. He must have dozed off, as well, because he woke up with a start. His mind was in such turmoil he was surprised he'd slept at all.

All these years he'd blamed her for betraying him, but he was the one who'd betrayed her. She'd been pregnant. It was hard to wrap his head around that. They were always careful, of course, but it had happened, anyway, and he hadn't been there to help her through the miscarriage. He'd been sulking like a teenage boy who couldn't handle real emotions.

He'd said he was sorry, but it somehow didn't seem enough. But at this late date it was all he had. The rattle of a key in the steel door alerted him. Levi immediately got to his feet, as did Myra. He pushed her behind him. "Let me do the talking."

One of the big doors at the top of the stairs opened and a woman stood there, silhouetted against the night in a black hoodie and a long negligee.

"Bonita," Myra gasped.

"Is that Marco's wife?" he whispered.

"Yes."

Bonita came down the stairs with the hood over her hair. "Come quick. We don't have much time." She spoke English.

"What are you doing, Bonita?" Myra asked.

"If you want to live, *señorita,* do not ask questions."

Without another word, Levi and Myra followed her up the stairs. The warm night air embraced them. A woman stepped out of the shadows; she was holding a baby.

"You brought Daniel," Myra said, and tried to rush toward the boy.

Bonita stepped between them. "Take the baby and leave. I cannot stand it in the house any longer. My maid—" she motioned to the Mexican woman standing there "—will take you to the gate. I'll turn the security system off and you'll have thirty seconds to get out. That's all the time I can give you."

"May I have the baby, please?" Myra asked.

"Take the *bastardo* and leave. Marco will not flaunt his *puta*'s child in my face."

"Thank you, Bonita." Myra lifted the boy from the maid. "Why is he so limp?"

"My maid gave him something to stop him from crying. I cannot tolerate the crying."

Bonita turned to Levi and pulled something out of her pocket. "Here are your passports. That's all I could get out before Marco returned. It will be enough to get you across the border. That is, if you can outsmart Marco. From your ID, Marco and his cronies gathered information on you. If you're caught, Marco will not hesitate to kill you. As a private investigator, you will need every skill you have."

He looked at the passports. "I need the baby's passport."

"I didn't have time to get it. Take what you are given, Mr. Coyote."

"Thanks." He shoved them into his pocket, knowing that getting across the border wasn't going to be so easy without Daniel's passport. "How will I know when you've turned off the security system?"

"My maid will know. And, Mr. Coyote, make no mistake, if that child is brought back here, I will kill it."

"Don't worry. I'll get everyone out. I could use a weapon, though."

Bonita laughed, a sound that seemed to chill the night. "I'm not stupid, Mr. Coyote. You have one chance to live so be grateful for that."

"Yes, ma'am." He wasn't looking this gift horse in the mouth or any other place.

Bonita spoke in Spanish to the maid. "Follow her."

Levi couldn't help but ask, "Will you be okay?" It wasn't Levi's concern, but if Marco found out Bonita had released them, she'd die a horrible death.

"All hell will break loose once they discover you're gone, but you see, I have been in bed being treated like I'm mentally ill." She laughed the crazy laugh again. "So I know nothing of what is going on. Go. Go. I have to return to my bed to hear the shocking news."

They followed the maid through the darkness. All seemed to be quiet around the warehouses. Two lights were on in the house, but otherwise there was no activity. Either Marco was waiting for daylight to deal with them or more pressing matters had come up.

Levi kept a close eye on everything. They made it to the concrete wall and crouched behind some bushes.

The maid spoke quickly in Spanish.

"What is she saying?" Levi asked.

"We have to wait until Bonita makes it back to her room," Myra translated. She kissed Daniel's face, which lay on her shoulder. "I can't believe our good luck. We're going to get out of here because of Bonita's pride."

"Just keep thinking those thoughts," Levi told her, and noticed the baby just had a T-shirt and jeans on, no shoes. "Is he okay?" he whispered. "He doesn't have many clothes on."

"It's September, it's warm. I'm worried about no food or bottle. When he wakes up, he's going to want a bottle."

They waited, side by side, by the wall. The moment seemed surreal. Out of place. Out of time. But the woman beside him felt more real than she ever had before. She was so natural with the baby, cuddling him and kissing his cheek to reassure him in some way. How could she not want children? Maybe that had changed. What difference did it make to him now?

"You okay?" he asked.

"I'll be much better once we're outside the gate," she replied.

The maid pulled a phone out of her skirt pocket and said something in Spanish.

"It's time to go," Myra translated again. "She'll undo the latch on the gate and then we're on our own."

"Got it." Slowly they inched toward the double wrought-iron gate. The red light on the security camera went out and the maid undid the latch and quickly disappeared into the darkness.

Daniel stirred in Myra's arms and she had to stop to change his position. Suddenly, a spotlight blasted on and caught them in its rays. In a split second guards with assault weapons stood around the perimeter. Marco stepped out of the darkness.

"Did you really think you could escape, Mr. Coyote? As soon as the security alarm is tampered with, a backup system alerts us, the way it did earlier in the night. You have many tricks, Mr. Coyote, but now you're a dead man."

Damn! He knew some systems had backups and it was his bad luck that the Mortez family had thought of everything. But why not? They had valuable inventory to protect. He wondered if Bonita knew of the backup alarm. If she did, she didn't care. Maybe she was hoping the Mexican henchmen would fire before asking questions. Levi had to bluff his way out of this somehow.

"Don't think so, Marco." He whispered to Myra, "While I have him distracted, slip out the gate with the baby and run."

"No. I'm not leaving you here."

"Damn it, Myra. Do what I'm telling you. You have to save yourself and the baby." He knew she wasn't going to make this easy for him and his mind whirled with a way to get them all out of here alive.

"I'm staying," Myra snapped. "Marco won't hurt his son."

"Myra—"

"Mr. Coyote, it's over." Marco motioned to the man on his left. "Take my son from that bitch."

Somewhere in the desperate region of his mind, a plan surfaced. He pulled the small phone from his pocket and held it up. "Nobody move. This is a detonator. I planted bombs near the warehouses and in the house. If I push this button, everything will blow up and nothing will be left but dust and chunks of concrete."

Myra gasped behind him.

The man stopped in his tracks and Levi felt Marco's

eyes pinned on him like a panther about to attack. "You lie, Mr. Coyote."

"Try me."

"Do not take me for a fool."

"I would be the fool if I did that. I know the warehouses are full of assault weapons just like the basement. I push this button and your inventory goes up in smoke. How will you explain that to the drug lords waiting?" He held the phone higher. "What's it going to be, Marco?"

It took a moment for him to answer and Levi kept scanning the areas on both sides of him. He didn't want anyone blindsiding him. It would be over in seconds then. A warm wind bathed his heated face and the muscles in his arm tightened, but he held his position with more confidence than he was feeling.

Come on, Marco.

"Give me my son and you are free to go."

He swallowed back an angry retort. "No deal."

"I'm giving you a chance to walk out of here alive."

"Now you see, Marco, you have that wrong. When I push this button, the house behind you is going to come down on you just like the ton of concrete that it is. *I'm* giving *you* the chance to live. Once again, what's it going to be?"

He was bluffing out both sides of his mouth and he was starting to believe himself. He prayed some of that bravado spilled over into Marco's thinking.

"Go, Mr. Coyote, but I will hunt you down. You will not leave Matamoras, and if you manage to do that, I will find you in Texas. I will make you pay for what you did here today. And, Myra, you will not escape, either. Watch your back. I'll be coming in the dead of night, or in the early-morning light or maybe in the bright sunshine of the day. But I'll be coming, Myra. Watch your back. This isn't over."

Levi waved the phone. "This detonator works from a hundred yards in case you're thinking of following. If I see one of your henchmen, I will still push the button. Just beware of that, Marco."

"Go, Mr. Coyote, but my son will be returned to me and soon."

"Slip out the gate," he said to Myra. He took several steps backward until the steel of the gate touched his back. "*Adiós,* Marco." With that he quickly followed Myra.

He caught up with her and took the baby. "Run. I'm right behind you." Through the darkness they ran. Mesquite bushes scratched their arms but they kept going. When they were quite a distance from the house, they sank to the ground to catch their breath.

"Did you really plant bombs?" she asked between gulps.

"It was just a bluff. Thank God we had the phone." The baby slept peacefully in his arms as if he was in his crib, safe and sound.

"Your mind is diabolical and I love it. I was trembling so bad I had trouble standing."

"You're one stubborn woman. Why didn't you go when I told you to? You said you'd follow orders."

"Let's don't argue, Levi."

"Yeah. We have more important things to worry about." Levi glanced toward the house and the spotlight was still on. A truck roared out of the gate, coming after them. "We have to go."

They made it to the truck, but the keys were in his backpack. "I could jump-start it, but it would take too long. We have to hide, and quick."

The darkness provided a shield as they walked through people's yards toward the town. It was very early and everyone was still asleep, so they hid in a cluster of bushes. Once the place came alive they could disappear into the crowd. Then again, Marco could find them easily enough because the Mexicans would be willing to answer questions for pesos.

They sat on the ground, gasping for air. A dog sniffed them but soon trotted off. Daniel was still sleeping. Myra brushed the baby's hair with her fingers. "When he wakes up, he'll be hungry and we have nothing to give him."

Her voice was soft as he'd ever heard it and he wanted to reassure her that everything would be okay, but he couldn't. He didn't know what was going to happen in the next minute.

"We'll think of something," was all he could say. He pulled the phone out of his pocket. "Let's see if it works here." The cell lit up. "Hell, yeah. Time to do your magic, counselor. It's too dangerous for Turner to fly into a residential area, so I hope you remember Steve's or Tom's number. They're the only ones who can get us across the border." He handed her the phone.

"You bet I do." She poked in a number. She tried Tom first and Levi listened to the conversation. "Shut up and listen," she said, and told Tom their situation. "We don't have Daniel's passport or we could walk across. Call Clarence and Steve and get everyone involved, even the Mexican police. We don't have much time. They're right behind us. This has to be done ASAP or they'll kill us….Okay. I'll wait for the call." She handed Levi the phone. "He's handling it, but it will take time."

Shouts echoed in the distance. He handed Myra the baby. "Stay here while I check it out." He crept from the bushes and glanced down the street and saw two trucks coming their way. The men had flashlights and were shining them in the bushes and around the houses to check for them. He squatted. "We have to go. They're getting close."

He gathered the baby out of her arms and noticed she was trembling. "It's okay. We'll make it."

"How? They'll cut us off before we reach the border and the U.S. officials can't get here in this short amount of time."

"Come on." He stroked her cheek with the back of his hand and the smooth softness spun delightful memories across his mind. "You can't give up on me now. You trusted me to find the baby and you have to trust me to get us out of here. Can you do that?"

"Levi…"

"Can you trust me?"

"Yes."

He couldn't see her eyes clearly, but he didn't have to. She trusted him again and that was all he needed to hear. Earlier, he was unsure of how this was going to go down. Now he knew. He would protect her with his last breath.

CHAPTER TEN

"WE HAVE TO go." Levi stood, holding Daniel against him. Myra rose on shaky legs. Did she trust Levi? Yes, with her life. Trusting him with her heart was something else entirely—but his question wasn't about forever. It was about now and she had just put all her tomorrows in his hands.

"Encontrarlos" echoed from the street. "Find them" was the order.

Crouching low, she followed Levi through a dark, cluttered neighborhood of small houses. A dog barked and shouts followed them as they crept farther away. She had no clue about their direction, but she was sure Levi did. They came to a business section of the town and rested against a concrete wall.

"The border crossing is not far," he said. "If our luck holds, we'll make it there before Marco's men."

Daniel stirred in Levi's arms. "Uh-oh. He's waking up."

Myra looked around at all the closed buildings. "We have to find a place that's open so we can get him a bottle and milk. He's going to start to cry and he's pretty loud."

"I believe there's a grocery store around the corner. Let's hope it's open all night." Levi stood and she quickly trailed after him through the streets and down an alley into a parking lot. In the distance was a store with lights. It was open.

"I don't even remember seeing the store when we came in," she told him. "You have an uncanny memory."

"It's gotten me out of a lot of jams."

They sat against the building and Levi shoved a hand into a pocket of his jeans and pulled out money. "That's all I have. You know more of what to get than I do, so I'll stay with Daniel."

"Do you know how to handle a baby?"

Even in the darkness she could see one eyebrow raised. "I have two friends with kids, and yes, I can handle a baby."

"How old are the kids?"

"Ethan's son, you remember Ethan?" Ethan had worked for the Austin Police Department back then, and still did.

She nodded.

"His son is three months and I've changed his diaper and carried him around many times. And my other friend Carson, his wife died in childbirth and I was there to help him with the baby when Carson was barely holding it together. Why are you doubting my abilities with kids?"

"I don't know. It just seems at odds with your tough-guy persona."

"I'm not always tough."

She knew that. At times he could be the most tender, the most gentle man alive.

Daniel rubbed his face against Levi's shirt. "You better go before he's wide awake."

"I'll need your bandanna." She slipped it from his head, untied the knot, placed it over her hair and tied it under her chin. "A little disguise."

"Very little."

The bandanna had a soapy, sweaty scent but she didn't find it offensive. It was Levi.

"I can see you the whole time. In case you run into trouble, I'll be watching."

"Okay." She had no idea what Levi would do if Marco's men found her in the grocery store, but she'd never underestimate Levi.

"If I have to move," he was saying, "I'll still be watching you. I'll whistle so you can always find me."

"You'll whistle?"

"Yes." He whistled.

She laughed.

"You find that funny?"

"A little. I just never heard you whistle."

He sighed. "Go, Myra. We're wasting time."

She knew she was. Maybe she just wanted this moment with Levi holding Daniel to stay in her mind forever—that picture of him with a child safe and sound and the outside world completely oblivious to their existence.

Walking across the roadway, she made sure to stay out of the streetlight. Not seeing Marco's trucks anywhere, she darted into the store. She got what she needed and exited just as quickly.

When she reached the spot where she'd left Levi, he wasn't there. She looked around and then she heard it. A whistle. She suppressed a laugh. She felt like howling with laughter and it was a welcome sensation. Following the sound to the next building, she found Levi sitting with Daniel behind some garbage cans.

She sank down beside him. "I have to remember the whistling trick."

"Can you whistle?"

"Sure. Just put your lips together and blow, but I could never do it as sensually as Lauren Bacall."

"Who?"

"Never mind." This was not the moment to talk about old movies.

"I had to relocate. The trucks came by," Levi explained. He sat with his back against a wood fence, his knees drawn up, and Daniel sat in his lap, wide-awake. And not crying.

"I hope you found something for him. I'm running out of tricks." Daniel stood up and flailed his hands at Levi with grunting, bubbly sounds.

Myra took bottled water out of the bag and poured it into a baby bottle. She then opened a can of baby formula and, using the scoop inside, added some to the water. Replacing the nipple, she shook it and rubbed it with her hands to warm it a little.

Daniel saw what she was doing and begin to bounce up and down on Levi's stomach and his baby sounds grew louder.

"He's hungry," Levi commented.

Daniel held out his hand for the bottle and grunted loudly.

"Hold on, buddy, it's coming." Levi's voice was soothing, comforting, and she could see why Daniel was so calm with him. Daniel trusted him, too.

Once she had the bottle ready she took the baby into

her arms. He sucked greedily, holding on to it with chubby hands. The milk wasn't warm like it usually was, but Daniel wasn't complaining.

"You're very natural with him," Levi said.

"I've had a lot of practice with Jessie's boys. Of course, she nursed them at first, but later I got to feed them with a bottle."

"If you had a baby, would you breast-feed?"

Her muscles tensed and there was an awkward pause. "Since I'm not having children, I haven't thought about it."

"I've never understood why you don't want children."

She shifted uneasily. "I'd rather not talk about this."

"Why not?"

"Because it doesn't have anything to do with the present. We're running for our lives. Let's concentrate on that."

"I was just curious."

She knew he was thinking about the miscarriage and what could have been. But no one had invented a time machine where they could go back and erase god-awful mistakes. Maybe there was a reason for that. People needed to remember the bad and the good so they could learn and grow and become whole. She was still waiting for the metamorphosis.

Levi patted his shirt pocket. "The cell is vibrating."

He handed it to her. "It's Tom."

She maneuvered a pacified Daniel into Levi's arms. "Myra, we're on our way in a police helicopter. Steve is with me. We're about an hour away."

"They're searching for us and we're hiding behind trash cans. You need to get here fast."

"I'm doing the best I can. Just hang tight. It would be a good idea if you tried to get as close as you could to the border crossing. Just stay safe. I'll call you when we land. The Mexican police are dragging their feet on this, so it might be touch and go, but we're pulling out all the stops."

"Daniel Stevens was kidnapped on Texas soil. Call the governor's office. Call whoever you have to so we won't be shot down like animals as we try to cross the border. Believe me, Marco Mortez will do that in plain sight. The Mexican police have to get involved. That's the bottom line."

"Okay. Calm down. I have papers to identify the child, so we're hoping the security guards will work with us, and the FBI is backing us up. Like I said before, just stay hidden until we get there."

"Sometimes you're an ass, Tom, and sometimes you're a pretty damn good cop."

"You got it, sweet cheeks."

She gritted her teeth and clicked off.

"They're on the way?" Levi asked.

"About an hour away."

"Damn it. It'll be light soon."

Dawn flickered like a candle, bathing the Mexican town in a warm effervescent glow. Slowly, voices echoed and engines revved as the town began to wake up.

"Tom said for us to get as close to the border crossing as we could."

"It will be difficult in broad daylight, especially carrying a baby."

Daniel was asleep in Levi's arms, the bottle empty. He was satisfied and that was good. Maybe he would sleep until this was all over.

"Daniel needs his diaper changed," Levi remarked.

"We're out of money and an hour is not that long, really."

"We better move." Levi stood. "This is part of a restaurant and they'll be using it soon." He handed her the baby. "We can't be seen together. We'll be spotted too easily. I'll go first and you follow."

She settled Daniel against her shoulder. "Where are we going?"

"To the border. Keep the bandanna on your head to throw them off."

"Okay." She forgot she had it on. He started off down the street with his long strides. "Do I whistle if I need you?"

He stopped and looked back at her with a glint in his eyes. "I'll know where you are at all times."

She gave him a thumbs-up sign and he grinned. Funny how one little thing could make her feel so much better even in a moment of crisis.

Even though it was early, people were out and about, getting ready to sell their wares. She could see Levi up ahead. He was taller than the rest and easy to pick out. Slowly and carefully they made their way toward the border. As she waited to cross a street amid a crowd, she saw the white truck coming toward her with two men in the bed of the pickup and two in the front seat. And she knew they were armed.

She immediately ducked her head and turned around, walking toward a shop that was opening. It sold sombreros, clay pots and everything imaginable, even liquor. A Mexican lady came from the back and Myra exited before she reached her. She had to find Levi.

"Looking for me?"

She swung around and Levi stood there. "You startled me."

"The truck has moved on and we have to go."

Her pocket vibrated and she held Daniel with one hand and fished the phone out with the other. Daniel thrashed about so she handed the cell to Levi.

"Okay. We're about a half a mile away," Levi said, and slipped the phone into his pocket. "We're almost there. Are you ready?"

"Yes." This time there was no doubt that Levi would get them across.

They started off again with Levi walking ahead. Daniel grew heavy in her arms and her muscles ached, but she kept going, trudging through the many people. The noises, the scent of tortillas cooking, the rapid chatter and everything else crowded in on her.

Levi came running back. "One of the trucks is at the road leading to the border crossing. They're waiting for us."

She shifted Daniel in her arms. "Now what?"

Levi pulled out the phone and spoke to Tom. After he shoved the cell in his pocket, he said, "They're about twenty minutes out and are talking to the Mexican authorities. We have to wait or get across on our own."

Myra could see the border entrance to the bridge. They were close, but not close enough. She hoped Levi had a few more tricks up his sleeve because, this time, Marco would not let them live.

THOUGHTS WHIZZED THROUGH Levi's head. He didn't have many options without the help of the Mexican authorities. How did they get past Marco's men?

"Walk ahead and look at the stuff the vendors are selling on the way to the crossing," he said to Myra.

"Where will you be?" She waved a hand. "Never mind. You know what you're doing. I'm just nervous."

"Go ahead. I'll follow." He didn't want to tell her he was nervous, too. If they were spotted, Marco's men would shoot first and not ask any questions.

Daniel was wide-awake and looking around at the strange surroundings. He seemed content. Levi hoped that held for the next few minutes.

Myra searched through the goods the Mexicans offered as they tried to make a sale before the tourists reached the border. Up ahead, the white truck had jumped the curb near the entrance to the crossing and Marco's men waited outside, checking the cars as they went by. The other truck and crew were at the entrance as they waited for a signal that Levi and Myra had been spotted. There were Mexican police all around, but he was sure they wouldn't be of any help. Some were probably even on the Mortez payroll.

Levi glanced at the people milling around the stalls and saw another truck identical to the others. Two men in the truck bed were slowly scanning the crowds. Marco had people everywhere. They had to get out of Matamoras quickly or they wouldn't get out alive.

He spotted a young couple chatting over cheap jewelry. They couldn't be more than eighteen years of age, and gullible, he was hoping.

"It's, like, way too expensive, Amber," the boy said.

"But it's so totally cool. I gotta have it."

"We're supposed to be, you know, responsible and not spend money foolishly. Isn't that what we told our parents?"

The girl rolled her eyes. "Sometimes you're a total egghead."

Levi walked up to the boy. "Are you from Texas?"

"Yeah. Corpus Christi."

"I'm Levi Coyote...."

The boy laughed. "Do they call you Wile E. Coyote?"

"Not twice."

"Oh." The boy paled. "I'm sorry. I didn't mean to offend."

This was going to work, Levi thought to himself. The boy was a little unsure and nervous, yet respectful.

"None taken. As I was saying, my name is Levi Coyote. I'm a private investigator from Austin, Texas." He thumbed over his shoulder. "The lady with the baby is Myra Delgado, an assistant D.A. in Houston. She's holding a baby who was kidnapped from his mother in Houston. I was hired to find him." He stopped for a moment. "Are you following me?"

"Hey, dude, it kind of like freaked me out when you said private investigator and an assistant D.A."

The girl was listening closely by the boy's side.

"Okay, I'm going to make this short. The people that kidnapped the baby are trying to prevent us from crossing the border. I could use your help."

"Oh, wow, this is so cool. Like a movie or something. I'm, like, totally freaked."

Levi did a double take at the girl's enthusiasm. "This isn't a movie. It's real and could be dangerous."

"Like with guns?" the boy asked.

He took a moment before answering, but he had to be honest. "Maybe."

"Oh, sick. Like hero stuff. We gonna blow away the bad guys?"

What was wrong with today's youth? He'd just told the boy this could be dangerous and he was all excited. Did kids fear nothing these days?

"What's your name?"

"Aaron."

"Aaron and Amber." The girl singsonged the names over and over, waving her hands. "Isn't that wicked?"

"Whatever. Listen, when you meet strangers and they ask something of you, you should really ask for ID." He had no idea why he was trying to teach them a lesson. He certainly had more important things on his mind, but something about their carelessness and naïveté bugged him.

"Oh, okay," the boy said. "I'm totally on it. Do you have ID?"

"No, but I do have our passports." He pulled them out of his back jean pocket. "You can't be too trusting."

"Are you gonna give us a lecture, yo? You kind of, you know, sound like our parents."

"Here's the deal." Levi got down to business before his nerves snapped from pure frustration. "Can we borrow your car to cross the border?"

"Whoa, *hombre,* that's over the line."

Levi glanced at Daniel. "That little boy's life depends on us getting him to Texas safely."

"I'm cool with that. But, you know—"

"Aaron, look at that totally cute baby." Amber linked her arm through the boy's. "Your car's a piece of junk, you know. Maybe he'll, like, wreck it, you know, and your dad has insurance and you'll, like, get a new one. And it will be, like, so romantic, just the two of us walking across."

Levi shook his head. The parents of these two must be worried out of their minds, letting them loose on the world.

"Okay," Aaron said. "You can use the car." The boy looked at the girl and shrugged. "We're cool."

"Do you have a phone?"

Aaron laughed. "Sure. Doesn't everyone?"

Levi didn't respond. It took all of his patience to deal with these kids, but they were doing him a big favor, so he had to do one for them in turn. "I'm going to give you a couple of numbers in case something happens to the car." He looked at his phone and got Tom's number. "One is mine, the other is a police officer. I want to make sure you get your car back and want them to know what a brave young man you are."

"Ah, dude, can you, like, say that to my parents?" Aaron tossed him the keys and, arm in arm, the two walked toward the bridge.

Levi turned to Myra. "Did you hear?"

"Yes. Unbelievable."

"Let's go. This is our last chance."

Levi took the wheel, but he had to push the seat back

to fit his long legs. Myra crawled into the backseat and buckled Daniel in with her. He cried until she kissed him and cooed to him. She was so good with the baby, the way she would be with her own kids. Why couldn't she see that?

"Hang on," he said, and started the engine. Rap music blasted from the stereo, loud enough to shatter the windows, and Levi immediately switched it off. Daniel started to cry again.

"No, no, it's okay," Myra soothed him. "It was just noise. It's okay."

While Myra dealt with Daniel, Levi shifted into gear and pulled away from the vendors. He didn't want to get too close behind a car and give Marco's men a chance to open a door. The tan car in front of him was almost to the entrance before he picked up speed.

"Here we go."

He passed the truck on the curb and thought he was home free when he saw a Mexican waving his arms in the rearview mirror. "They spotted us. Damn it!"

Two Mexicans with guns stood in the road. "I'm going through. Hang on, and hang on to Daniel."

"Levi…"

"Stay as low as you can."

He pushed his boot down on the pedal and the car picked up speed. His heart pounded and he gripped the steering wheel, willing the two men to move out of the way. They didn't. He kept driving straight for them.

Levi's ears roared as he barreled down on the two. About twelve feet from them, one man dove out of the way and a split second later the other followed, except he came up shooting. Bullets pinged off the vehicle. Zooming through a Mexican checkpoint, Levi slammed on the brakes. The car jumped a curb and spun to a stop about six feet from a small building. That's when all hell broke loose as all of Satan's little helpers finally appeared.

Guns were pointed at him from every angle. Where in the hell were Tom and Steve?

"Are you okay?" he asked Myra.

"My heart is in my throat and Daniel is about to let out a scream."

On cue, the baby wailed loudly.

"I'm getting out. Stay inside until we find a friendly face."

He raised his hands and a security guard opened the door. "We have a baby inside," he said in Spanish.

"Out," he was ordered.

They opened Myra's door and she was ordered out, too. But she wasn't going down easily. "My name is Myra Delgado and I'm an assistant district attorney in Houston. This baby was kidnapped by his Mexican father from his mother in Texas. The baby is an American citizen."

"Sí, señorita."

"We have passports. Now if you will kindly let us through."

"They're in my back pocket," Levi said, reaching for them.

A guard flipped through them and then handed them to another guard. He looked up from the passports. "The baby's passport?" The man spoke English.

"We don't have one."

The guards conversed among themselves and Levi kept listening for the sound of a helicopter. They had no proof who the baby was. If Tom and Steve didn't arrive soon, they would be arrested and taken to jail.

CHAPTER ELEVEN

THEY WERE ESCORTED into a small building, and Aaron and Amber were there. Seeing the shooting, they probably decided not to walk over the bridge and instead wait for their car. When they tried to talk to Levi, the guard forced them back. Myra and Levi were led into a small room with a table and chairs. Daniel began to fuss and rubbed his head against her.

"I have to make him a bottle. He's hungry," she told the guards in English since they all seemed to speak the language. "His formula is in the car."

"*Señorita,* there are more important—"

Daniel released a loud howl that stopped the conversation. "Please," she begged, "he just needs a bottle." She hoped it would calm him, but since he'd already had a bottle, she wasn't sure. In fact, what she was doing was stalling for time.

The guard in charge motioned to another one and he left the room. Myra tried to soothe Daniel, but he wasn't having any of it. Seeing Levi, he held out his arms for him.

"Hey, buddy." Levi lifted the crying baby into his arms and he immediately stopped at the sound of Levi's voice. "It's gonna be okay. I know you're tired and wet. Soon, though, you can go home to your mother. How about that?"

Daniel stared at Levi as if he understood every word and then let out another wail. Levi patted his back until he stopped. A guard came back in and handed Myra the bag.

She looked at the guard behind the desk. "Is there somewhere I can rinse out his bottle?"

He motioned to another guard and he took the bottle. After a moment, he was back with a clean one. Daniel saw the bottle and began bouncing in Levi's arms and reaching for it.

"Hold on, Daniel." Myra poured water in the bottle and worked as fast as she could. Giving it a good shake, she handed it to him and all was quiet as he sucked hungrily.

A female guard entered the room.

"She'll take the child now," the man at the desk said.

"The baby has been through a horrific few days and I'm not letting him out of my sight." She didn't know who worked for Marco or who didn't, and she wasn't taking any chances.

The guard folded his hands on the desk. "*Señorita,* you are not in charge."

She looked him in the eye. "The baby stays with me."

He stood, his dark eyes challenging. But before he could say anything, the door opened and Tom and Steve walked in. Tom made the introductions and laid papers on the desk in front of the man. "This identifies the baby, and the FBI is here to see that we take him back to Texas."

The guard looked through the papers. "I have to meet with my superior."

Tom glanced at Levi holding Daniel. "Damn, Coyote, I never thought you'd find that baby. Ol' Stu was right about you."

"Mortez didn't do a very good job of hiding him because he thought no one here would touch him. Now it's your job to get us out of here."

"Yeah, but sometimes these officials can be hard-nosed."

"You better find a way to unhardnose them," Myra told him. "I'm dirty, I'm tired and I don't have any patience left, so do your job the way you're always bragging about."

Tom held up a hand. "Cool down, Myra. This isn't over. I'm just letting him think he's in control."

"You're doing a damn good job of that."

"Everybody calm down." Steve joined the conversation. "We'll take this one step at a time and hopefully we'll find an understanding person."

Two men entered the room. The new man was thin with a pencil mustache. He shook Steve's hand. "We seem to have a problem, Mr. FBI Agent." He spoke English, too.

"You're not gonna complicate this, are you, Sergio?" It was clear the two knew each other and Myra relaxed a little.

Sergio went to the papers on the desk. "The woman's and the man's passports are in order, but there is the matter of the way they drove into the checkpoint parking area. We do not tolerate reckless driving."

"We didn't have a choice," Levi said, rocking a sleeping Daniel in his arms. The peaceful picture seemed out of place compared to the danger they were facing. "Mortez's men were after us and two were waiting at the entrance with guns. They fired at us. Speed was the only way to get in here alive."

The man fingered his mustache. "I have only your word for that."

"Give me a minute." Levi handed Daniel to Myra. "May I go outside, please?"

Sergio nodded to the guard and he followed Levi out. Myra had no idea what he was going to do or how he could prove they had been in danger. In less than five minutes, he returned with a phone in his hand. He laid it on the desk in front of Sergio and pushed a button.

Leaning forward, Myra could see a video playing of them driving in and Marco's men shooting at them; the whole scene was there. The kid who owned the car must have taken it. Probably to put up on YouTube.

"I apologize for any inconvenience or disturbance this may have caused," Levi said. "As you can see we were literally racing for our lives."

"*Sí.* We like to maintain a good relationship with our friends in Texas and with the FBI." Sergio tapped his fingers on the desk. "You and the child are free to go, but do not return to Mexico anytime soon."

"Thank you. *Señor,* I hate to ask another favor." Levi picked up the phone from the desk. "But the car belongs to a young man who is outside. I borrowed it from him to get here. Can he please have it back? He knew nothing of what was happening."

Sergio sighed heavily. "His car will be waiting in the parking lot."

Levi held out his hand. "Thank you." They shook hands and everyone added their thanks and appreciation. After exiting the room, Levi rushed over to the young couple and returned the phone. Myra was amazed at his ability to convince and con people, but in Levi's case, it was always in a good way. He was genuinely concerned about Aaron and Amber.

Steve cleared them through U.S. customs and they wasted no time in making their way to the helicopter. Daniel woke up as they boarded. His schedule was so mixed up; he was sleeping in spurts.

The chopper lifted off and Myra sagged with relief. They were back in Texas. Going home. And they had recovered Daniel just like they had set out to do. But it would never have happened if it had not been for Levi's cunningness. He was an amazing man. She'd known that, though, from the first moment she'd met him years ago. How she wished there was a way to go back and undo all her mistakes.

But life wasn't that easy.

THE EASY RHYTHM of the chopper was relaxing and the knot in Levi's stomach unclenched. Daniel would go back to his family, and Levi and Myra would say goodbye. The way they both knew it had to be. The last twenty-four hours had proven to be an exorcism of all the pain and heartache from their relationship. They were two strong-willed people and neither had been willing to bend to save their love. He would never get over not being there for her when she'd needed him the most.

"Oh." Tom interrupted his thoughts. "I called Stu to let them know you found the baby and were trying to get him across the border. That's how I got all the information on Daniel. He sent some of the baby's things in case you needed them." He pointed to a bag on the floor.

"Why didn't you say something?" Myra snapped. "His diaper needs changing."

"I was hoping that smell was the baby," Tom joked.

Myra laid Daniel on the bench seat between herself and Levi and pulled the bag forward. Levi placed his hand on Daniel's chest to hold him steady, but he was content chewing on the nipple of the bottle. He'd only drunk about half of the formula.

Myra pulled baby wipes and powder out of the bag with a diaper. She removed his jeans and dirty diaper and quickly cleaned his bottom. In a few minutes, Daniel had clean clothes and smelled better. It was obvious to Levi that Myra had done this many times.

Holding Daniel in her arms, she asked Tom, "How's Natalie?"

He shrugged. "No change."

"And Stu?" Levi inquired.

"Stu's going to hang on until his family is safe. Seeing his grandson is going to help him a great deal."

Levi felt good about that. It was always rewarding to repay an old friend. He sincerely hoped Stu found some peace.

"Will you be able to drive us to my apartment?" Myra wanted to know.

"Will do, sweet cheeks."

"I'd appreciate that."

Tom eyed Myra. "I must say that grungy gang look is not working for you."

Steve snorted. "You just can't help sticking your foot in it."

"Hey, I'm being nice. She was throwing her clout around back there and I saved her ass."

Steve groaned.

Levi knew by the fed-up expression on Myra's face she was about to unload on poor old Tom.

"If you call me 'sweet cheeks' one more time, I'm going to knee you where your clout lives. Got it?"

"Come on, Myra. You know I'm always joking."

"Well, stop it, or you'll be singing soprano for a while."

"Yes, ma'am."

Myra's pride and her temper were her two worst enemies and sometimes they were her best assets. She was cool in a crisis, compassionate to a fault and stood firm in what she believed in. Why hadn't she believed in them?

He shifted uneasily and wanted to say something to Tom, but she didn't need him to fight her battles. She did fine all by herself. And Levi had to wonder if Myra had ever really needed anyone.

Daniel played with the bottle and babbled to himself. Everyone watched and it was a soothing, welcome release from the tension.

Before they landed, Levi told them about Marco's vowed retaliation. They planned to meet later to discuss the situation. In the meantime, Levi would make sure Myra and Daniel were safe until the police had everything under control.

They landed at police headquarters and Tom drove them to Myra's apartment in his personal car. Very little was said.

Levi was surprised to see a car seat in the vehicle

and more surprised to learn Tom had a kid. Levi knew he was a good cop, a little rough around the edges, but Stu trusted him and Levi did, too. He just didn't like his arrogant attitude.

While Myra showered and changed, he watched the baby. Daniel crawled around on the white rug, babbling. He pulled himself up on the glass coffee table and beat his chubby fists on it, leaving streaks. This immaculate apartment wasn't designed for a baby. Or a man, he couldn't help but think.

Daniel was occupied, so he pulled his briefcase out from under the sofa and opened his laptop. Since he had all his information saved, and had an autodelete app on his lost hardware, he wouldn't have a problem setting up a new iPad and iPhone. He needed to do that as soon as possible.

Myra came down the stairs in a formfitting multicolored dress and heels, looking like her old self. And looking dangerous to his peace of mind. He always liked her in dresses. The skirt swayed above her knees, showing off her smooth legs.

He hurried upstairs to shower. He didn't have any clean clothes, so he had to wear his old dirty ones. But his top priority was getting the baby to his mother and Stu.

Ready to go, he was once again surprised to see a car seat—this time in Myra's car. At his startled look, she said, "I have it for Jessie's boys."

"You're a puzzle, Myra Delgado, and I'll never understand you."

"Good. It's sexy to leave a little mystery."

"Well, lady, you have it in triplicate."

Her face grew somber. "Not really. You know everything about me."

He buckled Daniel in. "No, I don't know why you don't want children when you're obviously very fond of them."

She handed him the keys. "It's not that hard to understand. I have a very busy career and a child needs attention, especially from its mother."

"A lot of women with careers have children."

She got in on the passenger's side. "Well, I don't want to be one of them. Could we drop the subject, please?"

Levi got in and adjusted the seat. "Mmm. Fancy car. I'm not sure if I can drive it."

"It's a car, Levi. I'm sure you can figure it out."

He glanced at her as he backed out. "You're rather testy."

"It's been a harrowing time and I just want to get Daniel to the hospital."

The trip was made in silence. Something was bugging Myra and he wasn't going to push her. Right now, they had other important things to consider.

As he negotiated traffic, a store caught his eye and he whipped into the parking lot.

"A thrift store? Really, Levi?"

"I need clothes and I'm not picky. My jeans and shirt smell like refried beans from those trash cans."

"Don't take long."

"Ten minutes tops." He left the engine running and jumped out.

He darted into the store, found his size in jeans and grabbed a couple T-shirts off the rack. He then quickly tried them on and was out of the store in less than eight minutes.

"I'm impressed," Myra said as he got back in the car.

"And I feel and smell a hell of a lot better."

"I didn't think men worried about things like that."

"Only in the extreme." He backed out and headed for the hospital.

Levi stayed in the waiting room with Daniel while Myra went to check on Natalie. In a minute, Myra was back. "The doctor said you can come in, too."

He wanted to tell her there was no need, but she might need help with the baby. Natalie lay lifeless in the bed, hooked to machines. Dark bruises covered one side of her face and neck. Myra took Daniel to the bed.

"Daniel's here, Nat. He's safe and sound and looking at you with big brown eyes." She gently sat Daniel on the side of the bed and touched his little hand to his mother's. "Can you feel him, Nat? He needs his mother."

There didn't seem to be any change in Natalie and Daniel was fidgeting around, so Myra lifted him from the bed. Daniel pointed to his mother.

"Yes, that's Mommy." Daniel's puzzled look showed he wasn't quite sure. He turned and held out his arms to Levi and Levi gathered him close.

"I think this might be too much," he whispered to Myra. "It's confusing. She looks different to him."

"I know," she said in a low disappointed voice.

"We'll meet you in the waiting room."

Myra came out looking defeated.

"You can't expect a miracle the first time," he told her.

"She has to wake up soon or…"

Daniel whined.

"It's probably time to feed him again," she said absently. "The bag is in the car."

Before they could leave, the doctor came in. "Good. I caught you. There have been some subtle changes in Ms. Stevens's condition and tomorrow we're going to try to take her off the ventilator and see if she can breathe on her own."

"Oh, that's wonderful!" Myra exclaimed.

"We're hoping for the best."

"Thank you," Myra said. "What time?"

"Around eight in the morning."

Daniel let out a wail, demanding attention. The doctor walked off and they hurried to the car to make a bottle. Myra was on a high now, her face flushed with excitement as she talked.

"Natalie's going to make it. Stu's going to be so happy."

"He'll get to spend more time with his daughter," Levi said as he pulled into the nursing home.

He pocketed the keys. "After we see Stu, where do we take the baby?"

"What?"

"Natalie can't take care of her son and neither can Stu, so who keeps him?"

"I've been so concerned about Daniel's safety I hadn't even thought about who will keep him. He stays in day care while Natalie works, but other than that, there's no one."

"No close relatives?"

"None that I know of."

"We'll have to discuss this with Stu."

Stu was waiting for them, sitting in his recliner, flipping the TV channels. He turned it off when he saw them and held out his arms for Daniel. Levi placed the baby in his lap.

"Look at this boy. Isn't he something, Levi?"

"Yes, you have a fine-looking grandson, Stu."

"I thought I'd never see him again." Stu wiped away a tear. "You guys really came through for me and Natalie."

"You'd do the same for us," Levi said.

Stu started coughing and Levi took the baby.

"Tell…tell me everything that happened."

Myra took up the story before he could and she made him sound like a real hero.

"Nat forced his hand about marriage?" Stu asked.

"That's what Marco told his father," Myra replied.

"That bastard." Stu drew a ragged breath. "He thinks he can come to Texas and take Daniel again?"

"Those were the last words he screamed at us."

Stu pointed a finger at Levi. "You have to be on top of this. Hell, what am I saying? If I know you, you have a foolproof plan in mind."

"Right now my concern is who's going to care for Daniel."

Stu scratched his head. "That is a problem."

"I have some time off," Myra said. "I can keep him for a while, or at least until things cool off and Natalie is better."

Levi thought of that white apartment and wondered what she was thinking or if she was thinking at all, other than to please Stu.

"Myra, you have to be careful," Stu told her. "Marco's a coldhearted killer and he'll stop at nothing. I'll talk to some friends in the department and see if we can set up some guards."

"I'll look out for them," Levi said without thinking it through. This not-thinking thing must be contagious. He had to go back to Willow Creek. He had a job, a family, a woman who loved him.

"Now, that's what I like to hear." Stu sucked in oxygen and struggled to breathe. "I can rest better knowing you're caring for my grandson."

"Stu, Levi has a life in Willow Creek. I think we can handle things from here." Myra must have sensed his conflicted feelings and tried to change the plan.

Stu shook his head. "You have to let people help, Myra. You can't do this all on your own. Levi's here and willing, so let's not take his help for granted."

There was a long pause. After that, the silence grew a little awkward, as if no one knew what to say.

"You've always been one stubborn jackass," Myra said.

"Yes, ma'am, so don't argue with me." Stu gulped for air and they waited until his breathing eased.

Myra kissed his cheek. "We'll have to get Daniel some things from Natalie's apartment."

"The keys are on my dresser. Take whatever you need so the baby will be comfortable. Nat would want that." Stu had another coughing fit, so they left him to rest.

Myra picked out what they needed for Daniel from Natalie's apartment. She got permission to enter from the police and since she was an assistant D.A., there was no problem. There were still bloodstains on the rug in the living room and Levi noticed Myra avoided looking at them.

They took the stuff back to Myra's apartment and set up a Pack 'N Play. But first Myra gave Daniel a bath, fed him some baby food and put him down for a nap. Levi watched all of this with keen interest.

"Are you sure about keeping the baby here?" he asked while she rinsed out a bottle.

"Yes, why?" She gave him a narrow-eyed look.

He glanced around the apartment. "It's not exactly designed for a baby."

She shrugged. "It will do, Levi."

"If something happens to Natalie…" He had to state the obvious.

"She'll be fine." Those dark eyes flashed at him and he knew a whole lot of attitude was coming his way.

"You deal in facts, Myra. Face the facts. Child Protective Services needs to be involved."

"Shut up. I'm not listening to this."

"You told me earlier that your job is very demanding and a baby needs a full-time mother. Did you change your stance on that in a split second?"

"No." She turned to the sink, not looking at him. "You don't understand."

"Myra…"

She swung back. "I promised Natalie I'd look after him."

That threw him. "When?"

"When I found her in the apartment after the beating. She was conscious for a few seconds and she begged me to take care of Daniel. Those were her last words before going into the coma. I don't think she realized Marco had taken him."

He leaned against the cabinet, watching the stubborn lines of her face. "I'm not going to say anything else, but you have to realize that your apartment will be the first place Marco will look. And his goons will be coming."

"I'm aware of that."

"That's good to hear. We meet with Tom and Steve this afternoon and we'll figure out something. While Daniel is sleeping, I'm going to get a new iPad and iPhone. And a razor to shave off this beard." He started for the living area.

"Levi?"

He looked back.

"Do you think I'd make a good mother?"

Her dark eyes begged an honest answer. "Not if it's out of some guilty obligation you feel you owe Natalie. You're not doing yourself or the baby any favors."

She ran past him for the stairs. Damn! Who knew she was this sensitive? In the old days, she gave as good as she got. What was going on in her head?

CHAPTER TWELVE

MYRA WAS IN a foul mood and she didn't understand why. She'd gotten what she wanted—Daniel was safe and back in Texas. But as Levi had said, she was a person who dealt with facts and, right now, she was ignoring them. She needed to get her head on straight. Maybe some days she was allowed to be optimistic and a dreamer because, above everything else, she wanted her friend to get better. To take care of her child. To have the life she wanted.

If she didn't...

Myra had to be prepared to do what was best for Daniel. At the moment, she couldn't see herself being the best choice to take care of him. She'd never planned on being a mother. It wasn't her thing. But why not? That's what was bugging her. And then there was Levi, who was annoying the crap out of her. He was so natural with Daniel, as if he'd been taking care of the child all his life. But then Levi was planning to be a father and wanted to be a father.

Why didn't she have those feelings? Oh, she didn't want to open her heart and feel the pain. She wasn't going that deep right now. Other thoughts took precedence and everything circled back to doing what was best for Daniel.

Everyone said she was a strong, independent woman.

Where was that woman now? It wasn't like her to be so conflicted. But then, she'd never had a child's life in her hands and Levi judging her.

She had to stop thinking and beating herself up. Things would work out and she would handle it the best way she could.

On the way to the police station, she and Levi were quiet. Myra knew there was a lot both of them wanted to say but that would come later.

Levi had Daniel in a carrier and they made their way to the police chief's office where Tom, Steve and Clarence were waiting. Chief Greg Gilmore frowned when he saw the baby. "What's he doing here?"

"Sorry, chief, we don't have any place to leave him right now," Myra explained.

"Carla!" He bellowed for his secretary and she appeared in an instant. "Watch the baby for a little bit and call CPS."

"No, please." Myra stopped her. "They're going to take Natalie off the ventilator in the morning and then she can tell us what she wants done with the baby."

"I didn't realize she was that much better," Clarence said from his perch by the chief.

"I'm just repeating what the doctor said and I'd rather the baby stayed with me until then."

"Watch him in your office," Greg told Carla.

For the next thirty minutes, Levi and Myra explained what had happened at the Mortez house.

"There's no basement in the plans we have of the house." Steve's fingers zoomed across the keyboard of his laptop and then he raised his hands. "No basement at the Brownsville house, either."

"Have you ever gone into the house in Brownsville?" Levi asked.

"Yes. We've raided it several times. Since there was no basement on the house plan filed for tax purposes with the county tax assessor-collector, we didn't even look for one. We will now."

"The one in Matamoras was huge and stockpiled with guns."

"I heard César telling Marco a shipment had arrived and for him to take care of it," Myra added.

"Can't say we saw any drugs, though. It was dark and I was more worried about our lives than finding things we could use to nail Marco to the wall," Levi continued. "I don't know how they plan to move the guns, but have you done a check of Ava and her family?"

Steve clicked keys on his laptop. "Yes. The yachting business. We haven't been able to connect it, but you've given us more information."

"My concern now—" Levi leaned forward and rested his elbows on his knees "—is the safety of Myra and the baby. Marco was really pissed off and threatened revenge. He vowed to get his son back."

"Marco's wife is the only reason we're alive. She got us out of the basement and brought the baby to us because she doesn't want him in the house." Myra shifted in her seat. "She is seriously unbalanced and actually hates Daniel. From the little she said, I assumed her father was also in cahoots with the Mortezes. And he wouldn't be pleased about Marco flaunting his bastard child in front of his daughter. I got the feeling the

Mortez family was trying to pacify her. Sane or insane, I'm grateful she got us out of there."

"We can't ignore these threats," Tom said.

"We'll put a guard on Myra and the baby and someone at the hospital." The chief made the decision.

"Thank you," Myra said.

A loud cry sounded outside the door. Myra got to her feet. "I better get him. His life's been turned upside down and he's confused with seeing so many different people."

In the secretary's office, she lifted him out of his carrier and patted his back and he immediately calmed down, blinking at her with watery eyes. "It's okay," she cooed at him, giving him his Binky, which he hadn't had in days. Happy, he smiled at her.

"I tried to talk to him but he cried that much louder," Carla said.

"He's confused about what's going on." Myra carried him back into the chief's office. The moment Daniel saw Levi, he held out his arms. Myra experienced a moment of disappointment. Maybe she *would* make a terrible mother. She'd known Daniel since he was born and yet he preferred a man he'd just met. She didn't have those motherly instincts or Daniel just didn't recognize them. The depressing thoughts weighed her down.

Levi bounced Daniel in his arms. "I think we'll take him back to Myra's so he can play and be quiet without being carted around to any more strange places."

Tom got to his feet. "We'll have guards at Myra's apartment and, if you leave, they will follow you, so rest assured someone is always watching you. There'll be guards at the hospital, too."

Steve closed his laptop. "The agency will have people on the ground in Matamoras. We'll know when the Mortez family leaves the compound whether by car or by plane. We'll do our best to keep this under control and maybe put this drug family out of business."

They shook hands and Levi and Myra made their way to her car. Levi strapped Daniel in and then joined her in the front seat. Her participation wasn't required.

Back at the apartment, Levi was on the phone talking to his friend about his truck in Brownsville. The truck in Matamoras they wrote off as a loss. Daniel played in the Pack 'N Play with his toys.

"How are you going to get your truck?" she asked when he put his cell in his pocket.

"Turner's brother is going to fly him there and then Turner will drive it to Houston. I've notified the car dealer in Brownsville. Turner'll call when he makes it here."

"That's a very good friend."

"I've known Turner and his brothers all my life and they've always lived just a little bit outside the law."

She held up a hand. "Don't tell me. I'm very big on not breaking the law."

He smiled and her stomach trembled with familiar awareness. "You've always been a little uptight about that."

Curling up beside him on the sofa, she said, "And you haven't?"

"Okay. We're two tight-asses."

"We're alike in a lot of ways."

He looked into her eyes and she wanted to glance

away, but she couldn't. "Except in what really matters. Home. Family. Kids."

"Yeah." She stood, ignoring the ache in her stomach. "I'm hungry. How about you?"

He nodded. "Food would be nice, but you have nothing to eat in this place."

"I'll order pizza." She placed the order and sat on the sofa again.

"You didn't ask what I wanted." He gave her a puzzled look.

"Meat lovers?" She lifted an eyebrow.

"You remembered." That wicked smile sent her blood pressure soaring. "Did you order coffee? I need coffee first thing in the morning."

She jumped up. "You're such a baby." She marched upstairs and got her Keurig machine out of her office and carried it downstairs.

His eyes opened wide when he saw it. "You have one of those?"

"In my office. Sometimes I work late and the coffee helps me to stay awake."

"Mmm. You failed to mention that the other morning."

"Because you weren't being nice. In my apartment, you have to be nice. That's the rule." She set the K-cups on the counter in the kitchen and plugged in the Keurig. "I only have caramel vanilla cream, French vanilla and French roast."

"French roast will have to do, and for your information, I'm always nice."

She sat on the sofa again. "I'll admit it might be me. I'm out of sorts."

"Why? Daniel is here safe, and tomorrow they'll take Natalie off the ventilator. That should lift your spirits."

She smoothed the fabric of her dress over her knees. "I just keep thinking about Natalie. What if she can't breathe on her own?"

"You have to be prepared for that," he told her.

"We risked our lives to save Daniel and Natalie has to be okay. That's all I can think."

Levi looked her in the eye. "When Stu was a cop in Austin, I remember him talking about Natalie and how good her grades were and what a bright future she had. The last I heard, she was accepted into Texas University. What I can't understand is how she got mixed up with someone like Marco. I mean, this woman has a good head on her shoulders."

"Stu said the divorce hit Natalie hard and she began to take risks, acting out and doing things to get back at him. They had one of those tense relationships. But after Natalie's mother died, she moved here to Houston to be closer to Stu. They were getting along, or at least I thought they were."

"Did she date Marco to get Stu's attention?"

"I'm not sure. Stu did a background check on him but Natalie wouldn't listen to a thing he said."

"Would she listen to you?"

"Sometimes, but I didn't want to alienate her, so I closed my eyes to what she was doing. I didn't like it, but I thought she would come to her own conclusions that Marco was bad for her." She curled one hand into a fist. "Then she started coming to work with bruises and I tried to handle it as delicately as possible. But the moment I said anything she became defensive, so I backed off, wanting to be there for her if she needed me."

"But she never asked for your help?"

"No."

"So you're feeling angry at yourself for not stepping in."

She glanced at him, wondering if he could read her mind.

"Maybe."

"She would have chosen him over you," he stated confidently. "That's the way it works. I've never seen it happen any other way since I've been a cop or a detective. She would have resented you and broken off all contact. And this little guy's life—" he thumbed toward Daniel "—would have been cut short by Marco's deranged wife. Pat yourself on the back. Daniel is safe."

"But how long can we keep him safe?"

He frowned. "Are you Myra Delgado? The prosecutor who faces hardened criminals and puts them behind bars?"

"That's different."

"Maybe, but the police department and the FBI are doing everything they can to protect us. What's really bothering you?"

Fear. How could she tell him that? She'd promised Natalie she'd take care of Daniel and the fear inside her was telling her she'd make a terrible mother. Those weren't normal feelings, and if she said the words out loud, she'd look like the monster she felt like.

The intercom buzzed. She jumped up. "The pizza is here."

"Wait a minute." Levi was on his phone, talking to

the guard. He clicked off. "Buzz him through." Levi opened his briefcase and pulled out his Glock. "We have to be prepared."

Myra trembled with the reality of their situation. On the security panel in the living room, she tapped in a code to open the gate for the pizza guy. Grabbing some money out of her purse, she took a deep breath and headed for the door. Levi was already there. When the doorbell sounded, he looked through the peephole.

"Open it," he said, standing behind the door.

A kid about seventeen handed her the pizza. She gave him some cash and said, "Keep the change." She had no idea the amount she'd given him, but she knew it was more than enough.

Levi closed the door and she carried the pizza to the kitchen. In a moment, he followed her. She opened a bottle of wine and poured two glasses. Sitting at the bar, they dived into the pizza only to be met with a loud howl from the living room.

"Oh, someone's feeling left out," Levi said.

"We should have fed him first."

"You think?" He charged into the living room to get Daniel.

When he brought the baby back, Daniel had big tears in his eyes. Myra searched through the baby's food to find something for him. "How about sweet potatoes and creamed chicken?"

Levi made a face, but she ignored him and opened the jars. She had never really fed Daniel, but she'd watched Natalie a number of times. To be on the safe side, she pushed the jars and a spoon toward Levi. Since he helped with his friends' kids, he probably knew how to feed a baby.

He slid off the bar stool and went into the living room to get Daniel's carrier. He set it on the bar and strapped Daniel in. Daniel waved his arms when he saw the food. Scooping a spoonful of sweet potatoes, Levi slipped it into Daniel's mouth. The baby smacked his lips, wanting more, and Levi continued to feed him.

"I'll fix a bottle for him," she said, needing to do something. "It's close to his bedtime, so he'll probably go to sleep after we feed him."

"He doesn't like this chicken crap but I'm sliding it in with the potatoes."

Myra watched as if mesmerized. Levi was a natural father. He seemed to know what to do and Daniel responded to him.

"I'll put a quilt in his Pack 'N Play and get towels so we can bathe him." She hurried upstairs feeling more inadequate than she ever had before. Once she had Daniel's bed ready, she went back into the kitchen.

She stopped short when she saw the baby. He had food all over his face and clothes—orange food.

"He got a little happy with the food," Levi explained.

"I have his pajamas and towels."

Levi lifted Daniel out of the carrier and carried him to the sink. Between the two of them, they managed to get his clothes off, which was a mistake. Daniel peed, the stream shooting onto Levi and the countertop.

"Whoa, boy." Levi held him out like a football. "That's a no-no. I'm almost positive you're not supposed to pee on Myra's granite countertops."

Myra quickly filled the sink with water. Levi sat

the baby in it before any more damage was done. She handed Levi the washcloth and baby soap. He scrubbed Daniel thoroughly, even putting his head under the faucet, and Daniel didn't seem to mind. He actually giggled and splashed around in the water, having fun.

"Ready?" Levi glanced at her.

"Yes." Levi lifted the baby out of the water and she wrapped a big towel around Daniel. Levi whisked him into the living room and laid him on the sofa.

They got him into a diaper and pj's quickly. Levi gave him his bottle and the baby fell asleep in minutes. Once Levi laid him in the Pack 'N Play, Myra flicked off the light and they went back into the kitchen.

"The pizza's cold," she said, sliding onto a stool.

"I like cold pizza." He picked up a big slice and nothing was said for a few minutes.

She sipped her wine. "You're very good with the baby."

He pushed back from the island as if he'd been stung by something. "Damn! I forgot about the pee. Oh, well." He picked up another slice and downed it. "I'm too hungry to think about it."

In that moment, besides the obvious, she was very aware of the difference between a man and a woman. A woman would have stopped eating immediately. A man adjusted his way of thinking. That was her problem. She had a hard time adjusting her way of thinking. Maybe she just needed to watch Levi and take a page out of his book.

But sometimes the genes could not be denied. Setting her wineglass aside, she stood up and got the cleaning supplies out from beneath the sink and disinfected the counter.

Levi's eyes bore into her back, but she refused to look at him. "This apartment is not going to be the same after a couple of days with a baby in it. Where are you putting the dirty diapers?"

She swung around. "I don't know, Levi. The trash. Isn't that obvious?"

"Whoa." He held up both hands. "A little touchy, aren't you?"

She put the cleaning supplies away. "I'm going to bed." She started toward the living room and then stopped. "I have to clean up the rest."

Levi looked up. "It's just leftover pizza. I think I can handle it."

She had no idea what she was being snippy about, but his reply made her even snippier. "You can do everything, can't you? You're supermom. Superdude."

He stared at her with narrowed eyes and she quickly backpedaled. "Never mind." She reached for her wineglass. "I should really take Daniel upstairs."

"He's fine where he is. I'm a light sleeper, and if he wakes up I can take care of him."

"Fine." She stomped upstairs and slammed the door.

She drained the wineglass and then took a deep breath. What was wrong with her? Too many emotions fought for dominance. She was being an ass for no reason other than she didn't appreciate the fact Levi was better at taking care of Daniel than she was. She needed to apologize to him, but first she'd take another shower. After not bathing for days, she needed it to feel normal again. It would also help to calm her and gather the remains of her composure.

Fifteen minutes later, she felt much better. She could get through this. She wasn't a weak woman, unable to handle a crisis. With that thought, she headed for the stairs in shorty pajamas and a tank top. At the top of the stairs, she heard Levi's voice and paused.

"I should be here a couple more days, at least," Levi was saying. "I miss you, too, but I got caught up in this thing and I have to see it through."

Evidently, he was talking to Valerie and she should tiptoe away and let him have his privacy. She didn't understand why she couldn't make her feet move.

"I'm at Myra Delgado's, guarding her and the baby."

A long pause.

"No. That's not part of my job. Why are you grilling me?"

Another long pause.

"Yes, I dated Myra years ago, but now we're just acquaintances trying to help a good friend and his daughter. That's all it is. You have no reason to be jealous."

This time the silence lasted so long she thought he'd ended the call.

"I'll be home soon and we'll have a really long weekend….What? Where am I sleeping? Come on, Val. You're not that paranoid."

Finally, good manners and common sense chimed in. She went back to her room, pulled back the comforter and sheet and crawled in. Acquaintances? They were acquaintances. It took her a moment to digest that, but after all they'd been through, she supposed it was a good description. Two acquaintances who had loved deeply, created a child together and parted badly. There was no way to resurrect all those feelings that had torn them apart. Nor did she want to.

Thinking that, she had to surmise her feelings for Levi were now a result of guilt. Guilt she couldn't shake. Guilt kept her company at the oddest of times. And guilt that she'd made all the wrong choices for all the right reasons. How did she shake the annoying guilt?

Seeing Levi again hadn't done it. Talking to him hadn't accomplished it and baring her soul had only deepened the guilt. So where did she go from here? Levi had moved on and she had to do the same.

In the past seven years, she'd dated, but no one came close to touching her heart like Levi had. How did she forget his smile? His touch? His love? She flipped over and buried her face in her pillow. Maybe she was destined to love him forever. While he loved someone else.

Oh, please, she wasn't that neurotic. She was just feeling lonely, an emotion that seemed to be a part of her. That's why she worked so many long hours—to avoid the loneliness of coming home to an empty apartment. Coming home to nothing but thoughts of him.

She flipped back over. "Pity party over." The situation with Natalie was making her overly sensitive. Tomorrow was a new day and Natalie would get better. She had to.

There was still the matter of Marco coming after her and Daniel. She had to concentrate on their safety and forget about all those old feelings Levi had awakened.

How did she do that?

CHAPTER THIRTEEN

DANIEL WOKE UP twice during the night, crying. Levi picked him up, gave him his pacifier and cuddled him for a minute and he went right back to sleep. The little guy's whole world had been turned upside down and it would take time for him to get back into a normal routine.

Levi was up at five and made coffee. Then he put clothes in to wash. He wasn't going one more day without clean underwear or socks. By the time Myra came down, he and Daniel were dressed and he had the baby fed. His breakfast was leftover pizza. He had no idea what kind of mood she would be in this morning. Last night was a whole new Myra to him.

The woman he'd known was confident and strong, and *insecurity* was an ugly word to her. But the cracks in her facade were very visible. It was nice to see her vulnerability, but not so nice when she took her frustrations out on him.

"Daniel's dressed," she commented.

He glanced over to her. She was dressed as she normally would for work in heels, a black skirt that came demurely above her knees and a tan blouse that had some kind of frilly ruffles on the front.

"Yes," he replied. "I even washed my clothes and

some of Daniel's." He rested his hands on his hips. "Superdude and all, you know."

"I'm sorry about…" She glanced at Daniel to avoid looking at Levi. "I was a little stressed out last night."

"A little?"

Her eyes swung back to him. "I'm worried about Natalie and today and Marco and everything else. It's just a little too much."

"It's good to know you have some limits."

Before she could retort, Daniel pulled up in the Pack 'N Play and held out his arms to her. "Mmm. Mmm. Mmm," he mumbled.

Levi couldn't figure out the expression on Myra's face. She appeared surprised that Daniel wanted her to hold him. She couldn't be that insecure.

"Good morning," she murmured to Daniel, picking him up. "How did he sleep?" she asked Levi.

"He was awake twice, but went back down easily."

Daniel twisted his head and smiled at Levi, holding out his arms.

Myra's expression changed. This time she looked hurt. A lot was going on with her and they didn't have time to get into it now. They had to go to the hospital.

"I didn't pack his diaper bag or his food."

"I'll do it." She walked into the kitchen and Levi stared after her, perplexed by her behavior.

"We have time if you want to eat something," he said.

"I couldn't eat a thing," she replied, filling Daniel's bag with diapers and food from the box they'd brought from Natalie's.

Levi's cell buzzed and he shifted Daniel in his arms

to answer it. It was Tom about the schedule for the day. He talked for a minute and clicked off.

"I told Tom we were getting ready to leave."

"I heard you."

Damn, she was still in a testy mood. It was like dial-a-mood with her these days.

"I'll take Daniel to the car and strap him in first. We don't want to stand out in the open too long."

"Okay," she replied without any fuss.

They got in the car and headed for the hospital. Levi drove and Myra seemed lost within herself. Clearly, conversation was not welcome. He really hoped this day went well for Myra and the Stevens family.

Tom had arranged for them to go in the back way and it was relatively easy and out of sight. He got Daniel's stroller out of the trunk, which was easier for Daniel, too.

There were two guards and Levi recognized them immediately. Since he was in the business, he could pick them out without a problem. One went up with them in the elevator. They didn't speak. There was no need. He was there to guard them. Another stood in the hall as they got off the elevator.

Stu and his orderly waited for them in a room. The hospital administration was aware of the danger, so they were taking special measures to keep everyone safe. Stu was very pale, almost gasping for breath. The morning would be rough on him, too. Levi pushed Daniel to his grandfather and the baby babbled, slapping the front of the stroller.

"Hey, son," Stu said, leaning over to ruffle the baby's hair.

"Have you heard anything?" Myra asked, sitting next to Stu.

"No. We just got here."

"I can go check," Levi offered, but before he could move, a doctor came into the room. Levi pushed the stroller out of the way.

The doctor shook hands with everyone. "I'm sorry, Dr. Grossman has an emergency in the E.R. so we'll be delayed about an hour."

"Dr. March, how's my girl this morning?" Stu asked.

"As I told you before, Mr. Stevens, your daughter took quite a beating to her head and to her chest. Problems could pop up at any time. But we're being positive. She's young and will heal quickly. Her tests are improving as are her brain functions. That's the reason for removing the ventilator. Say a prayer and hope for the best."

"Thank you. We'll keep waiting."

Stu turned to the orderly. "Colin, see if the cafeteria has coffee and sweet rolls or something." Stu handed him some bills out of his pocket.

"I won't be long," Colin said.

The waiting was the hardest thing and the hour dragged. Daniel grew fussy and Myra extended the back of the stroller to make a bed. She gave him a bottle and some baby food and he went to sleep. Everyone was nervous and Levi was beginning to think they'd forgotten about them when Dr. March entered the room again.

"Okay. We're ready to remove the ventilator. I think it would be best if you waited outside her cubicle. These things aren't easy to watch."

"That's fine," Stu said. "Myra and I'll go with you." Stu glanced at Levi. "Take care of the baby, and if Natalie asks for him, you can bring him in."

"Got it. Good luck."

Sensing that something wasn't right, Daniel woke up crying. Levi changed his diaper and got him out of the stroller. He held him and Daniel laid his face against his chest as they waited. Levi felt a heaviness around his heart. This little boy needed his mother.

Myra came back in, her face flushed with excitement. "She's breathing on her own. It's wonderful."

He gave her a quick hug and she held on to him a little longer. That tantalizing scent he associated with her wafted around him. Whenever he smelled gardenias, he thought of her, delicate and sensual.

Last night, when Valerie had asked where he was sleeping, he hadn't answered the question, not that he would lie, but old memories were as tempting as the gardenia scent. Memories of the little cooing sounds Myra made when she slept. Memories of her soft skin. Memories of the feel of her body against his. Memories he should have forgotten. Why hadn't he?

He quickly brought his thoughts under control. "That's great. Is she awake?"

"No." She drew back. "I came to get Daniel."

Levi handed her the baby and she walked out of the room. Thank God. Everything was going to work out. He sat down and took a long breath. Now they just had to worry about Marco.

Suddenly, he heard loud voices, someone screamed and running feet pounded against the tile. What was going on?

Myra came back into the room with Daniel. Her skin was white and she was visibly trembling. He jumped to his feet.

"What happened?"

Daniel held out his arms and he took him because he had a feeling Myra was about to drop him.

Myra gulped a breath. "Natalie…died."

"What?"

"She had some kind of seizure. Her body was shaking and then she just stopped. Everything stopped. She's…gone."

He took her arm and guided her to a chair. She sat there, staring off into space. Levi didn't know what to do. She'd retreated into a place where he couldn't reach her.

He gave Daniel his Binky and put him into the stroller with some Cheerios on his tray. Then he went to Myra.

What did he say? He'd told her to face facts; reminding her of that now would be cruel. He put his arm around her shoulders and she rested her head on his chest, much like Daniel had, needing comfort.

"She's gone, Levi, just like that. I…I…"

"Where's Stu?"

"He wanted to sit with her for a while and the doctor allowed it." She straightened up and Levi could see she was gathering her courage, which had been scattered to the far corners of her mind. "She had too many internal injuries. I…I don't know what to do now."

"We'll do whatever we have to and I'll be here for you."

She looked at him. "Do you mean that?"

"Of course. You're going to need help with Daniel. Stu is going to need help. I wouldn't abandon you or Stu."

Myra looked at Daniel stuffing Cheerios into his mouth. "Oh, Daniel. He just lost his mother. How do we tell him that?"

"We don't. That's Stu's job." He rubbed her shoulder. "I'm sorry, Myra. I know you were good friends and I know this hurts."

"Yes," she replied quietly. "I did everything I could and…"

"Shh."

Colin wheeled Stu back into the room. The man's eyes were red as he gulped in oxygen. "That bastard killed my girl, my baby. I want him dead, Levi."

"I know you do, Stu, but that's up to the authorities now. I'm sorry for your loss."

"Thank you. But it doesn't ease this hole in my gut. I want Marco Mortez dead in the worst way."

At the rough voice, Daniel let out a wail and then several more. Levi took him out of the stroller and tried to calm him. After a couple of hiccups, he settled down.

"Sorry, Danny boy, Grandpa's a little upset."

Myra stood by Stu. "We all are."

Stu squeezed Myra's hand. "Thanks, kid, for all you did. I'll never forget it."

Myra hugged Stu. "You would have done the same for me."

Stu ran a hand over his face and took a couple of deep breaths of oxygen. "I should have been the first to go. She had her whole life ahead of her and that monster destroyed it."

Silence filled the room with waves of sadness that no one could avoid.

A nurse came in. "We need someone to fill out papers."

Stu looked at Myra. "Would you mind?"

"No, of course not."

Daniel revved up with more cries, rubbing his eyes with his fists. Levi tried to soothe him, but nothing worked.

"Levi, why don't you take him back to Myra's where he'll be more comfortable until we can make better arrangements."

"Sure, Stu. No problem."

Daniel laid his head on Levi's shoulder.

"The little guy has made a connection with you."

"Yeah. We seem to speak the same language."

Stu nodded. "I trust you with my grandson."

The weight of the tragedy weighed heavily on Levi. It wasn't a responsibility he wanted, but he wouldn't let his friend down. Stu was dealing with enough and Levi knew Daniel's future was uppermost in his mind.

Levi strapped a whimpering Daniel into the stroller. "Myra, I'll come back and pick you up when you're through helping Stu."

"There's no need." Tom walked into the room "We'll get her back to her apartment. Keeping Daniel out of sight is the best thing."

Levi looked into Myra's dark eyes and all he saw was pain. "Are you okay with that?"

"Yes. I'm fine." The words sounded hollow and forced.

Levi didn't feel good about leaving her, but Daniel was crying so he had no choice. And Stu needed someone.

Back at the apartment, Daniel crawled around and played. Levi paced. He would have made something to eat but there was no food besides yogurt. Even though he'd told Myra to be prepared, he found that he wasn't, either. He hadn't planned to stay in Houston this long. Now he had to make the best of it, especially since Marco and his men would be coming for Daniel and possibly harm Myra, too.

Finally, he fed and bathed Daniel. The baby played in the water and smiled at him, showing off his two bottom teeth, oblivious to what had happened today. He was just a baby, but years down the road, he would wonder about his mother. Who would tell him about her? Stu's days were numbered. It was a sad fact, but it was true. And Levi had to wonder what Stu's plans were for Daniel now.

Would Myra offer to raise him? Nah. She seemed almost afraid of the baby. Yet, she was so different in Mexico, loving and caring. Now she was as stressed as he'd ever seen her. And considering her stance on having children, the likelihood of her taking Daniel was nil.

So where did that leave this little boy? Maybe Stu had some relatives who would be interested in keeping him. All of this would be dealt with later. Right now, Stu needed their help to get through the loss of his daughter.

He was putting Daniel's jammies on him when he heard Myra's key in the door. She came in with two bags. "I brought dinner and supplies for Daniel."

Levi put Daniel in his bed and gave him his bottle. "Did you go into a store?" he asked as he followed her into the kitchen, not liking that she was taking risks.

"No." She put items in the refrigerator. "I called a girl from the office and I gave her a list of things we needed. She picked up a salad for me and a chicken fried steak for you. I'll just go upstairs and change. It won't take long."

"Myra," he called before she could leave the room. "How did things go with Stu?"

"Fine. We made the funeral arrangements and it will be as soon as possible."

Looking at her, he was puzzled by her cool demeanor, so different from the emotional woman earlier in the day. "You're talking like this is some case you're preparing. Your friend just died. It's okay to be sad, to show emotion."

"I'll be back in a minute," she said, as if he hadn't spoken.

He shook his head. What was wrong with her? She wasn't acting normal. But then again, maybe she was. Myra had always been closed off with her emotions in public, but never with him. He had a feeling she was headed in a bad direction. She had to talk and soon or she was going to explode from all the feelings she was holding inside.

He found silverware and napkins, poured two glasses of wine and waited for her at the kitchen island.

She slid onto the bar stool next to him in shorts and a tank top. The scent of gardenias played with his senses like a cat with a mouse. He took a deep breath and opened his container of food.

"How's Stu?"

"Tired and sad," she replied, pouring dressing onto

her salad. "He was asleep when I left and I hope he gets some rest."

"With his breathing problem, I don't think he sleeps much."

"Yeah." She picked at her food.

"You need some rest, too."

"I'm not very hungry." She pushed the salad aside. "Think I'll go to bed. I want to be at Stu's first thing in the morning."

"Sure. I'll clean up down here."

She slid off the bar stool and looked at him, her eyes dark and sad. Tears weren't far away and she was fighting it. His gut curled into a knot. One thing he remembered about Myra—she never cried. He always thought that was odd. But now he could see the floodgates were about to open.

"Thank you" was all she said, and she walked into the living room.

He stood and watched her pause by the Pack 'N Play. She leaned over and put the Binky back in Daniel's mouth. Then she squatted and watched him. Tears were about to erupt, but again, she surprised him. She ran up the stairs and he heard her bedroom door close. Maybe she needed to cry in private.

He wanted to help her, but he wasn't sure his help would be welcomed—too many hurtful memories and too much sadness. He'd just wait around and be there for her, just like he'd told her. His heart was hurting and he didn't want to take time to analyze it or question it.

After he cleaned up the kitchen, his cell buzzed. It was Carson.

"Hey, Carson, what's going on?"

"That's why I'm calling. I haven't heard from you since you left for Mexico."

Levi kept his voice down so as not to wake Daniel, and told his friend what had happened.

"So you're a bodyguard now?"

"Seems like it. I can't leave until Daniel is safe."

"What about Myra?"

"Hell, man, I don't know. Life is getting very complicated."

"You're still there, so that must mean something."

"How's Pop?" Levi quickly changed the subject because they were getting on to a topic he'd rather not discuss. He didn't understand it himself, so how could he explain it to his friend?

"Smooth." Carson laughed. "Pop is Pop and cranky as ever, but he's taking his meds."

"Thanks for checking on him."

"Anytime. Call if you need anything."

Levi shoved his phone back into his pocket, feeling better at hearing a familiar voice.

He fished Daniel's dirty clothes out of the diaper bag and carried them into the utility room. After stripping off his, he put everything in to wash and laid his wallet and phone on the dryer. With a towel around his waist, he went back into the living room. Daniel sat up and made whimpering sounds. Levi immediately picked him up before the baby woke up completely.

Sitting on the sofa, Levi held him, gently rocking, until Daniel went back to sleep. Soon he laid him back in the bed and covered him with a blanket.

Like Myra had earlier, he watched the baby sleep,

feeling a weight of helplessness resting on his chest. This little guy deserved more.

His cell beeped and he hurried to the utility room to get it. A text from Valerie. Hope u r coming home tomorrow. Miss u. Love u. V.

He should call her, but he didn't want to be grilled again. He knew his feelings for Valerie were changing and that was a whole lot of misery he didn't want to get into right now.

After putting the clothes in the dryer, he decided to take a shower. Hurrying upstairs, he wondered if that was a good idea. If Myra was sleeping, the shower might wake her. But her door was closed, so he'd be okay, especially if he closed the bathroom door.

It didn't take long and he made sure to put the dirty towel in the hamper before wrapping a dry one around himself. On his way down the hall, he heard a sound coming from Myra's room. He stopped and listened. Was she crying? If she was, he was sure she wanted to be alone. He took a couple steps and stopped. The thought of her crying her heart out alone bothered him. Maybe she needed to talk. Maybe she needed someone.

But not him.

Even that thought didn't stop him. At one time, they'd meant a great deal to each other and he couldn't let her go through this by herself. He couldn't help that feeling.

He opened the door slightly. "Myra, are you okay?"

No response.

He opened the door wider. "I know you're crying."

"Just…just go away."

Against every sane thought in his head, he walked to

the bed and sat on the edge. The room was almost completely dark except for a glow coming from the night-light in the hall. "You did all you could. You have no reason to feel guilty."

Sniffles came from the bed. "Then why do I?"

"You tell me."

She rolled toward him and scooted up against the headboard. "I've always stuck my nose in where it doesn't belong. Just ask Jessie. I should've done the same with Natalie. I should have confronted her and made her see reason."

"It wouldn't have worked. It's why you didn't keep pressing her, so put the guilt away and grieve for your friend."

"Then there's Daniel. I told Natalie I'd take care of him."

"That bothers you?"

"Yes. That's why I wanted to find Daniel, so his mother could raise him. I know nothing about kids and never planned on having any."

"Why is that?"

She didn't answer.

"It's just you and me, here in the dark. What we say here stays here."

She shifted restlessly. "It's not like I have a deep dark secret in my past. My decision just evolved over the years. My mother was shocked I wanted to go to college and did everything she could to talk me out of it. It cost a lot of money and they didn't want Mr. Roscoe to pay for my education. That was what she felt and my dad backed her up. It was crazy. She wanted me to get married and have children. In her mind, that was the only way a woman could be happy."

"But you knew different."

"My parents' focus in life was keeping Jessie safe and I understood that, but at times I felt very alone and left out—left out of my parents' affections."

He always sensed that her need to be strong and independent stemmed back to her parents. "So you decided to show them."

Drawing up her knees, she replied, "It wasn't that. I don't know. I guess I wanted to be more than a mother. And I wanted to show them I could make it on my own, without a man, and be a success. I enjoyed the challenge of working with men, proving myself and being judged for the quality of my work instead of whether I wore a skirt. When I'm working a case, I'm totally absorbed in it, day and night. It takes over my life, my energy, and there's not much room for anything else. Then I met you and—"

"What?"

"I began to think I could have a career and a marriage, too, but I screwed that up so badly I thought I'd never find my way back. And I messed up with Natalie, too. I seem to make all the wrong choices for the right reasons and I...I..."

Loud sobs racked her body and he did the only thing he could. He came closer and gathered her into his arms. "Why do you feel you have to take the blame for everything? We're both to blame for what happened between us. It's sad, but Natalie made her own choices." He stroked her hair. "Please stop crying."

"Hold me. I just need someone to hold me."

As he held her, an old familiar longing surged through him. Her smooth, curved body made him weak and strong at the same time.

She kissed the warmth of his neck. "Stay with me tonight. I need you."

"Myra..." he groaned, the scent of her trapping him in a never-ending cycle of need—a need only she could fulfill. He was headed down a one-way street going the wrong way and he had no desire to stop.

Not tonight.

CHAPTER FOURTEEN

"Myra—"

"Shh." Myra wrapped her arms around his neck and ran her fingers through his damp hair, loving the warmth of his skin against hers. "Don't talk. Make the hurt go away for tonight." She kissed the side of his face, breathing in his soapy scent and trailing kisses to his mouth. "Please."

She'd lost all train of thought and pushed her qualms to the back of her mind. Her chest was about to crack in two from sadness and she couldn't be alone. She needed Levi more than she'd ever needed anyone in her life. She knew it was wrong. He had someone else in his life, but her brain was not working rationally.

Or maybe not at all. She sensed he wasn't participating and she pulled her lips away, feeling as if she'd finally reached the outskirts of hell where nothing existed but the pain and the regrets.

Then, slowly, his hands were at her waist and he slipped the tank top over her head, exposing her breasts to his hands and lips. He pushed her back into the mattress, his lips finding her skin as he explored and renewed an acquaintance with her body. She trembled from the sensation of his tongue licking, tasting secretive, sensitive places that he had branded. Needing to be closer, he removed her shorts in an instant and they were skin on skin and she welcomed the hardened planes of his body. It had been so long.

But she hadn't forgotten a thing: the broad shoulders that could shut out the world or the tiny scar where a bullet had grazed him, or those impeccable abs or the strength of his loins. She breathed in the fresh scent of soap and shampoo mixed with his manly aura and she was lost in memories of early-morning sex and late-night romps that went on until the wee hours. She missed him and the way he made her purr with the touch of his hand, which he was doing now.

With a sigh, he rolled them over and she straddled him, loving that feeling of empowerment as she stroked and caressed unbelievably strong chest muscles and fitted her body against his hardness. Just when she thought she would explode from the blood pounding through her veins, he flipped her onto her back again and their hands and lips began a frenzy of touching and kissing, as if they couldn't get enough.

"My-oh-my-oh-My," he moaned, familiar words he'd often used when they made love.

When his fingers teased her, she cried out from sheer pleasure. His lips caught hers in a fiery kiss that went on and on until her sweat-bathed body yearned for more. She needed more. His hardness pressed into her side and her hand stroked the bulging muscle until he rolled onto her. She opened her legs to welcome him.

She moaned as he slid into her and the big, sad world started to float away. With each thrust, she wrapped her arms and legs tighter and tighter around him until they were one, moving, rocking together. When pleasure rippled through her in spasms of release, she cried out his name.

He took her mouth in an earth-shattering kiss as his body shuddered against her. And then waves of bliss washed over them. Easing to his back, he carried her with him and she lay replete on his chest, her head tucked under his chin. He stroked her hair away from her face and he softly kissed her before they fell asleep.

When Myra awoke, it was early morning and Levi wasn't in the bed. She sat up and pushed hair from her face. A feeling of warmth and relaxation settled over her…along with a load of guilt.

What had she done?

Sadness had clouded her judgment. She should never have asked Levi to spend the night. Maybe somewhere in the back of her mind, she hoped he'd realize he still loved her, but his absence this morning proved that wasn't true. Memories. Wonderful, powerful, sensual memories were about to kill her. What could she say to him now?

Seeing the time, she scurried from the bed and took a quick shower. Her tears mingled with the water and she knew she had to pull herself together. She wasn't a weepy person by nature and she had to stop with the waterworks, find her courage and face Levi.

Hurriedly, she dressed in brown linen pants and a white-and-brown layered blouse. After brushing her hair, she clipped it at her nape and let it hang loose. She applied a little makeup and slipped on brown heels.

Reaching the bottom of the stairs, she saw Daniel standing in his bed wearing a diaper. He held on to the rail, babbling. He smiled when he saw her.

"Morning," she cooed to him, kissing his head.

She looked up and saw Levi standing in the doorway to the kitchen. That shattered look on his face spoke volumes. Her heart fell to the bottom of her stomach and she had the feeling she'd had seven years ago when she'd tried to tell him about the pregnancy. He wasn't going to listen; he'd made up his mind.

She cleared her throat. "I'm sorry."

He shrugged. "That doesn't change anything and, once again, you're taking all the blame. I was there, too."

Her hands were clammy. "I should never have asked you to stay."

"No. You used me and our past feelings for each other, and the sad fact is, it was just sex. I don't love you anymore and you don't love me."

I don't love you anymore.

But I love you. I will always love you. Why can't you see that? Why can't you feel it?

Her throat closed up. She didn't expect him to be this blunt. This honest. This hurtful. But he was protecting himself. She should rant and rave, call him a few names in Spanish, but she'd done enough damage. It was time to let Levi go—for good.

"I'll get Daniel dressed. I'm sure Stu will want to see him this morning."

"Myra—"

She swung around. "You said what you had to say, so just stop. I can't take any more."

"I didn't say it to hurt you."

She placed her hands on her hips. "Really? You said it to boost my confidence?"

He ran a hand through his hair. "Damn it, Myra. I had my life all planned and now it's muddled. I cheated on someone I care about. I'm just like all those guys I chased down who cheat on their wives. I'm not like that. I'm not that person. It's just when I'm with you…"

"What? I tempted you? I'm the reason you cheated on Valerie? You might want to think about that." She waved a hand. "I really don't want to talk about this anymore. I have to get going." But something in her wouldn't let her take the high road because he was right. She'd used him, but if she told him she loved him, he would be more stressed, so it was best to leave it alone. But, again, she couldn't. "I'm really sorry, Levi. I know that doesn't change anything and I take full responsibility. It happened. Maybe it's time you went back to Willow Creek. I'll talk to Stu and make arrangements for Daniel's safety. You've done enough."

Levi glanced toward Daniel. "All of a sudden you've changed your mind. You're going to take care of Daniel?"

She didn't have a response for that. Her stomach was tied into knots. "I'm just thinking about getting through the funeral. Stu and I will figure out what's best for the baby."

He stared at her for a long time and she resisted the urge to squirm. "So you're choosing your career over Daniel. Look at him, Myra. He needs you."

Sitting on the sofa, she pulled baby clothes out of a suitcase she'd brought from Natalie's, desperately trying to ignore him. But she knew she'd have to make a decision soon. She wasn't sure what she was so afraid of. For a woman who knew her mind most of her life, she was suddenly as indecisive as a ten-year-old.

Without looking at Levi, she lifted Daniel out of the bed and quickly dressed him.

"Do you ever wonder why you're so good at that? Fears are just fears, Myra, and they're beatable. Just look at the reward."

Her hands shook as she placed Daniel back in the bed. Levi was pushing her and she couldn't take that right now. She had to end it with him. They both had to move on and there was only one way out. She had to wipe him from her mind and heart forever, just as he had done with her.

She looked directly at him. "I would make a terrible mother."

His eyes narrowed. "You don't know that."

"Yes, I do." She drew in a deep breath and prayed for courage. "Seven years ago when I found out I was pregnant with your child and you wouldn't speak to me, I didn't know what I was going to do. And when you repeatedly walked away when I tried to talk to you, my first thought was—" she took another breath "—my first thought was abortion."

"What?" He paled.

"It crossed my mind, so, you see, I'd make a terrible mother. I put my feelings above my child's. I was afraid to face the future as a single mother. I deserved to lose that baby. I deserved all the pain I went through… alone. I…"

He didn't offer any solace and she didn't expect any, but the silence that stretched was as painful as when the doctor had said, "You've lost the baby." Because now she was losing her last link to Levi.

"What made you change your mind?" The words came out low, but she heard the anguish clearly.

She bit the inside of her lip until it bled. "Because there are some things even strong, independent women can't do."

Before he could say a word, someone pounded on the door. "It's Tom. Let me in."

Levi stared at her for an extra second and then went to answer the door. Tom hurried into the living room.

"What's up?" Myra asked. For Tom to be here this early, she knew something must have happened.

"Two of Marco's henchmen crossed the border about an hour ago. Agents are following them and they're headed straight for Houston. Pack your things. You and the baby have to go to a safe place."

Levi joined them. "I suppose he heard about Natalie's death and Marco has sent them for his son."

"That's our guess," Tom said. "Hurry, Myra, we don't have much time."

Tom's cell buzzed and he answered it. "Yes. I'm here.…Okay. I'll put you on speakerphone." He pushed a button on the phone. "It's Stu."

"Levi, are you there?"

"Yes, Stu, I'm listening."

"That bastard is coming for my grandson. You have to stop him."

"Stu, I'm not a cop anymore."

"I know that. I'm just asking you to keep Daniel and Myra safe until the cops can catch these guys."

At the conflicting thoughts on Levi's face, Myra stepped in. "Stu, it's time for Levi to go back to Willow Creek. The cops will guard Daniel and me."

"I don't trust anyone but Levi."

"Thanks, Stu," Tom joked.

"You know what I'm talking about."

"Between the FBI and the police, we'll be safe," Myra tried to convince him.

"I've been a cop for too many years and I know there are snitches. It just takes money. Marco found out very fast that my daughter had passed away. Levi, don't let me down."

The look on Levi's face said it all: honor and loyalty would win this round.

"Okay, Stu, I can take them to the ranch. They'll be safer there until the situation is resolved."

"Thank you. I owe you big for this one."

"We're paid in full," Levi told him.

"Stu, I'm leaving for the home now. I'll see you in a few minutes," Myra interrupted. "And don't argue. I'm staying for Natalie's funeral. I have to be here for that. Please understand."

"I knew you would. We'll talk when you get here."

"Do you want me to bring Daniel for a moment?"

"No. I want Levi to get him out of Houston as fast as he can. Okay, Levi?"

"Okay, Stu," Levi replied.

Tom turned off the phone. "Myra, pack your things and take them with you because you won't be coming back here." He looked at Levi. "What's your plan?"

PLAN?

Levi's whole world had just caved in and he was trying to find his way through the rubble. His mind was still focused on Myra and everything that had happened between them. He needed to talk to her in private. They needed to sort this out, but first, he had to think of a way to keep them both alive. That took precedent.

"Damn, I forgot about my truck."

Tom frowned at him as if he'd lost his mind. "What about your truck?"

"It's in Brownsville. A friend was supposed to get it back to me, but with everything that happened yesterday, I forgot to call him. Hold on." Levi reached for his phone.

It rang several times before Turner answered. "Hey, Turner, I forgot to call you yesterday about my truck."

"Don't worry, friend. I have it handled." Turner's voice sounded sleepy. He must've woken him up.

"What do you mean?"

"I brought the truck back late last night. It's parked here at my office."

"Great, man. Thank you."

"Where are you?" Turner asked. "I'll deliver it."

"How will you get back to your office?"

"I'll take a cab."

"You've done so much I hate to ask anything else of you."

Turner laughed. "Who knows? I might need a detective one of these days and I expect a big discount."

"You got it."

Levi gave him the address and told him about the security gate. "My friend's bringing my truck. It won't take long."

"Then what?" Tom asked.

"Well, the faster I get Daniel out of Houston, the

better. But I'll need his baby bed and stuff out of his room at Natalie's."

"I'll drop Myra at Stu's and pick up the stuff from Natalie's apartment. Maybe your truck will be here by then."

"Now we've got a plan."

Myra came down the stairs with a small suitcase, her face set into a mask of anguish. He forced himself not to react. They were both to blame and they would sort it out later when their tempers had cooled.

"Is that all you're taking?" Tom pointed to the suitcase.

"Yes. I don't plan on being away that long."

Tom shook his head. "Stubborn, thy name is Myra."

Levi knew he had to do something. Myra was going to resist all the way. She didn't want to spend any time with him and the feeling was mutual, but they didn't have much choice. Of course, she wasn't going to admit that. So he had to make things clear.

"This is how it's going to happen." He stared into her dark eyes. "I'm taking Daniel to Willow Creek and you will help Stu at the funeral. Afterward, Tom or a guard will escort you to the ranch. You will stay there until this is resolved."

She glared at him, her eyes as fiery as the depths of hell. "As long as Daniel is safe, that's all I'm worried about. I can stay at a safe house and I will be closer to Stu and to work."

"To hell with work." She'd said the one thing that could set him off. And it did. "Did you see how badly Natalie was beaten? These guys won't even think twice about doing that to you or worse and then they will leave you with a bullet in your head. Does that sound attractive to you?"

"Hey," Tom intervened. "That's a little harsh."

"It's the only thing that's going to get through her hard head." Levi swung away for a second before his anger got the best of him.

"I don't know what's going on here—" Tom looked from one to the other "—but whatever it is, it has to stop." Tom focused on Myra. "You don't have any choice here. So let the tempers subside and let's get on with the business of keeping you and Daniel alive."

"Fine." She picked up her purse. "But Willow Creek is the last place I want to be."

"Noted," Tom said as they headed for the door. Myra didn't look at Levi and that was just as well. His emotions were helter-skelter and all over the place. He was always a man in control, but Myra had managed to take even that from him. Or maybe he'd let her.

As the door closed, he ran his hands over his face and sank onto the sofa. He was thinking of marrying one woman and having sex with another. That wasn't him. When he tracked down cheating husbands and saw them cavorting with women half their age, he knew deep down he wasn't that kind of a man. Once he made a commitment, it was final for him. So what the hell had happened?

Maybe some things just weren't black-and-white like he'd always believed. And he had to stop blaming Myra. He could have walked out of her room and then he wouldn't be going through this turmoil today. In retrospect, he was actually the one who went into her room in the first place. He could have kept walking. Oh, God!

He didn't want to think about it anymore. Keeping Daniel safe was his top priority. Myra, too.

"Mmm. Mmm. Mmm." Daniel held out his arms to him.

"Hey, buddy." Levi lifted him out. "Are you tired of being caged up?" He set him on the floor and Daniel shot off crawling. Levi sat back on the sofa and watched him. Daniel sprinted over to him and pulled up on his jeans, and then pointed to the Pack 'N Play.

"Oh, you want your Binky?" He stood and fished the pacifier out of the playpen. Daniel immediately latched on to it, sucking away.

"Mmm. Mmm. Mmm." Daniel held out his arms.

Levi lifted him into his lap. "What's the matter, buddy?"

Daniel just stared at him with rounded dark eyes.

"We're going to a new place where there are cows, horses, a dog and a cat in the barn. Just be prepared for a grouchy old man, but he's got a really big heart. Ready to go on a trip?"

His cell buzzed and he had to juggle Daniel to reach it in his pocket. Daniel thought it was a game and laughed a bubbly baby laugh. First time Levi had seen him do that. The little guy was a cute kid and Levi would do everything humanly possible to keep him safe.

Turner was on the phone and Levi opened the gate for him. He was glad to see his truck was still in one piece. Levi thanked his friend and Turner left. The next hour was busy. Tom arrived with his car filled with

Daniel's belongings. He'd taken the baby bed apart and stored it in his trunk. They transferred everything into the bed of Levi's truck. They installed the car seat in the back and strapped Daniel in for the trip.

He shook Tom's hand. "Thanks for your help."

Being a cop, Tom had questions and he didn't hesitate to ask them. "I take it you and Myra know each other from way back?"

"Yeah, you could say that. But that's all I'm telling you."

Tom got the message and returned to business. "As soon as the funeral is over, I'll get Myra to Willow Creek even if it takes the whole department."

Levi slid into the driver's seat. "It might."

"Watch your back," Tom said as Levi closed the door. He pulled out of the apartment complex and headed for I-10. It was a little over a three-hour drive. Daniel fell asleep quickly.

With nothing but the highway and music on the radio, Levi had a lot of time to think. He'd screwed up. He'd hurt Myra and he'd never meant to do that. It wasn't like him to be unkind. He didn't know where they went from here, but of one thing he was sure: he would protect her just as he had in Mexico. And maybe she wouldn't hate him for being an ass.

The trip was long for Daniel. When he woke up, he wanted attention. Levi pulled into a roadside park and changed his diaper and fed him. His gun was never far from him as he walked around with Daniel in his arms. If anyone was following him, and he was sure they weren't, but on the off chance, he was careful not to stay in one spot too long.

Finally, he reached U.S. 290 and headed for Willow Creek and home. Crossing the cattle guard, a feeling of peace came over him like it always did when he returned home from a trip. But that peace may not last. Now he had to explain Daniel to Pop. He could have called, but then, Pop wasn't known for answering the phone. Telling him face-to-face was best, anyway.

He pulled to the side of the house and into the carport. Pop was sitting on the front porch in his rocker. John Wayne barked and ran out to greet them. Yep, he was home.

He unstrapped Daniel and got him out. Seeing the dog, he began to wave his arms and bounce excitedly. The baby liked dogs. He carried him to the front porch and Pop frowned when he saw what Levi had.

"Lord, boy, where'd you get that baby?"

"It's a long story."

"Well, you better shorten it."

Levi opened the screen door and Pop followed him inside. He explained as best he could about what had happened.

"So now you're bringing your work home with you?"

"Kind of." He sat Daniel on the floor and the baby crawled quickly to the screen door, looking for John Wayne. Levi hurried over and locked it so Daniel couldn't get out. "I have a lot of stuff to get out of the truck. Do you think you could watch him for a few minutes?"

"What do you mean, 'watch'?"

"Make sure he doesn't pull something over on top of himself or put something in his mouth he shouldn't."

"Oh, no, I'm not Walt. I'm not taking care of a baby. I'm too old."

Daniel scurried over to Pop and pulled up on his jeans. "What's he doing?" Pop growled as if Daniel was going to bite him.

"Standing up."

"Why does he have to stand here?"

"Hell, I don't know. Maybe he likes you."

"Mmm. Mmm. Mmm." Daniel held out his arms.

"What does he want?"

"He wants you to hold him."

"Oh, no. That's how it starts. They wrap their little hand around your heart and then they yank it out by the roots."

Levi couldn't help it. He laughed. "So that's what happened to it?"

"Does Valerie know about this baby?"

"Why?"

"She's bringing a casserole out for my supper and she'll be here any minute."

Damn. Now he had to face her and tell her what he'd done. As Pop would say, the shit was about to hit the fan. And his world would never be the same again.

CHAPTER FIFTEEN

MYRA STOOD BY Stu as the casket was lowered into the ground. No one was there but Stu, Myra and Colin. For safety reasons, the burial was top secret. A man from the funeral home read a couple of verses from the Bible. It was a sad ending for a beautiful young woman who'd had her whole life ahead of her.

"I failed her," Stu said, brushing away a tear.

Myra couldn't contradict him because she felt as if she had failed Natalie, too. If only she could go back. If only... But no one had that option.

"When I was coming up through the ranks of the department, I always told myself I needed to make time for my kid. But, sadly, that was left up to her mother. I was building a career and now I'm wondering for what. Everything and everyone I love is gone." He looked up at Myra. "It's not worth it. If I had been closer to my daughter, I could've talked to her. I could've reasoned with her, but with our tenuous relationship, she was always on the defensive. That was my fault." Stu wiped away more tears and gripped tissues with a shaky hand. "If I had been the father I should have been, she wouldn't have looked for comfort from someone like that bastard Marco Mortez."

It started to drizzle and Myra glanced toward the sky. Dark thunderclouds were gathering. "We better go."

"It doesn't matter, Myra. Nothing much matters any-more."

She took a deep breath and tried to deal with all the sadness and heartbreak inside her and found it wasn't an easy task. It was too much even for her, especially on top of her situation with Levi. This morning should have been magical. A reuniting after years of being apart. And that's where fiction and reality collided.

A pink spray of roses had been removed from the casket and laid on the ground. Myra walked over and plucked two stems from it. She handed one to Stu. Colin pushed him closer and he threw the rose on top of the casket.

"Goodbye, baby girl. I'll be joining you soon."

Tears blurred Myra's vision and she threw her rose on top of Stu's. "Goodbye, my friend. Rest in peace."

Colin pushed the wheelchair to the van and soon they were on their way back to the home. She sat in the back with Stu. Rain pelted the vehicle with a steady rhythm, enclosing them in stoic silence.

Stu had trouble breathing and had to relax to take in his oxygen. The rain suddenly stopped and through the window Myra saw a black car she knew was the guards following them. Tom had beefed up security and it made her aware of how much danger she was in. She kept thinking about what Levi had said this morning and a chill ran through her. Even though it was cruel, he had spoken the truth. She didn't know how she was going to manage staying with Levi and his grandfather for several days without revealing her true feelings. Because that was one thing she couldn't do. She couldn't come between Levi and Valerie any more than she already had.

She knew Levi well enough to know that he would tell Valerie everything. Things were going to be rather tense around the Coyote house. And Myra had to take the blame for all of it. Sometimes life was just too damn cruel.

When they reached the home, Colin helped Stu into his recliner. He was pale and breathing hard. She sat beside him.

"It's not worth it, Myra," he said.

She shifted uneasily in her chair. Stu was trying to tell her something.

"Natalie was ten when her mom left me. She said I was never home so we didn't have a marriage and she was right. I spent more time with the guys at the station than I ever did with my wife and my kid. But I wanted to be more than my old man, who was a beat cop all his life. In the process, I lost everything that was important. I barely knew my daughter. A couple of weeks in the summer and the odd weekend did not make me a father."

"But you and Natalie reconnected when she was a teenager," she reminded him.

"Yeah, she wanted to go to college in Texas and I was thrilled, but those old forget-me-not scars were there and Natalie brought them up every time she was angry with me. Pointed out numerous times what a lousy father I had been and that I had no say in her life. But I hung in there, determined not to let her down this time." He took a big draw of oxygen. "Look how it turned out."

She reached over and hugged him. "I'm sorry, Stu. Natalie never had a chance to really get to know you. But she loved you, I know that. And she was very proud of you."

"But all she could see was the father who was never there for her," Stu murmured.

"He was there for me," she told him.

Stu smiled. "I remember that terrified young woman who interviewed for a job in the D.A.'s office in Austin. She put on a brave face, but I could see through it."

"I would have never gotten that job if you hadn't spoken to the D.A."

"Hey, kid, you were the minority pick that month. Didn't you know that?"

It was good to see Stu teasing her like he had so many times in their past. He said she took herself too seriously. Maybe she did.

Stu touched her hands. "I'm sorry about you and Levi, kid."

"We just keep hurting each other."

"Why?"

She stared into his dull blue eyes. "He doesn't trust me."

"Good God, Myra. You two need to get past what happened in Austin."

"It's more than that. I did something he can't forgive me for again."

Stu lifted an eyebrow. "Now, I wonder what that could be?"

"It's complicated."

"Mmm. I'll simplify it for you. You're both scared shitless that love will somehow change who you are.

You've worked for years building your career and at the back of your mind you're worried you might not be the woman Levi wants. And Levi, all he's ever wanted was a home and a family, and he's not sure that's what you want. So instead of talking about it, you two do some crazy things. Talk, Myra. That's what you need to do. I know. I never did that with my wife. So listen to a man of experience. Lay it all on the table, like you do in court. It comes down to what you're willing to give up for love. Can you change? Can he change? If you or Levi are not willing to compromise, it's not love. And it's time to move on. It's that simple."

Myra wished it was that simple, but Stu didn't know the whole truth. He didn't know about the pregnancy, the miscarriage or her lack of judgment last night. He was right about one thing, though. She and Levi had to talk.

The door opened and Tom came in. "Ready to go?" he asked Myra.

"I suppose," she replied.

"She's ready." Stu nodded. "Any news on the two guys from Mexico?"

"They're about thirty minutes out of Houston, so we have to go." Tom gave her a sharp look and she got to her feet.

She hugged Stu. "Take care of yourself and I'll call once I reach Willow Creek."

"You better. I'll worry until these guys are behind bars. And I won't rest until Marco Mortez pays for what he did to my daughter."

She picked up her suitcase and followed Tom out the door.

"You're being rather docile," Tom said as they got into the car.

"Don't get used to it."

He glanced at her. "You know, you're not too bad. Most of the time I think of you as a tight-ass bitch."

"Thank you," she replied drily. "You're not too bad, either. And in case you're wondering, I think of you as a macho asshole all the time."

Tom laughed and she settled into her seat and rested her head back. In no time, she was sound asleep. The night had finally caught up with her.

WHEN LEVI HEARD the car, he put Daniel in the Pack 'N Play. The baby protested at first until Levi gave him his pacifier. Then he sat down and played with his teddy bear.

Pop looked at him. "Valerie doesn't know about the baby, does she?"

"No. Could you watch Daniel while I talk to her?"

"Do I look like a babysitter?"

"No, you look like my grandfather, who is known to help me whenever I need it."

"You're going to need more help than I can give you."

"Pop…"

"Okay. I'll watch the little booger."

"Thanks."

His grandfather stared at him. "You're nervous. I've never seen you like this. What else have you done?"

He took a long breath, unable to lie to his grandfather. "Something I'm not proud of."

Henry held up a hand. "That's between you and Valerie."

"Thanks, Pop." Levi hurried to the window to make sure it was Valerie. He watched her get out of her car, her long blond hair swirling in the wind. She was beautiful, sweet, compassionate, loving, everything he wanted in a woman. But she wasn't Myra. The thought hit him like a sucker punch and he struggled with the revelation.

The knock at the door brought him out of his stupor. He opened the door and she rushed in with a casserole in her hands. She stood on tiptoes to kiss him.

"You're home. Why didn't you call me?"

"I was just about to."

"Hi, Pop. I brought supper. I'll put it in the kitchen and…" She stopped when she saw the baby in the Pack 'N Play.

He took the casserole from her. "I'll put it on the stove."

"Where did the baby come from?"

He stepped back into the living room. "This is Daniel, the little boy I rescued."

"The drug lord's son?"

"Yes."

"Why is he here?"

"Let's sit on the porch and I'll explain." He looked at his grandfather and Pop winked. Levi ignored him.

He held the screen door open as they went out.

"Why did you bring that Mexican baby into your home?"

Levi was getting a little tired of her tone. Before this case, he'd never seen this side of Valerie. As a nurse, she worked with all nationalities, but only a few were obviously included in her close-knit circle.

He sat on the swing and she sat beside him. "He's just a baby and I've agreed to protect him until it's safe for him to return to his grandfather."

"You mean those drug dealers could come here?"

"Val, I agreed to protect this baby and I will."

"I didn't realize that was part of your job." She flipped back her hair in an angry gesture.

"Not usually, but this is a special circumstance."

She scooted closer to him. "Why are we arguing? I haven't seen you in days."

"I'm wondering that myself."

"It was just such a shock seeing that baby."

"You say 'that baby' like he's contaminated or something. His mother is white. His father's Mexican. Do you have a problem with biracial children?"

"Of course not."

But he could see she did and that surprised him. He thought he knew her and her heart, but it seemed he didn't know her at all and he was beginning to wonder what was real and what wasn't.

She curled into his side. "I've missed you. Let's have a quiet dinner at my apartment tonight."

"I'm not going anywhere until the situation with the baby and his safety is resolved."

She raised her head. "You mean you have to stay here all the time?"

"Yes."

"Can't the police handle this?"

He looked into her blue eyes. "We have to talk. I thought we had something special, but the vibes I'm getting from you about a half-Mexican baby are bothering me."

She stroked his chest. "You know I didn't mean anything."

"It's not only that. Something happened while I was away and I need to tell you about it."

She shifted away from him. "It's about that woman, isn't it?"

"If you mean Myra, yes."

"You slept with her."

He took a deep breath and never realized it would be so easy to admit. "Yes."

"I could see there was something between you the day she came into the barn. The tension was so thick I had to leave because I knew she was someone from your past. Someone you had known before me. Someone you had loved."

"Yeah."

"Was it a one-time thing?"

Ever since he had woken up this morning, he had been feeling like a cad, the worst kind of man because it felt like he'd cheated on a woman who loved him. After his confession, he was expecting tears, anger, hurt and disillusionment, but what he was seeing was someone almost detached from the situation. Her reaction was not normal, he was almost positive.

He told her about Natalie's death and how upset Myra was.

"So you were just consoling her?"

Where was the anger? The betrayal?

"It was more than that." He had to be honest.

"But you're not going to see her anymore?"

"She'll be coming here, and I'll protect her and the baby until it's safe for them to return to Houston."

Valerie drew away. "Isn't that lovely?" she said sarcastically, and got to her feet. "You know, Levi, you're not the only one who has been tempted."

"What does that mean?"

"It means men hit on me all the time, but I love you and—"

He stood. "I'm sorry, Valerie."

"How could you do this to us?"

He exhaled deeply. "I don't have an explanation. It just happened. Since it did, maybe it's best if we took a break."

Her eyes opened wide. "No, we can get through this."

He was taken aback for a minute by his own words. This was not what he was expecting and now he had to carry it through. "Valerie…"

Almost as if she knew what he was going to say, she stepped forward and wrapped her arms around his waist and laid her head on his chest. "You do your job and I'll call you later."

"Val…"

She placed her fingers over his lips. "Get her out of your life, Levi." After saying that, she ran to her car.

He was thirty-four years old and he'd dated, been serious more than once, but he'd never encountered anything like this. Valerie was willing to forgive him. Why? He couldn't forgive himself. His investigator instincts told him something was not quite right. He always heard that love was about forgiveness and knowing when to compromise. Still, something about this was too easy.

He walked back into the house. Pop had Daniel in his lap and Daniel was sticking his hands into the pockets of Pop's western shirt.

"He was fussy so I got him out," Pop explained.

"That's okay." Levi sat on the sofa across from his grandfather. "I don't understand women."

"Really? Well, join the rest of us sorry bastards. No man understands a woman. It just don't come natural. We just learn to cohabitate because the benefits are pretty damn good."

Levi rubbed his hands together, needing to talk to someone. Usually he kept things bottled up inside, but this was eating at him. He told his grandfather what had happened.

"Lordy, boy, you got yourself in a mess. You young guys don't know how to keep your pants zipped."

Daniel grew tired of playing with Pop's pockets and climbed down to the floor, crawling to Levi. The baby played around his feet.

"I don't need a lecture."

Pop eased to the edge of his chair. "Valerie didn't get angry?"

"Not until it interfered with our time together."

"Hell, your grandma would've slapped me, kicked me and ripped off my balls if I had told her something like that."

"I don't understand her reaction. She said she'd call me later, but I don't think we have anything left to discuss."

"Give it some time. She may be more upset than you think."

"I don't know, Pop. Things just aren't right between us now."

Pop shook his head. "It'll kill you trying to please two women."

"I don't have two women," he snapped.

"Really?"

Daniel wedged himself between Levi's knees and Levi picked them up. "Hey, buddy."

"You said Myra's coming here, too?" Pop asked.

"Yeah. Later today." Levi thought about his grandfather's safety. "It might be best if you spend a couple of days with Walt."

"I'm not leaving this house. Besides, Walt would drive me crazy."

"If Mortez's men locate Myra and the baby, I don't want you to get hurt."

"Well, I got my shotgun and I can take care of myself. Besides, I'm not leaving you and Myra alone. You've gotten yourself into enough trouble—womanwise."

"Do you ever listen to what I say?"

"Sometimes." Pop got up and headed for the kitchen. "I wonder what kind of casserole girlfriend number one brought."

"Pop…"

"What?"

"This is not a joke."

"Seems kind of funny to me. I mean, girlfriend number two is on her way and we're going to have a casserole for supper that girlfriend number one made."

Levi got up and put Daniel back in his playpen,

which wasn't exactly what Daniel wanted. He let out a howl. Levi gave him his Binky but big fat tears still rolled down his cheeks. Levi reached for some kind of melt-in-your-mouth cereal puffs out of Daniel's supply of food and gave them to him. That made him happy. He sat down to poke them in his mouth, which he did rather rapidly.

Levi heard the sound of the car and hurried to the window. Myra was here. Against every sane thought in his head, his heart raced like a stupid teenager's and he knew he was in big trouble. Pop was right. His life was a mess.

MYRA STRAIGHTENED IN her seat. "Sorry. I didn't realize I was that tired."

"No problem," Tom said.

She glanced around and saw the ranch land, the barn and the Coyote house. "We're here."

"Yes. We made good time."

Tom stopped at the chain-link fence. "This really is small-town Texas. Are you ready for country life?"

"As ready as I'll ever be."

"This really is best, Myra," Tom said as if he needed to reassure her, and she wanted to laugh. Tom was not considerate or caring. Not like Levi.

John Wayne barked from the front porch and they got out. Levi opened the door and came onto the porch. His tall, lean frame and rugged good looks squeezed her heart until she wanted to cry. So many years of loving that man and all she'd managed to do was hurt him. And it wasn't over.

"Hey, Levi. We made it," Tom called, opening the gate on the fence. "You really do live in Hicksville."

"The best place in the world," Levi replied.

As they walked up the steps, Tom's cell rang. "Hold on." He stepped aside.

There was a tense moment as they waited. There really was nothing left to say. They'd reached an impasse and Myra didn't relish the next few days of tense silence and awkward moments.

Tom swung back. "That was Steve. Mortez's men stopped at a Mexican nightclub and had drinks and a meal. They are now parked outside Myra's apartment, waiting."

Goose bumps popped up on her skin and she rubbed her arms, really grateful she wasn't there.

"I spoke with the constable here, Carson Corbett, and he said he would patrol the road. He knows Willow Creek and the vehicles and he would know if a strange car was hanging about."

"I talked to Carson a while ago," Levi said. "He'll be on top of things."

"That's good to know." Tom slipped his phone in his pocket. "The only people who know Myra and the baby are here are Stu and myself, so any chance of a leak is impossible."

"What's the plan concerning Marco's guys?" Levi asked. "Is the FBI just going to watch them?"

"Steve feels sure that later tonight they'll break into Myra's apartment and then they can grab them. He also feels they're not planning to hang around. They're here to do a job and they'll do it as quickly as possible." Tom glanced at his watch. "I have to go. If they bring the men in, I want to be at the station."

Levi and Tom shook hands. "I'll be in contact," Tom said, and glanced at Myra. "Don't give the man too much flak."

Myra lifted an eyebrow at him. She didn't have enough energy to do anything else. Tiredness clung to her like a day-old hangover.

Tom walked away to his car, and she and Levi were alone. "I'm sorry," he said in a soft tone, completely blowing her stance to be as cool as possible. "I was way out of line this morning."

"It was my fault. I take full responsibility."

"Will you stop taking the blame for everything," he said, his voice changing in an instant.

She held up a hand. "Please, can we not do this tonight? I'm tired, sad and completely spent."

He stared into her eyes and a weakness assailed her when she wanted to be strong. When she needed to be strong. But what she felt was a heartache that encompassed every part of her and she had no idea where to go from here.

CHAPTER SIXTEEN

THE MOVE-IN WENT smoothly. Levi showed Myra to her room. She was quiet and looked incredibly sad, which made him want to hold her.

"How's Stu?" he asked instead.

"Coping as best as he can." She glanced around the room and he was aware how drab the iron bed and bare hardwood floor must look compared to her fancy digs. He wished he'd had time to wash the sheets, but honestly he hadn't even thought of it until now. The house had three bedrooms and the spare bedroom was rarely used.

"I can wash the sheets if you'd like," he offered.

She laid her bag on the patchwork quilt his grandmother had made. "Why? Are they dirty?"

"No, but probably not too fresh."

"They'll be fine." She kicked off her heels and placed them by the nightstand. Removing the pins from her hair, she shook her head and the long waves of her hair fell down around her shoulders. His muscles tensed as he remembered running his fingers through it last night. "I'm going to play with Daniel for a little while."

"Okay." He blew out a breath. "The bathroom is at the end of the hall."

She stopped at the door and faced him. "I can find my way around, and you don't have to wait on me."

"And you can lose the attitude. I'm only trying to help."

She swallowed. "Okay, truce?"

"We're going to be spending a lot of time together so a truce would be nice."

"Good." She walked off down the hall to the living room. Seeing her, Daniel bounced up and down in the Pack 'N Play and she picked him up. She sat on the floor and Daniel crawled all over her. She seemed to have a need to touch him.

"Supper's ready," Pop said from behind him.

The meal was quiet except for Daniel jabbering in his high chair. Myra fed him his food while eating hers. Pop didn't mention girlfriend number one or two and he was grateful for that. Afterward, they gave Daniel a bath in the bathtub and put him down for the night.

"I put his bed in my room so if someone tried to take him they'd have to go through me," he told her.

"If he cries during the night, I'll get him," she said.

"Okay, but I'll probably hear him first. Try to get a good night's rest."

She ran a hand through her hair. "I'll take a quick shower and go to bed, then."

Levi walked into the den. Pop was watching TV. Levi sank onto the sofa, feeling drained and wondering if he and Myra could ever find some sort of middle ground. They were talking and acting like strangers when they were really so much more. How much more was yet to be seen.

God, he had two women he needed to talk to and he wasn't sure who to talk to first. But he knew which one was tearing him up inside.

"She go to bed?" Pop asked.

"Yeah."

"She don't talk much."

"She just buried her friend."

"Yep, that'll sap the life right out of you."

"Levi," Myra called from the hallway, and he immediately went to her.

"In the rush, I didn't bring anything to sleep in. Can I borrow a T-shirt?"

"Sure." He went into his room and pulled out a white V-neck and carried it back to her.

"Thanks," she said.

The sadness on her face twisted his gut. "Are you okay?"

She shrugged. "I don't know. It's been a rough day."

He had the urge to hold her again, to let her know she wasn't alone, but that would only cause one more problem. "If you need anything else, just let me know."

He went back to the living room, and soon he and Pop both went to bed. Around midnight, Daniel woke up crying. Levi jiggled him, talked to him, changed his diaper, but nothing helped. The baby even spit out his pacifier.

"What's wrong?" Myra asked, walking into the room. Her hair was tousled and her eyes were sleepy. He'd seen her like this so many times and it triggered memories of better days.

"Let me have him. I'll take him to bed with me and maybe he'll calm down." She took the baby and went into her room, but the wails continued. She got up and walked with him. That didn't help, either. Daniel continued to cry heart-wrenching sobs.

Myra kissed the baby's forehead. "It's almost as if he knows he's lost his mother."

Levi couldn't deny that. Daniel had seen too many strange people and been in too many strange places. It was normal for him to be upset. They just had to figure out a way to calm him.

Pop stomped out of his room in his cowboy boots and boxer shorts.

"Pop, where's your robe? We have company."

"I don't know. I can't find it. I'm not even sure I have one."

"I gave you one for Christmas a few years ago."

"Ah, who knows."

"So you decided to put on your cowboy boots instead?"

"It just seemed right."

Levi shook his head.

Daniel's wails continued with intermittent hiccups. "Let me have the boy," Pop said.

"If we can't calm him, how do you think you can?"

Pop took the baby from Myra. "Because you're young and I'm old, and I know a hell of a lot more than you do."

Pop stomped off to the living room with a crying Daniel. Sitting in his recliner-rocker, he began to rock and sing to the baby. "Booger was a bumblebee with a stinger on his butt. Buzz buzz buzz, all day long…"

"Oh, no."

"What?" Myra asked, standing next to him. A whiff of gardenia reached him and he had trouble thinking for a second.

"It's a god-awful song he made up when I was a baby. It doesn't even rhyme."

"Does it work?"

"I have no idea. I just remember it."

Pop continued to sing and Daniel's crying turned to hiccups and then silence. "Booger was a bumble-bee with a stinger on his butt. Buzz buzz buzz, all day long, looking for a bud to bust." Pop's voice rose. "Oh, no, Booger can't get me. Buzz buzz buzz." Pop used his hand and fingers as the bee buzzed around. "Buzz buzz buzz. Booger can't get me." Pop's hand came down and tickled Daniel's stomach. "Oh, no. Booger just got me. Buzz buzz buzz-z-z-z-z."

Daniel cackled out loud, his little chest shaking with laughter.

"I guess laughing is better than crying," Levi said, the childish laughter filling the room.

"You guys go to bed," Pop said. "I got this."

"You have him wound up," Levi told him. "He'll never go to sleep."

"Go to bed, Levi."

He knew that tone…the one that said Henry Coyote wasn't going to budge.

"What do you think?" he asked Myra.

"Daniel's not crying, so I guess we go back to bed."

They turned toward their rooms. Levi stopped at his door. "I'll check on them in a little while."

"Daniel's just upset. He was crying like that at the compound. Poor little thing just wants his mommy and I—"

"Myra…"

"I'm okay." She walked into her room and Levi knew

she wasn't okay. It was going to take a whole lot of healing before everyone could move forward.

At two, Levi got up and went into the living room. Everything was quiet. Pop and Daniel were sound asleep. He lifted the baby out of his grandfather's arms and carried him back to his baby bed. Pop stirred and went to his room. The rest of the night everyone slept.

The next morning they slept in and it was the first time Levi realized they were going to be confined here until this was over. But then when would it be over? Marco would continue to fight for his son and that put Myra in extreme danger.

As they finished breakfast, Tom called and Levi spoke to him for a minute.

"What did he say?" Myra asked, wiping Daniel's mouth.

"The two guys stayed outside your apartment until two and then went to a motel. They're back there this morning. They'll continue to watch them."

"They'll soon figure out I'm not there."

Levi got out of his chair. "We'll wait and see what they do then."

They could hear the sound of a vehicle and Levi immediately went to the door. "It's my friend Ethan. I had him pick up some stuff for me in Austin."

Levi met Ethan at the gate.

"How's it going?" Ethan asked as they stood by his truck.

"It's rough and could get rougher," he replied. "Did you get everything I asked for?"

"It's in a box in the backseat."

"Thanks." Levi got the box out of the truck. "I'm

adding some security measures just in case. Sensors at the cattle guard will let me know through my phone when a vehicle crosses it and I'm putting sensors on every door and window so I'm not caught by surprise."

"Carson's keeping an eye on the road."

"I knew I could count on my friends."

Ethan thumbed over his shoulder. "Myra Delgado's inside?"

"Yeah." Levi didn't mind talking to his friend. They'd shared a lot since they were kids and Carson and Ethan knew all about Myra. They'd kept him sane during that rough patch. "It's a little awkward, but we don't have any choice."

"You were crazy about her," Ethan commented.

Levi shook his head. "Don't go there." He placed the box on the hood of the truck and told his friend what had happened.

"Damn. You're supposed to be the sensible one."

"I'm wondering if I have any sense at all at the moment."

Ethan slapped him on the back. "Love does that to you. Call if you need anything else."

As Levi opened the screen door, he heard, "Buzz buzz buzz..." Pop was teaching Myra the song and Daniel sat in her lap, clapping his hands and cackling every time the bee tickled his stomach. It was a Kodak moment and one that would stay with him long after Myra had left his life.

"Want to sing with us?" Myra asked with a twinkle in her eye. She was much better today and he was glad to see that. Or maybe not. She was just that much more tempting to a man who obviously didn't have much willpower.

"I'll pass. I'm going to be installing some extra security, so I'll be outside most of the day."

"Man has no taste in songs," Pop grumbled.

By the time he finished putting sensors at the cattle guard, on the doors, windows and barn entrance, it was late. Myra and Pop were cooking supper and seemed to be getting along, which was odd because it took a while for people to warm up to Pop. He had his own unique annoying personality and Levi loved him for that—most of the time.

Dressed in jeans and a knit top, Myra looked young and eye-catching as she hurried around the kitchen to do Pop's bidding. Daniel was in his high chair, waiting for food. They seemed like an ordinary family and a small part of him, the part that had loved Myra seven years ago, wished it were so.

After the kitchen was clean, they gave Daniel a bath and put him in his stroller and went out to the front porch, hoping to tire him out before putting him to bed. Daniel bounced up and down with glee when he saw John Wayne, and when the dog barked, Daniel tried to do the same.

He and Myra sat on the porch swing. "Have you talked to Tom any more today?" she asked.

"Just that the two men have made no move to enter the apartment and that at noon they left for the courthouse, I guess trying to catch you at work. Tom hasn't called since, so I assume everything is the same. He did say that Steve was stymied. He was sure they would've made a move before now."

"I did, too. I talked to Stu and he said to keep my ass here, but I have the Dawson trial that starts in a month and I need to be back in my office soon. And Clarence informed me that if I'm not back within the week, he has to appoint a new prosecutor."

"That bothers you?"

"Yes. That creep killed two teenage girls and he deserves to spend the rest of his life behind bars."

"What about your life?" The swing moved gently as the shadows deepened across the ranch.

She looked toward the barn, a faraway look in her eyes. "I don't know. My life has been turned upside down."

"It might be time to rethink your life." He hadn't meant to be so blunt, but the words just slipped out.

She pulled her feet beneath her and sat facing him. "It's nice here. Peaceful and quiet."

"What did you expect?"

She shrugged. "I have to be honest. When you talked about it years ago, I thought it would bore me to tears."

"And now?"

MYRA ROLLED THE answer around in her head and wondered if honesty was the way to go. In truth, she felt as if she'd found the missing part of herself, the one she kept trying to fill with a career, with long days and little sleep, and a schedule that would kill a younger person. Stu said it wasn't worth it and now she had to weigh his words concerning her own life.

What did she want out of life? The career? Or a family?

She couldn't ignore all the years she'd put into her

career. And she couldn't ignore the yearnings she experienced just being here with Levi and his grandfather. It was hard for her to get away and relax, but today, even with Marco's henchmen on her trail, she felt more relaxed than she ever had.

Instead of answering, she asked, "Did you talk to Valerie?"

He ran his hand along the chain that held the swing in place. "Yeah, yesterday."

It was hard to ask such a personal question, but she had to know. "Did you tell her?"

"Yes, and she was understanding and forgiving."

Myra was surprised. "Oh. I'm, um, happy for you."

He looked at her and the darkness of his eyes rivaled the warmth of the night. "Really, Myra?"

"What do you want me to say?"

"I think we're both going to have to admit that there's a lot of feelings left from the old days. Also, we have to acknowledge that we're still attracted to each other. And that we still have different goals. Your life has always been about your career and you're a damn good prosecutor, but someday you're going to have to decide if that's all you want."

She had already figured that out for herself. What she wanted was sitting next to her. She wanted him in her life and in her bed. That was called having it all. For her to accomplish it, she had to make some changes. Her heart had always known what it wanted. But how would she manage a career and a family? The thought created more doubts and fears.

She decided to steer clear of her inner turmoil. "So you think you and Valerie can make a go of it?"

"I'm not sure. Right now my focus is keeping you and Daniel safe."

She reached out and touched his forearm, feeling his taut muscles. "Thank you for everything you've done for us."

"I'm sorry I got so angry about the abortion thing." His dark eyes begged for forgiveness.

"Well, I think I told you every dark secret I have. Jessie doesn't even know, so you can blackmail me anytime you want." She was trying to bring levity to a tense situation, but it only created a different kind of tension.

His eyes held hers with unwavering honesty. "You make me crazy sometimes."

"Sometimes?"

His mouth curved into a smile and she was lost for a moment in everything she had thrown away. The squeak of the swing was as soothing as a baby's lullaby. It wrapped them in warmth unequaled by anything she'd ever felt. But it was only temporary. Danger lurked just outside their comfort zone.

Suddenly, the porch light came on and Pop came outside. "What are y'all doing sitting in the dark?"

"It's not dark yet. It's dusk," Levi told him.

"Same thing." Pop looked down at Daniel, who was leaning out of the stroller trying to touch John Wayne, who was stretched out on the porch. Every now and then the dog would lick his hand.

"I've lost my dog to the little guy," Pop said. "Maybe we need to get him a puppy."

"He's not going to be here that long," Levi reminded him.

"Ah, every boy needs a puppy."

Levi's cell rang, interrupting the conversation. Pop grabbed the handle on the stroller. "I'll take the little guy inside and put him to bed."

"I'll go with you," Myra said. "He takes a bottle before bed." They left Levi talking on the phone.

With Daniel asleep, she walked into the living room. Levi sat staring at his phone.

"What happened?" she asked. From his angry expression she knew something had.

"That was Tom. He said Marco's guys spent some time at the courthouse waiting and then one went inside and asked for your office. Someone told him you were out for the week. Damn it!" He stood in an agitated movement.

"What's wrong with that? They just know I'm not there."

"That's not all. They lost track of the car. The last time they saw it, the two hoods were headed for I-10."

"What does that mean?"

"We're trying to figure it out, but the obvious is they found out where you are and they're coming this way."

"But they couldn't. No one knows."

"Marco has money and resources and he probably found out where I live. They put two and two together. Now we have to be ready."

A shiver ran through her.

Pop came in and sank into his chair. Levi told him what had happened.

"Son of a bitch! We gotta make sure they don't take that baby."

Levi ran a hand through his hair and she could see his mind was working overtime with ways to protect them. "Everyone do exactly as I tell you. And, Pop, I really need you to listen to me."

"I'm listening with both ears."

"Okay. It would be best if we slept here in the living room tonight so we're together. Myra, you take the couch. Pop, I know you can sleep in your chair."

"You bet. Spend half my life in this chair."

"We'll also bring Daniel in here. We can't leave him alone in the bedroom."

For the next few minutes, they rushed around and got pillows and blankets. Myra gathered Daniel out of his bed. He whimpered, but he didn't wake up. She padded his Pack 'N Play with a big quilt and she then laid him on it. Levi had moved the coffee table and they put the Pack 'N Play in the middle of the room.

Pop got his shotgun and Levi brought a rifle and more ammo for his Glock. Myra had a small Smith and Wesson she kept in her purse for protection. She lay on the sofa with it beneath her pillow and they settled in for the night. Myra thought she wouldn't sleep. So much was happening and all she could hear was Marco's words: "I will find you."

She must have fallen asleep because the buzz of Levi's phone woke her. He was immediately on his feet and she wondered if he had slept at all. Pop stirred in his chair, but Daniel was still sleeping.

Sitting up, she asked, "Who is it?"

"The sensor at the cattle guard just went off. Something has triggered it. Get into the hallway. Now! And don't turn on any lights."

A shiver of alarm shot through her. She grabbed

Daniel and ran. Pop followed with his shotgun in his hand. Levi hurriedly brought a chair for his grandfather.

"Thanks, son. I can't stand on this arthritic knee too long."

"Do you want a chair?" he asked her.

"No, thanks. I'm fine."

In that moment, when fear was crawling along her spine like a killer scorpion, she marveled at how thoughtful and considerate Levi was of others. That personality trait was the reason he was involved with her and now fighting for his life and theirs.

"Stay here. No one move until I tell you. If they start firing, and I don't think they will because they won't take a chance of hitting the baby, I want everyone safe as possible."

"John Wayne," Pop cried. "Don't let them hurt him."

"I'll let him into the house, but the next few minutes are very crucial. Everyone be very quiet."

Levi left and in a few seconds John Wayne joined them, sitting very still by Pop as if he knew danger was imminent.

Pop rubbed the dog's head. "I told you to stay in the house, didn't I?"

John Wayne whimpered in response.

Myra's legs grew weak and she sank to the floor with the baby. She could hear Levi on the phone, evidently talking to Tom. "Get a damn chopper out here. Your guys screwed this up. We don't have much time."

It was dark and Myra could barely see her hand in front of her face, but she could hear Levi moving around, agitated. And she could hear bits of conversation.

"No, I don't see any headlights. They're not stupid enough to turn them on at this time of the morning. It might alert us. If there are just two of them, I think I can handle it, but I'm going to need backup quick."

"Don't worry, missy," Pop whispered. "Levi'll take care of us."

She knew that. She knew Levi would protect them with his life and she prayed that wouldn't happen. Clutching Daniel, she prayed like she'd never prayed before. They sat waiting and raw terror crept around them in chilling silence.

The hum of the refrigerator sounded like an eighteen-wheeler. The clock in the dining room ticked with the urgency of a bomb. Myra held Daniel a little tighter and waited.

And waited.

Then Levi was there.

He squatted close to her. "If a sensor goes off, don't move from this spot. I'll handle it." He handed Myra her gun that she'd left on the sofa. "You might need this."

"You don't have to worry about us, son. We can follow orders. I was in the Korean War and I know that when there's danger, you follow orders."

"Thanks, Pop."

Levi's cell beeped. He looked at his phone. "Someone just opened the barn door. Damn it!" He ran to the living room, talking to Tom.

"They're in the barn for some reason. I need backup."

Myra trembled and gripped Daniel a little tighter.

"I'll see if I can spot a vehicle, but I don't want them to know that we're awake.... No. I can't see a thing. Wait. I see two shadows headed toward the house. Damn! It's fixing to go down, man!"

Levi was in the hall again. "They're probably planning to burst through the front door. If you hear shots, have your gun ready. Do not let them in the hallway."

"Got it," Pop said. "This old shotgun'll take 'em out in a minute."

"Just be prepared."

"Levi," she called. "Please be careful."

"I will, and don't fire unless you absolutely have to." He moved back to the living room with catlike movements and she waited for the sounds of holy hell, one arm clutching Daniel and the other her Smith and Wesson.

"This is it," Levi said. "They're coming in."

CHAPTER SEVENTEEN

LEVI STOOD WITH his arms outstretched, his right hand gripped tight around the Glock, his finger on the trigger. His feet were planted firmly on the hardwood floor. As he waited for Marco's thugs to come crashing through the door, his hand was steady, his nerves rock-solid. But all was quiet. All he heard was the pounding of his heart in his ears.

He counted in his head. *One. Two. Three.* They should be at the door. Maybe they were coming through a window or the back door. He took several steps backward, so he could get a better view of the whole house. Nothing.

Something was wrong.

Sensors monitored all the windows, so if one was opened he would know. But everything was silent.

Too silent.

His phone was in his shirt pocket and he had Tom on the other end. "Something's not right," he whispered. "They should have been here by now."

"Just stay put. We're almost there."

"I'm going toward the door to check things out."

"Stay put, Levi. Don't draw unnecessary fire."

Levi lowered his arms, but kept the gun tightly in his right hand. Myra, the baby and Pop were safe—for now—and he had to make sure they stayed that way.

His eyes stayed trained on the front and the back doors. Still nothing was happening.

His cell beeped. He drew it out of his pocket. "Tom, a vehicle just went over my cattle guard. For some reason, they're leaving. I never expected that."

"We're on it."

Levi shoved the gun into his waistband and went into the hallway. The early-morning light seemed to brighten up the house.

"It's safe to come out," he told them.

"Good." Pop got to his feet. "Because I got to pee." He disappeared into the bathroom.

He helped Myra to her feet. "Are they really gone?" she asked, her voice a little shaky.

"Yes. I'm not sure what's happening, but Tom and the highway patrol should be able to stop them. Maybe we'll have some answers then."

Daniel stirred and rubbed his eyes. Opening them, he smiled at Levi and held out his little arms.

"Hey, buddy, stay with Myra. I have some things to do."

Daniel stuck out his lower lip and Levi was hard-pressed not to take him. But to ensure their safety, he had to be ready at all times.

Luckily, Pop came out of the bathroom and Daniel's attention was diverted. "Missy, let's get some coffee going." He took Daniel from her. "I'll watch this little guy."

"He needs changing," Myra said.

"Dang it." Pop frowned. "Should have kept my mouth shut." He carried Daniel into Levi's room and flipped on the light.

"What do you think is going on?" Myra asked.

"I don't know. It might just be teenagers out for a joyride. We'll have to wait and see. In the meantime, I could really use some coffee."

She smiled and the stress of the night seemed to disappear. "I don't make coffee for just anyone."

"Who do you make coffee for?"

She looked into his eyes and saw everything he wanted, including the heartache and the pain, forgiveness and love. How did life get so complicated when it really should be so simple?

"For a big old guy who's willing to die for me."

His cell beeped and he dragged his eyes away to answer it. It was Tom. Myra leaned in close and he pushed the speakerphone button.

"I have you on speakerphone, Tom."

"Okay."

"Did you catch them?"

"We got them."

"Was it Mortez's men?"

"Yes. They've been booked into the San Marcos jail and I'm almost back to your house. Talk to you in a minute."

They could hear the sound of a helicopter as it drew closer and closer.

Pop came out of Levi's room, carrying Daniel, who wore nothing but a diaper. "What the hell is that?"

"It's Tom, the detective from Houston," Levi told him. "Daniel needs more than a diaper."

"Why? I'm fixing him breakfast and he just gets it everywhere. He's easier to wash than his clothes." Pop strolled off to the kitchen and put Daniel in his high chair. "There's no coffee," he shouted to Myra. "What have you been doing?"

Myra walked into the kitchen. "I'm not your personal maid."

"Damn." Pop grinned. "You can't blame an old man for trying."

She poured water into the coffeemaker and added grounds. "That's just because I like you so much," she said with a teasing light in her brown eyes.

"You know, I'm starting to like you, too. You got guts, missy."

Pop never knew when to shut his mouth, but Myra took him for exactly who he was: a grouchy old man with a compassionate heart.

The sound of the helicopter became deafening and they waited for it to ebb.

"I'll take care of the little guy," Pop said. "You two do what you got to."

After grabbing a cup, Levi joined Myra in the living room. He opened the door and Tom came in. "What's the story?" Levi asked.

"Man, I could use some of that." Tom glanced at the coffee cup in Levi's hand.

"Sure." Levi hurried to the kitchen.

Tom sat on the sofa and Myra sat beside him, sipping her coffee. "You're not going to believe this one," Tom said.

Levi handed Tom a cup and took a seat. "What were they doing in my barn?"

"They were eager to talk in order for protection."

"Protection?" Levi shook his head. "That doesn't make sense."

"They left their car not far from the cattle guard and walked in. They planned to hide in the barn until morning and jump you then. Their orders were to get the baby and to take Myra alive."

Myra gasped. "Then why didn't they?"

"They got a call from one of their buddies in Mexico. Seems Marco, his father and his mother were shot in their beds. They're dead."

"What!" Levi could hardly believe his ears.

"That's what they said. I called Steve to check it out. It's true. Antonio Guzman, Marco's father-in-law, has taken over the compound. An agent in Mexico confirms the bodies are those of Marco and his parents."

"So this friend from Mexico told them they better get lost and fast?"

"They figure Guzman is going to take out all of Marco's men unless they're willing to pledge their allegiance to him. These two seem to be Marco's right-hand men and they think Guzman's hoods will be after them."

"So they want the state of Texas to protect them?" Myra asked.

"That's the gist of it."

Myra stood. "Is Guzman to blame for the murders?"

Tom shrugged. "The housekeeper found the bodies. According to her, Bonita Mortez had been given something to help her sleep. When the housekeeper checked on her, she was still out, but alive. The housekeeper then contacted Mr. Guzman and he got his daughter out of there. No one knows where Guzman has her hidden and they never will."

"What's the motive?" Myra asked. "Could be drug-related. But why would they kill Ava Mortez, too? And why was Bonita spared?"

"Who knows?"

"Bonita was extremely upset about Daniel and Marco's unfaithfulness. Ava and César expected her to just accept it, but she wasn't in an accepting mood. Bonita has a very good motive, but it's not in my jurisdiction. Since I don't have to worry about Marco, I consider it more than a blessing for Daniel and me."

Tom got to his feet. "Do you want to come back to Houston with me and tell Stu? This is going to make his day."

"I'll get my bag." Myra headed for the hall and quickly turned back. She looked at Levi. "Can you bring Daniel later? I'm sure Stu is going to want to see him."

Just like that she was back to being Myra, the lawyer, the prosecutor, and her personal life had been shoved aside. He had been shoved aside. As had Daniel.

"Yeah. I'll bring him later. I have to find out what Stu wants to do about his grandson."

This is where she should say she would raise him because that's what Natalie wanted. But what she said was "I'm sure Stu has a plan."

He watched her leave with an ache in his heart. He'd been torn between two women, but he really hadn't. His heart belonged to Myra and she didn't want it. She didn't want a stable home and a family. She wanted her career.

Within minutes, she was back in the living room, her hair brushed and her eyes bright. She kissed Daniel as Pop was feeding him cereal. "Bye, sweetie."

Daniel held up a finger with cereal on it and tried to touch her face. She licked it and laughed. Daniel chuckled, too. Why couldn't she see what a great mother she would make? Maybe some things just weren't meant to be.

"Thanks, Levi," she said, her eyes holding his, and he could almost feel the gulf between them getting wider. "You seem to be saving my ass a lot these days and now I'll just disappear out of your life and make you happy."

Is that what she really thought? If she did, they really had nothing to talk about.

"I'll see you at Stu's," she called as she rushed out the door with Tom. In a few minutes, the whirl of the chopper accelerated and she was gone. As if she had never been here. As if she had never needed him.

LEVI HAD TO give Daniel a bath before he could dress them. Cereal was plastered in his hair and smeared across his face. The baby wanted to play in the water and wasn't too happy when Levi whisked him out. He wasn't sure of what to take with him to Houston, so he took just what Daniel would need for the day.

He wasn't moving that baby bed around until Daniel had a permanent home. With Daniel dressed and the diaper bag packed, he was ready to go.

"Where you taking him?" Pop asked.

"To see his grandfather."

Pop turned from the sink, his eyes narrowed. "But you're bringing him back, right?"

"Depends on what Stu says. He might have a relative willing to take the baby."

Pop's eyes narrowed to thin lines. "The boy needs a home and we got a home. He needs to stay here."

"I have to work."

"I can take care of him. I do a better job than you young folks, anyway."

Levi was at a loss for words for a moment. "Pop, I have to take him back."

"It's just like I told you. Rip my heart out by the roots. That's what you're doing. If you don't bring that baby back, I'll never..." He stomped out the back door and John Wayne slipped through the doggie door after him.

Forgive you. That's what his grandfather meant to say. Damn, this was getting out of control. He should've never involved his grandfather. Now he had to hurt the one person he loved most in this world.

Life was a damn bitch.

Daniel touched his face with a chubby hand and Levi looked at the cherub face. "It's all your fault. Your cuteness is affecting all of us."

Daniel clapped his hands and made a purring sound.

"Are you trying to say 'buzz buzz buzz'?"

Daniel clapped that much harder and Levi just smiled. How was he going to give Daniel back? Oh, yeah, this was going to hurt.

"We better go, buddy. It's a long way to Houston." The sound of a vehicle caught Levi's attention. Was that Pop's truck? He was probably going to Walt's.

Levi was about to go out the back when someone tapped at the front door. It couldn't be Pop. He went to see who it was. First, he glanced out the window.

It was Valerie. The last thing he needed today. But he opened the door.

She frowned the moment she saw Daniel. "Oh, you still have the baby."

"I was just taking him to Houston."

Her face relaxed into a smile. "Good. I was hoping we could go out tonight."

Daniel was babbling, "Buzz buzz buzz," or something similar, oblivious to the tension. Levi had to end it today and it wasn't something he would enjoy. "Sorry. I'll be busy getting Daniel settled."

"Can't someone else do it? Haven't you done enough?"

"Daniel's grandfather is a very good friend of mine. He supported me through bad times, and when I look at his grandson, I don't see a half-Mexican baby. I see a little boy who needs love."

"Levi, please, you know I didn't mean anything by my remarks the other day."

"When I opened the door, it was on your face the moment you saw him."

She flipped back her blond hair. "Okay. I might have a little problem in that area. But it doesn't mean I don't love you."

"What would you say if I told you I was thinking of adopting him?"

"You can't be serious!"

Levi had heard all he needed to hear. He wasn't thinking of adopting Daniel, but he knew he and Valerie would never make it as a couple. He'd thought they had the same views and goals in life, only to learn they were nowhere close to being on the same page.

"Valerie, I don't think you and I have anything left to talk about. I don't have any plans to adopt Daniel, but I can't be with a woman who resents a baby for his nationality."

"It's her, isn't it?"

How he wished he could say it was Myra. She had made her own choices and he knew he was not included in them. And it wasn't all Myra's fault. They just couldn't seem to connect the way they should. The way they used to.

"Now that the danger is over, Myra has gone back to her job in the city."

"Do you plan on seeing her?"

He glanced at his watch. "I have to go. Daniel's grandfather is waiting." He had no intention of answering her or fueling her jealousy.

"When you come to your senses, call me."

"I won't be calling." He didn't want to be that blunt, but she forced his hand.

Her eyes narrowed in anger. "I only went out with you as a smoke screen to cover up my affair with the doctor I work for."

"Excuse me?"

"His wife was getting suspicious and I needed a boyfriend quickly to throw her off the trail. You see, she's very wealthy and on the hospital board and could very well end his brilliant career. When I ran into you that day at the hospital, I knew I'd found my new boyfriend. At first, it was just a ruse, but it turned into so much more. Now you're throwing it all away."

He looked at this woman he thought he knew and saw someone who was just a figment of his imagination: the perfect woman who would love him the way he loved her. What a joke that was. He was beginning to question if he even knew what love was. It certainly wasn't what he felt for Valerie. He had a sick feeling in his stomach.

"Goodbye, Valerie. Don't ever call me again." He closed the door and walked away, feeling as if he'd escaped the biggest fiasco of his life.

From the helicopter pad, Myra and Tom went to the police station to get an update on Marco's men from the San Marcos police. Stu would want every detail. For information on the Mortez family, the FBI were discussing a deal. Myra left Tom to handle things. A cop drove her to her apartment and then she was on her way to Stu's.

A weight had been lifted and she felt as if she could float along the ceiling like a helium balloon if she didn't hold on to the handrails that lined the wide corridors of the facility. Marco was not a threat to her or Daniel anymore.

Without Levi, she wouldn't have been able to get through any of it. Normally, she was a strong person, but when it came down to life or death, she needed him. She really should have told him that. She should have told him a lot of things, but she was feeling her way through a minefield of emotions. Right now she had to focus on Stu and Daniel and sort her love life out later. It was more than her love life, though. It was her whole life.

Stu was sitting in his recliner, still in his pajamas

with a big smile on his face. "They got that bastard and he'll never hurt my grandson."

"Did Tom call you?"

"Nah. Very little happens in the police department that I don't know about."

"Mmm. I'm aware of that." She sat close to Stu. "I think Marco's wife, Bonita, did us a favor."

"You think it was the wife, huh?"

"She probably knew Marco had sent his men for Daniel. Because of her hate for the baby, Bonita helped us escape. The thought of the baby returning must have sent her over the edge. She seemed a little deranged. Since her father is Antonio Guzman, I can only imagine that they might have done it together."

"Well, kid, we're not going to analyze it too much. We're not going to question this gift, this blessing. Marco is dead and he can't take Daniel now. I can die in peace."

"Stu, please don't say that."

He patted her hands. "It's a fact of life. Don't be sad. I had a wild adventure while I was here. I have a lot to be grateful for. Also, I have a mountain of regrets. But it wouldn't be life otherwise."

Myra swallowed. "Have you made a decision about Daniel?"

Stu nodded. "Yes, so don't worry. He'll have a good life, the one I want for him filled with love and happiness."

Myra was taken aback. His answer surprised her. She'd thought he would have asked her to take Daniel. She didn't know how she'd manage with her job, but a big part of her was pulling her in Daniel's direction.

Now it seemed it didn't matter. Stu had made plans that didn't include her. She tried hard not to feel hurt. Then she thought of all the times she had told him she didn't want to be a mother, so she could only blame herself.

"Where is my grandson?"

"Levi's bringing him."

"Ah, Levi. Trustworthy Levi. There are a lot of men in this world and I've worked with a lot of cops, but when it comes to trust and loyalty, you'll never find a better man than Levi Coyote."

Her cell buzzed and prevented her from answering. Not that she had a response. She knew Levi about as well as she knew anyone and she couldn't dispute a single word Stu had said. Levi was the best.

She stood to talk to Clarence. "I can be there in about fifteen minutes. Oh, wait. I need to change. It'll be about forty-five minutes....Okay. I'll see you then."

Before she could click off, her cell beeped again. This time it was Steve. "I'll be in my office within the hour."

She stared at Stu's questioning eyes.

"What?"

He shook his head. "It's not worth it."

"Stu, I have a job and I've been away about a week now, so it's time to get back to work."

"Is that really what you want?"

She slipped her phone into her purse to avoid looking at him because he always seemed to know when she was lying. So she decided not to tell a big whopper. At the moment, she was struggling just to remember her name without Levi's face coming into view.

Swinging the strap of her purse over her shoulder,

she said, "Try not to celebrate too much today. I'll check back later."

"Aren't you going to wait for Levi?"

She glanced at her watch. "I really have to go."

She was running like a scared teenager. In the next few hours she would have to make a decision that would affect the rest of her life. Maybe somewhere in the maze of confusion, she would discover just what she wanted.

"Bye," she called, and rushed out the door. And ran straight into Levi pushing Daniel in a stroller.

"Oh, you startled me."

Daniel beat a fat fist on the front of the stroller and babbled something she couldn't make out. He smiled at her and for a moment the world made sense.

"Did you talk to Stu?" Levi asked.

Her eyes swung to his and suddenly her choices were very clear, and that just made everything more complicated. More emotional. And more heartbreaking.

She collected her thoughts. "Yes. He's very happy he no longer has to worry about Daniel's safety."

"Did he say what his plans were?"

"He said he had plans and I wasn't to worry. I'm assuming he's contacted a family member and they've agreed to take Daniel."

Levi frowned. "You didn't ask?"

"It's Stu's decision." Her cell beeped and she turned away. This time she was glad. Anger rolled off Levi in waves and it was all directed at her. "Yes, Clarence, I'm coming. I just spoke to Steve and he knows I'm running late. I'll be there as soon as I can."

"You're going back to work," Levi remarked.

"Yes." She slipped the phone back into her purse.

"The Dawson trial is moving forward and Clarence wants me there."

"What about Daniel?"

"Stu will fill you in." She started to walk off, unable to take any more, when he caught her arm.

"What about your promise to Natalie?"

She exhaled deeply. His fingers on her skin tripped her response in another direction and she was struggling to deal with her feelings. "I promised to look out for him and I've done that."

"I'm the one looking out for Daniel," he said sharply. "You're going back to work. There's a difference, Myra."

"Levi, please."

"What?"

When she didn't respond, he went on. "It always comes down to your job, Myra. So go. I'll make sure Daniel has everything he needs."

A piercing pain stabbed her in the heart. She was making all the wrong decisions and she couldn't help herself. She needed to talk to Levi, but she wasn't sure what talking would accomplish. They were still at a stalemate. She had to get her thoughts straight and the only way to do that was to be alone. Obviously, he didn't understand that. At times she didn't, either.

"What do you expect from me?"

"I expect you to tell Clarence to stuff that job and that you're going to do everything you can to give Daniel the life you promised Natalie."

Her legs trembled, so she knelt down to Daniel's level and kissed his cheek. "Bye, sweetie." She stood and ran down the hall toward the entrance and her car.

Once inside, the tears flowed. Tears of regret. Tears of shame. Tears of sorrow.

There was no way to go forward now.

Levi hated her.

CHAPTER EIGHTEEN

LEVI KNOCKED ON the door and pushed Daniel into Stu's room.

"There's my boy." Stu clapped his hands and Daniel bounced around excitedly in the stroller. Levi unbuckled the baby and placed him in Stu's lap.

"Look at that face, Levi. He looks like my Natalie. Hopefully, he'll have none of that bastard in him."

Levi took a seat. "A loving home is what Daniel needs."

"I couldn't agree with you more, my friend."

Levi rubbed his hands together. "I saw Myra in the hall...."

"Is that why you look like somebody just shot your horse?"

"Maybe. Things are kind of tense between us." Levi saw no reason not to be honest.

"Why? You two worked together to save Daniel and that should have brought you closer together."

"It's the same-old same-old."

"Her job?"

Levi sighed. "And the past. There's a lot of heartache between now and then." He didn't know how else to explain it. "Sometimes it takes more than love."

"You mean, if she quit her job that would prove she loved you more."

"What?"

"You want her to prove she loves you more than her job."

"No." That wasn't it. Was it?

Daniel held out his arms for Levi. "Mmm. Mmm. Mmm."

He lifted the baby from Stu and Daniel laid his head on Levi's shoulder.

"Now, I would be insulted if I didn't know you so well and that you cared for my grandson."

Levi padded Daniel's back. "The little guy and I made a connection and he's absolutely stolen my grandfather's heart."

"Old Henry's?"

"Yeah. Kind of hard to believe, isn't it?"

"Nah."

"Myra said you have someone to care for Daniel." Levi thought it was a good time to bring up the subject.

Stu adjusted the oxygen tubing in his nose and then had a coughing fit. It took a few minutes before he could speak. "I'm...working on it. Could you keep him a couple more days until I get everything set the way I want?"

"I don't mind, but whoever you've chosen should get to know Daniel as soon as possible. He's been handed off too much and needs a home."

Stu nodded. "I was thinking the same thing. The lawyer should have everything drawn up in at least two days. Will that work for you?"

Levi watched his friend. "What would work for me is that you stop being so cagey. Why can't you tell me who you're leaving guardianship to?"

Stu gave a half grin. "Always the cop, huh?"

"I get a little suspicious when people avoid telling me things."

"I…I don't blame you." Stu put a hand over his mouth and started to cough again, loud hacking coughs. "Sorry. Sometimes it just gets…hard to breathe."

Levi put Daniel back in the stroller and buckled him in. He'd known Stu a lot of years and the man had taught him everything he knew about police work. Stu had stood by him in good times and in bad and he couldn't have asked for a better friend when the higher-ups had wanted his ass canned all those years ago. For that reason, he would let Stu play out his little game or whatever it was. But there was something he needed to know.

"Have you asked Myra to take Daniel?"

Stu rubbed the arm of his recliner for a second. "No. She made a career choice years ago and she also made a choice not to have children. I respect that and wouldn't put the responsibility of Daniel on her shoulders. She's been too good to Natalie and me."

His response made Levi feel like an ass and he had a sneaky suspicion that's what Stu set out to do. Levi did not respect Myra's decisions. Staring at his friend, he had a revelation. He wanted her to bend to his way of thinking. It wasn't up to Levi to change Myra. It was up to him to accept her the way she was or get the hell out of her life and stop wanting her to be some-one she wasn't.

Levi held out his hand and Stu shook it. "Give me a call when you want me to bring Daniel."

"I can't thank you enough for everything you've done."

"No thanks required, but I think we're even now."

Stu shook his head. "We'll never be even. I'll never be able to repay my debt to you. You're the best friend a man could have and, Levi, I wish you nothing but the best."

"You're getting a little mushy." Levity was the only response Levi had for the years of friendship that required no thanks. "Catch you later."

"Bye, Levi."

Without another word, he pushed the stroller to the door.

"Levi," Stu called.

He glanced back at his friend.

"I'm going to give you a piece of wise advice. If you want things to work with Myra, tell her you love her and say you're sorry. Everything else will fall into place. Trust me. It's that simple."

Levi just nodded because there was nothing left he could say. It was now up to Myra. Not him. Like Stu had said, it was her choice and Levi had to respect that and stop wanting her to be mother of the year. He never felt about anyone the way he felt about her. So maybe he was the one who needed to change.

MYRA SPENT THIRTY minutes in a meeting with Steve. They were still working on a deal with Mortez's men and they'd raided the Mortez house in Brownsville and discovered a basement, as Levi had suspected. It was full of guns and drugs ready to be shipped all over the United States. The expensive cars were only a front.

The FBI was now checking into a snitch at the Brownsville border crossing. Someone was allowing the trucks filled with guns to cross. Steve was pleased with the progress being made. Finally, they'd caught a break.

From there, she met with colleagues to discuss the Dawson case. Jury selection started in a week. A wealthy boy of nineteen had raped and murdered two girls; one of them had ID'd him before she'd died. The boy's father had hired a high-priced defense attorney and gotten the boy out on bail. But Myra was determined to put him behind bars where he belonged.

Adrenaline rushed through her veins as always when she started a trial. She tried to concentrate, but voices went right over her head. What was wrong with her? Then she heard Levi's voice: *Do what you promised Natalie.* And then Stu's voice: *It's that simple.*

The sad truth was she wanted nothing more than to be Daniel's mother. It came back to her lack of confidence in herself as a mother. She could handle a murder trial and she was balking at raising a little boy. Suddenly, she knew what was wrong with her.

Under her breath she began to sing, "Booger was a bumblebee with a stinger on his butt. Buzz buzz buzz…"

"Myra. Myra!"

She glanced up and saw everyone staring at her.

"You were singing," Kyle said.

"Was I?"

"Something about a bumblebee."

She wanted to laugh at the expressions on their faces.

Cool, collected Myra Delgado was losing it right in front of them. She got to her feet.

"Well, I guess you're boring me to death. Take over, Kyle."

"But you're the lead prosecutor."

She lifted an eyebrow. Kyle was an eager beaver, dying to replace her, and she was about to make his day. "You can't handle it?"

"Damn right I can."

"Then have at it."

"Does Clarence know about this?"

She stepped a little closer to the young man. "Never question anything I tell you."

"Yes, ma'am."

She walked out and toward a future she wanted. But first she had to talk to Clarence. She couldn't leave otherwise.

The little shark receptionist was not at her desk and Myra tapped on Clarence's door.

"What?" came from within.

She walked in. Clarence was on his laptop and didn't even look up.

"I quit."

"Tell Kyle to sit down like a good little boy and everything will be fine."

"Clarence, I'm serious. I'll write up a resignation letter, but I really don't want to take the time. I have to go."

Clarence looked up, frowning through the glasses on his nose. "Are you serious?"

"I've never been more serious about anything in my life."

The D.A. leaned back in his chair. "Take a few more

days if you need to. You've been through a lot. I understand that."

"Thank you, but it's more than that."

"Myra, this is your life. That's why you're such a good prosecutor. You put everything you are into it and I don't want to lose you."

She bit her lip in thought. "Do you see me as a woman?"

"What?" Clarence looked confused.

"I'm a woman, Clarence, and I've been denying that part of myself. My biological clock has been silent for a long time, but now the sound is deafening. I've lost myself in this maze of fighting for the good guy. It's time to find me, the woman I should be, the woman I want to be."

Clarence removed his glasses and laid them on the desk. "You are serious."

"Yes. I'd like to leave right away, but I'll stay and work the Dawson trial if you prefer. I wouldn't be giving you my best, though."

"Do you think Kyle can handle it?"

"Yes. But you have to keep an eye on his enthusiasm, or maybe that should be his ego. It gets the best of him sometimes. He's a good lawyer, just young."

Clarence came around the desk and hugged her, which took her by surprise. He wasn't known for hugging. "You've given a lot of yourself to this department, so go, and I hope you find whatever you're looking for."

She hugged him back, fighting tears. All of a sudden she was a weepy mess. "Thank you."

"And for what it's worth, my wife has forbidden me to notice other women so, no, I never see you as one, just my prosecutor and I'm really sorry to lose you."

She walked out, leaving everything she'd worked for behind. She should be sad, but she wasn't. She actually felt a lot lighter from the release of the enormous responsibility she carried as a public servant.

It didn't take long to clean out her office and soon she was in her car, driving. She headed to the one person she could pour her heart out to and would understand what she was going through.

She went to Jessie.

As Levi drove up to the house, he saw Pop sitting on the front porch. Before he could get out of his truck, Pop was at the door ready to get Daniel out. He had to have a long talk with his grandfather and it wasn't going to be easy.

Pop carried Daniel inside and Levi followed with the diaper bag. Once Pop sat Daniel on the floor, the baby took off like a rocket, crawling just as fast as he could go straight to Pop's chair. He pulled up on the chair and glanced at Pop, babbling something that sounded strangely like "buzz buzz buzz."

"Is he trying to sing the bumblebee song?" Pop asked.

"I think so," Levi replied. "But I can't make sense out of it." He drew a deep breath and added, "Pop, we need to talk."

Pop waved a hand at him. "Nah, we don't. I acted like a crazy old man this morning. I know we can't keep him. It was just nice having a baby around, reminded me of you when you were little."

Levi put his arm around his grandfather's shoulders. "I know, Pop. It's going to be hard to take him back, but Stu's found someone who's going to raise him."

"How long is he going to stay here?"

"Probably a couple days."

"Don't you have to go back to work?"

"I left a message on my voice mail that I would be out of the office, but I have to get back soon. I have tons of calls to return."

Pop went to his rocker and Daniel was eager to climb into his lap. As Levi went into his bedroom, he heard, "Booger was a bumblebee…"

He opened his sock drawer and pulled out the sock in the back. For a moment, he stared at the mismatched socks and thought of all the times Myra had laughed at him because his socks never matched. For a man who paid attention to detail, she found that amusing. He didn't see that as something important. Socks were socks.

Sitting on the bed, he dumped the ring box into his hand and opened it. The diamond sparkled at him like a tear from bygone days. Seven years stowed away was enough. If he wanted a life with a woman he loved, today he started to change.

The box was too big for his pocket so he wrapped the ring into a handkerchief and slipped into his jeans. It would be easy for him to find a job in Houston. His problem would be his grandfather. How could he leave him? He was torn in two ways, but he felt sure he could find a compromise. Love was supposed to be magical and he could use a little magic right about now.

"You quit your job." Jessie was aghast.

"Yes." Myra got comfortable on the sofa, facing her friend. "I am now unemployed."

"What made you do that? I know you have a good reason."

Myra told her friend everything that had happened since she had last seen her, even the part about the night with Levi and about the miscarriage and thoughts of abortion.

Jessie just stared at her. "Am I supposed to be angry with you now? Is that what you're expecting?"

Myra tucked a strand of hair behind her ear. "I'm just being honest. Thinking about the abortion made me feel terrible and I still feel awful about it."

"Myra, you're a woman and you were faced with raising a child alone and having a stress-filled job. You're allowed those kinds of thoughts. Every woman has them."

"You don't."

Jessie laughed. "Oh, please. Some days when the boys are crying and fighting and nothing I do pleases them, I just want to pull my hair out. So I take a moment to regroup and remember how much I love them and how much they mean to me. Life is not about being perfect. Life is about adjusting and living it with as much zeal as you can."

"You've always had such a positive attitude even when your father had you locked up in your house."

Jessie made a face. "I think you have me confused with someone else. I was the one who cried and ranted and raved about all the injustice done to me. I don't remember being positive about much of anything. Just a desire to be a normal person."

Myra wiped imaginary specks from her jeans. "I think I have a tendency to put you on a pedestal."

"Yeah, and it's unrealistic and a little tiring, so please stop. I have flaws just like everyone else. I forced a man to marry me. Now, you can't get more desperate than that."

"I still can't believe you did that."

"I knew Cadde Hardin was never going to see me as a woman unless I forced his hand."

"How did you know he would fall in love with you?"

"I didn't. I just knew I'd loved him for a very long time and things needed to change, so I went after what I wanted, uncaring of his feelings. Does that sound like a perfect woman?"

"It sounds like a woman in love."

"Yes." Jessie clapped her hands. "Now you've got it. Sometimes we do crazy things in the name of love."

Myra looked down at her hands. "I'm not sure what to do now. I'm confused and conflicted."

"About what?"

"About loving Levi."

"From what you tell me, I have a feeling Levi feels the same way about you. You have to take the next step. Tell Levi how you feel and see what happens. You have to take a risk."

Myra still struggled with that demon inside her that kept saying she was biting off more than she could chew. "Do you think I'd make a good mother? Answer honestly."

Jessie threw back her head with a thoughtful expression. "Let me see how many years Myra Delgado guided me through every little turmoil in my life. She was my protector, my sister, my very best friend. She made me feel loved in a world where there was no love.

Or at least I didn't feel it until Myra showed me. So yes, I think you would make a wonderful mother. You'd give a child everything he or she would ever need, and why you think otherwise is beyond me. You have mothered everyone in your life. Now it's time for Myra."

Myra brushed away an errant tear. "I'm going to ask Levi to marry me."

"Now you're talking."

"And if he accepts, then we'll talk about adopting Daniel. That's what I want. I want us to be a family."

"Well, sweetie, you're telling the wrong person."

Myra jumped to her feet. "I don't know why I'm so indecisive. I've never been this way."

"Love makes us crazy. It's kind of like PMS, but so much better."

Myra laughed and it felt good. She could see a future just as bright as she wanted. All she had to do was say three little words to Levi and hope they were reciprocated.

SHE SAW HER parents' truck, so she knew they were home. If she didn't stop for a minute, she'd be in big trouble. She went in through the back door of the little brick house next door to Jessie.

"Mama, are you home?"

Rosa came out of the utility room, her eyes round. "*Mi bebé's* home." Her mom engulfed her in a big hug and then she ran into the kitchen for her cell and called Myra's father, who was at the barn. "Your father will be here in a minute."

There was such a difference in her mother these days. When they were guarding Jessie, they'd been cooped up in the house a lot and Rosa had cooked delicious meals, causing her to gain weight. Today, her mother was slimmer because they were out and about. Her parents walked five miles every morning. They were happier now than they had ever been, except their only child had been their biggest disappointment. Or at times Myra felt that way.

Rosa put on a pot of coffee.

"Mama, I really can't stay. I just wanted to say hi."

Rosa's eyes flashed in an old familiar way. "Then why come at all? You never think about your parents. So go to your big job. To your big life."

Myra was used to her mother's sharp barbs, but today they hit her the wrong way and she didn't come back with a sharp retort of her own. Instead, tears welled in her eyes.

Seeing the tears, her mother did an about-face. "Oh, *mi bebé,* what's wrong?"

"Nothing. I…I…" Heavens, what was happening to her? Maybe she did have PMS.

She exhaled deeply. "I quit my job."

Her mother's eyes grew even bigger. "What? Why?"

Before she could answer, her father came through the back door. A thin man with years of wisdom lining his face, he was dressed in worn clothes and a floppy hat.

"Felipe, Myra lost her job."

"Mama, I didn't lose my job. I quit. There is a difference."

Her father hugged her. "Whatever Myra chooses to do is her business." Oh, how she loved her father. "Your room is ready if you want to stay for a while or if you want to stay forever. Your room is always ready."

Tears gathered in her eyes again and she really needed to get control. For so many years, she always thought she'd been pushed aside or at least in her parents' affection. Their top priority had always been Jessie and her safety. Myra had felt left out.

Her need for independence and to show them she could succeed on her own stemmed from those feelings. She didn't need anyone, but life had proven her wrong. She needed her parents and their love and support. As an adult, she could see she'd never been left out of their affections. She was their daughter and she would always be their daughter.

She kissed her father's cheek. "Thank you, Papa. I'm taking some time to think about my life."

"Do you need some money?"

"No. Thanks. I really have to run."

But her mother couldn't let it go. "What's wrong, Myra? For you just to give up your job something has to be terribly wrong."

"I'm making some changes and I'll let you know as soon as I figure it out."

"Myra…"

"Rosa, stop it," Felipe chided.

"I'm sorry, *bebé*." Rosa hugged her. "I worry."

"I know, Mama. I'm fine."

"We're here if you need us, *bebé*," her father added.

She kissed them both and ran to her car, feeling their love in a way she hadn't since she was nine years old.

LEVI HAD A restless night. But he was still strong in his resolution to talk to Myra and the ring would stay in his pocket until then. He had to know one way or the other if they had a future, if somehow they could get beyond everything that had happened in the past. They'd forgiven each other, so they should be able to move on. With that in mind, he knew he had to make another trip to Houston. He hated to make the three-hour trip with Daniel. The little guy was crawling all over the house jabbering and Pop was one step behind him.

He was considering leaving the baby with his grandfather because he and Myra needed to talk in private. His friend Carson would check in on them. But he hesitated leaving the baby behind.

Daniel crawled up to him and pulled on his jeans, holding up his hands. "Hey, buddy. I need to change your diaper. You're a little smelly."

"Yeah. I was waiting for you to do that," Pop said from the sink. "And he's just about out of diapers."

"I bought some yesterday. I'll get them out of the truck."

By the time he had Daniel changed and freshened up, he'd made up his mind. He couldn't leave the little guy behind. His cell rang on the way to the kitchen. Placing Daniel on the floor, he answered it.

"Levi, this is Colin, the orderly who works with Mr. Stevens."

"Yes. Is Stu okay?"

"I'm sorry. Stu passed away about two hours ago."

The news hit Levi like a sucker punch to his chest and he sat down at the dining room table. "What happened?"

"The doctor told him on Monday that he didn't have much more time and I guess he was right. After Mortez was killed, Stu said he could die in peace and he did. I was with him when he passed and he said he was ready to join his daughter in heaven."

Levi swallowed hard. "Did he leave instructions for Daniel?"

"He signed papers yesterday to finalize everything."

"Where am I supposed to take the boy?"

"I honestly don't know. I wasn't in the room when the lawyer visited."

Levi was desperately trying to figure this out. "Did Stu ask you to call anyone else?"

"He wanted me to call Tom and Myra and his sister in Seattle."

A sister? The one he hadn't spoken to in years. "Did he recently reconnect with his sister?"

"I believe he did. They spoke on several occasions. The funeral is for ten in the morning."

"That soon?"

"That's what Stu wanted. He's had his funeral arranged for months."

"I'm on my way."

"There's nothing to do here. You might want to wait until the morning."

"Thanks, Colin."

Levi sat for a moment, lost in the pain of losing a dear friend. But Stu had known the end was near and still he hadn't mentioned guardianship for Daniel. He couldn't figure out what was going on. The only way to do that was to go to Houston to see what future Stu had planned for his grandson.

MYRA INTENDED TO go out for boxes to pack everything she would take out of the apartment. But first she fixed a vanilla-caramel-flavored coffee and started opening closets.

There weren't a lot of mementos, just clothes and linens and kitchen items. She spent very little time here, only to sleep and shower. Her whole life had been about fighting for justice and she had pushed her needs aside. But not anymore. A bubble of excitement ran through her and she couldn't wait to see Levi.

She looked around at the white-and-stainless-steel apartment and, for the first time, felt its coldness. This wasn't a home. This was a showplace. An interior decorator had picked out everything according to Myra's specifications. She hadn't even shopped for the items, just picked them out of a catalog. At the time, she was busy. But now she wondered why she never took an interest in her home. Because this wasn't her home.

She thought of Levi's old farmhouse with the stone fireplace, crown molding, hardwood floors and the antique furniture that was his grandmother's. It was warm and inviting. It was a place where people loved and lived. It was a place called home.

Her cell interrupted her thoughts and she ran to the living room to get her purse. It was Colin. Stu must want something.

"Good morning, Colin."

"Morning, Myra."

"What does Stu need this morning?"

"I'm sorry, Myra. Stu passed away."

Myra reached out for the sofa and sat down, feeling an ache inside that was indescribable. "I didn't expect this so soon."

"Stu knew the time was near. He just didn't want anyone else to know."

"Because he didn't want us to be sad," she replied.

"Yes. The funeral is at ten in the morning."

"What about Daniel?"

"I'm sure that's all been taken care of."

What, though? What had Stu done about Daniel's future? She should have talked to him. Now it was too late.

She bit her lip. "Is there anything I can do?"

"No. The funeral is all set, but Stu did want me to tell you something."

She swallowed the constriction in her throat. "What?"

"Never be afraid to open a new door."

"What does that mean?"

"I don't have a clue. It's just what Stu asked me to say to you. I assumed you would know."

"Thank you, Colin. I'll see you in the morning."

After Colin gave her the name of the funeral home, she laid her cell on the sofa. She curled up in a corner, remembering Stu and all the times he'd supported her and given her confidence in herself. She knew Stu wouldn't want her to be sad, but it was hard to control the tears.

She had to open the new door of her life with confidence.

LEVI PACKED DANIEL'S stuff. He didn't take the baby bed because he figured Stu's sister wouldn't want to travel with it. Picking out Daniel's clothes for the funeral was a chore. This wasn't his forte. He chose a white shirt and navy blue pants and the baby looked fine.

Pop had said his goodbye to Daniel and left for the barn. His grandfather was taking the parting hard and Levi knew today would be one of the hardest days of his life, too.

They arrived in Houston early and Levi had time to feed and change Daniel before the funeral. He kept looking for Myra and soon saw her dressed in a navy blue suit and heels. Like always, she looked gorgeous. He sat beside her and Daniel immediately went to her.

"Hi, sweetie," she whispered, kissing Daniel's cheek.

The funeral home began to fill up with police officers and people who had worked with Stu over the years. The memorial was short and poignant. There was no graveside service. It was over too fast with questions lingering in Levi's mind.

He walked to the back of the room with Myra. "Did you get a chance to talk to Stu?"

"No. I was shocked to hear of his passing. But he did seem paler than usual when I saw him and he coughed constantly. I guess I should've picked up on that."

"Colin said Stu had been talking to his sister in Seattle so I'm assuming she's going to take Daniel."

Myra looked at the people filing out of the funeral home. "I'm not sure what she looks like or even if she's here."

Daniel was tired of being confined and held out his arms to Levi. "Mmm. Mmm. Mmm."

"Hey, buddy." Levi took him and thought how right she looked holding a baby. Daniel wiggled to get down. He saw the funeral home as a new playground. They watched him pull up on a pew and didn't notice the woman walking up to them.

"Are you Mr. Coyote?"

He turned around to see a young woman possibly in her thirties. "Yes."

She held out her hand. "I'm Eileen George and I'm from Child Protective Services."

Levi was immediately on alert. There was only one reason someone from Child Protective Services would be here.

Myra came to stand by his side, still keeping an eye on Daniel.

Ms. George reached for an envelope in her purse. "Mr. Stevens left this for you. I am to act on your instructions."

Levi frowned, unsure of what was in the envelope. He ripped it open and pulled out a letter and began to read.

Dear Levi, you have been the best friend a man could ever have. I've asked more of you than a man should ever have to give. But I'm asking one more thing. I would like for you to raise Daniel. If you feel you cannot take on this responsibility, I ask that you find a loving family to place my grandson with. I know you'll do what's best for Daniel. Your old friend, Stu.

"What is it?" Myra asked.

He handed her the letter. "Stu wants me to raise Daniel."

Ms. George looked at her watch. "I just need an answer, Mr. Coyote. If you'd rather not have the responsibility, I can take the baby and find a home for him."

"No," he answered immediately. Daniel was not going to strangers. "I...I'll keep him."

"Then my work here is done. Have a good day." She reached down and ruffled Daniel's hair. "I love it when people are willing to step up."

She walked away, leaving Levi and Myra staring at each other and both wondering what to say.

"Stu chose the right person," Myra said. "You'll make a good father."

He heard the pain in her voice and wanted to hold her and tell her everything would be okay, but at that moment Daniel disappeared under a pew and he had to rescue him. When he stood up, Myra was gone.

MYRA WENT INTO her apartment with a heavy heart. What did she expect? She'd told Stu numerous times she didn't want to be a mother. He had no way of knowing she'd changed her mind and that raising Daniel would mean the world to her. Now Levi would raise him—without her.

Kicking off her heels, she sat on the sofa and told herself she wasn't going to cry. She'd cried enough, but her heart was breaking and she did what every woman did when there was nothing left. She curled into a ball. Right now she needed a really big hug from her mother and she hadn't needed one of those since she'd been a teenager or even then. She'd always been independent, strong and vocal. Well, now she was broken and all her dreams were like fairy-tale dust.

She must've fallen asleep because a pounding woke

her. Someone was at the door. Dragging herself off the sofa, she went to look through the peephole.

Levi stood there with Daniel.

She couldn't talk to him, not now. If she didn't open the door, he'd go away.

On the way to the living room, she heard a sound and stopped. She listened closely.

He whistled.

A smile tugged at her lips and the weight of rejection lifted.

I'll whistle so you can always find me.

It brought back memories of their time in Mexico, the danger, the fear and the closeness they'd shared. He'd risked everything for her.

"Myra, c'mon. We need to talk."

He had her. She unlocked the door and walked into the living room. Levi followed. He placed Daniel on the floor and the baby scurried off, searching new territory. She sank onto the sofa again and Levi sat beside her.

"I can't do this alone, Myra. Daniel needs a mother and I know and I think you know Stu wanted you to be that mother. You and I carried that baby out of Mexico and we both need to carry him into the next phase of his life. Your job is important to you but I'm sure we can work out some kind of solution. What do you think?"

She narrowed her eyes, feeling a fire burning in her chest. "You think we can find a solution? That's all you have to say?"

Levi ran a hand through his hair. "I don't know, Myra. I'm a little overwhelmed at all this and feeling my way."

"Well, when you figure it out, you let me know." She made to get up, but he caught her arm.

"I'm getting this all wrong. Maybe this will be better." He reached into his pocket and pulled out a handkerchief. Unfolding it, he took out the most beautiful diamond ring she'd ever seen, and for one of the few times in her life she was speechless. "I bought this ring seven years ago. I was going to give it to you the night of the shooting. You know what happened after that."

She fought to breathe. "You kept it all these years?"

He shrugged. "I don't know why. I should have returned it, but I stowed it away in my sock drawer. You know, the one with all the mismatched socks."

She smiled through her tears.

"I can easily get a job here, but we'll have to go to Willow Creek often to check on Pop and—"

"I quit my job." The words burst from her throat without her even realizing it.

"What? When?"

"Two days ago."

He stared at her with hope in his eyes, a hope she'd been longing for. "Does that mean…"

"It means I love you. I can't seem to stop."

He held up the ring. "Myra Delgado, will you marry me? I've tried to stop loving you, but it hasn't worked. I can't seem to stop, either. I love you more today than I did seven years ago and I'm not sure how that happened since I've been mad at you for so long. But I think I'm one of those guys who only gives his heart away once."

Myra just stared at him, her eyes watery, but she saw everything she wanted on his face. That look of forever suited him.

He held up the ring. "So what's your answer?"

"Y-yes."

He slipped the ring onto her finger and kissed her, a deep, everlasting kind of kiss that went on and on until neither of them knew where they were or what they were doing. They just needed to touch and hold on to make sure that never again would either of them hurt the other.

"I love you," he whispered, pushing her into the cushions on the sofa. She sighed and they were lost in each other until a piercing cry broke them apart. Daniel was crying at the top of his lungs.

"Hey, buddy. I'm not hurting Myra. Come here."

Daniel crawled to the sofa and Levi picked him up with one arm and brought him up beside them. "Meet your new parents."

Daniel gave a wobbly grin and wanted down again. "I hope that's a good sign."

Myra noticed the baby's socks. "His socks are mismatched."

"No, they're not," Levi insisted. "They're white."

She lifted Daniel's feet. "One has ducks on it and the other has teddy bears."

"Well, that makes him my son, then." He kissed her briefly.

Daniel climbed down and Levi pulled her into a sitting position. "Are you ready to start a new life as a wife and a mother?"

"As long as you're with me."

"You got it. Let's go home and make a grouchy old man happy."

As Myra packed the rest of her things, she couldn't

help but feel Stu had planned everything. He knew her weakness and Levi's. She would forever be grateful for his caginess.

The new door was wide open and she smiled as she stepped into this life with Levi and Daniel. It was exactly what she wanted.

EPILOGUE

Three months later...

AN OLD LOVE slept with his arms around her, his hand on her heart, his soul touching hers. In the past seven years, they'd come full circle and when the circle was complete, they'd found happiness and it was more than either of them had ever imagined because they'd learned how to forgive with love in their hearts.

Myra caressed the hand beneath her breasts.

"You awake?" Levi whispered into her neck.

"Mmm." She turned to face his sleepy-eyed look and loved everything about him, from his five-o'clock shadow to the twinkle in his dark eyes. "We have to get up. It's Christmas morning."

"Not just yet." His lips found hers and she melted into every inch of his hard masculine frame. They were lost in each other for the moment as the world waited outside their door.

They didn't want to move from the warmth of their bed, the warmth of their love, the warmth of each other as they lay skin on skin with their hearts in their eyes.

"I love you. Merry Christmas," he said.

She stroked his dark stubble. "Merry Christmas. I love you, too. Now let's wake up our son and watch his excitement as he opens his gifts."

"I heard him moving around earlier, but he must have gone back to sleep." Levi slipped from the bed, pulling her with him.

Myra reached for her robe. "He's going to be so excited, we'll never be able to calm him down. But it's Christmas, so anything goes."

Arm in arm, they went across the hall to Daniel's room. The bed was empty. Myra looked at Levi, trying to calm her erratic heart rate.

"Don't get upset," he warned. "He has to be here somewhere."

They hurried into the living room and stopped short. Pop sat sleeping in his recliner, a fire blazed in the fireplace and Daniel was beneath the Christmas tree in his red reindeer pajamas, asleep on John Wayne.

"Get the video camera," she whispered to Levi. "That's adorable."

Pop woke up and blinked at them. "'Bout time y'all got up."

Levi came back with the video camera. "Pop, how did Daniel get out of his bed?"

"He's a big boy and—"

"Pop." Levi stopped filming and looked at his grandfather.

"Okay. I heard him moving around so I got him out of his bed. I let him run around a little bit and he tore some paper off packages and went to sleep. It's Christmas. That's what kids do."

"If their great-grandfathers let them," Levi remarked with a tone of amusement.

Myra sat down by the tree and gathered her baby into her arms. He stirred and rested his head on her chest and she wondered why it taken her so long to realize she needed this connection in her life—someone to love, someone to mother.

She caught Levi's glance and smiled. He knew exactly what she was thinking and she loved him all the more because he could read her mind. Without him, none of this would be exactly what it was—happiness.

Levi sniffed the air. "Do I smell coffee?"

"Yeah," Pop replied. "Rosa was over here and put a turkey in the oven and she made coffee, too. She's cooking a ham in the trailer and a whole bunch of other stuff. Does she know there's only five of us? She's cooking enough to feed an army. I'm not complaining. I'll give it my best cowboy try."

"There'll be eight of us. Nine with Daniel," Levi reminded him.

"Oh, yeah, I forgot."

Levi's mother, stepfather and sister were coming. Feeling blessed and loved, Levi had let go of the resentment toward his mother and they'd been talking on the phone. He'd invited them for Christmas, wanting them to meet his wife and son. This day would be filled with love.

After the first of the year, they would be renovating the house to make it larger so they could have a master bedroom and bath. They would have to be out of the house, so they bought a mobile home to live in in the meantime.

"I'm sorry we're tearing up your house, Pop." Myra rubbed Daniel's back.

"It's not my house. I signed everything over to Levi years ago."

"Still, it's your home."

"Aw, that's just woman stuff, missy." He waved a gnarled hand. "I can live in that trailer y'all bought."

"You will not. This is your home." Myra made that clear. "My parents will be using the trailer for when they visit."

"Aw," was Pop's grumpy reply.

Her parents had come in last night and were staying in the trailer for Christmas. It still felt a little strange to realize for years she thought she'd disappointed them. When, in fact, they were just waiting for her to accept them into her life. What a way to learn a lesson. Her parents were ecstatic for her and over the moon about Daniel, their first grandchild.

Levi glanced at his grandfather. "You have your robe on this morning and your cowboy boots."

"Yeah. Thought I'd better since we got company. You know things are changing around here."

Levi sank down by Myra. "Yep. It's not just the two of us anymore."

"Fine by me."

"Fine by me, too."

There had been a lot of changes in the past few months. Adjusting to marriage and small-town life had been the easiest thing she'd ever attempted. But she didn't leave her old life completely behind. Levi had a friend who was a lawyer, a child advocate attorney, and Myra worked for her two to three times a week. There was a playroom in the office and it was easy to take Daniel with her to work.

Her mother insisted, though, that she keep Daniel at least one day a week. That brought out a little tension between Pop and her mother, but they were working on getting along and being grandparents together. Everyone was making the relationship work.

There'd been changes for Levi, too. He'd closed his P.I. office and was now an investigator for the D.A. of Travis County. He basically had a nine-to-five job. They were a normal couple raising a family together.

"Let's tell him," she whispered to Levi.

He smiled that smile that made her stomach weak. "Pop, we have news for you."

"I'll use the phone, okay? Just don't give me any other kind of fancy thing I have to learn."

"It's not about the phone you won't use. I don't think you'll have a problem with this."

Myra could hardly stand it and blurted out, "We're having another baby."

"Hot damn. Now we're talking. I guess it was time to make this house bigger. I'm happy for y'all. Wait till I tell Walt." The old man's eyes were watery and Myra knew the little ones were putting a little sugar in his grumpy. "Do Rosa and Felipe know?"

"No," Myra replied. "I'm telling them this morning."

"I knew I was the favorite." Pop grinned. "Now wake up the little fellow and let's have Christmas."

"We have to wait for Mama and Papa."

"What for? The real grandfather's already here."

"Be nice, Pop," Levi said.

Rosa and Felipe came through the back door and hurried into the living room to watch their grandson. Daniel woke up and looked around, his mouth forming a big O as he looked at the tree with all the lights and the brightly colored packages.

Levi gave Rosa the camera and he and Myra helped Daniel open his gifts. He giggled and laughed and was a happy little boy. His parents were happy, too. It truly was a magical day.

Pop had redone an old wood wagon of Levi's and it was Daniel's favorite toy as he pulled it around the living room with John Wayne yapping at him.

Easing into his chair with a smile on his face, Pop said, "A letter came in the mail yesterday and no one has opened it. It's on the counter."

"I didn't see a letter," Myra said, and went to find it.

"It came while y'all were visiting your friend Jessie."

She found the letter and brought it to Levi.

"It's from a law firm," Levi said, and ripped it open. Inside was another envelope and on the front was written "Levi and Myra Coyote." "It's from Stu."

Myra wrapped her arm around Levi's waist and he kissed her cheek because they knew what was inside would touch both of them.

Slowly, he opened it and they read: "It really was that simple. Merry Christmas, Stu."

* * * * *

Karl Milek is a by-the-rules guy...except for that
one night in Vegas when he ended up married
to Vivian Yap. Come morning, they both agreed
to a quickie divorce and he returned to Chicago.
But now, weeks later, Vivian has some news....
Read on for an exciting excerpt of the
upcoming book

A Promise for the Baby
By Jennifer Lohmann

"I'm sorry to drop in on you like this," Vivian said, gesturing
to the luggage near the door. "I didn't feel I had any choice."

"Were the terms of our divorce not sufficient?" Karl's elbows
rested on the arms of the chair and he'd laced his fingers
together in a bridge over his charcoal-grey suit. Vivian was
certain Karl must have soon-to-be ex-wives drop in on him all
the time, since he managed to remain so self-possessed about
the whole thing.

But his absolute composure was the reason she'd answered
"sure" on that fateful night in Las Vegas when he'd gestured
to the doors of the wedding chapel, and asked, "Shall we?"
with that half-smile on his face. She had wanted to be a part
of his stability then, so she supposed it was unfair of her to
be irritated by it now. And if she also longed for the passion

they'd shared…well, that had gotten her into this mess in t
first place.

"Yes. I mean, no, they were fine. I mean, I don't want
divorce—at least not right now."

If she'd shocked him, he didn't let it show. His only reacti
was to lean back in the chair and lift his left foot to rest on l
knee. Vivian was glad he hadn't sat on the couch next to h
She felt crowded enough by his presence without having
make room for his knees, elbows *and* infinite placidity—whi
took up far more space than any single lack of reaction shoul

"I'm pregnant and I want to keep the baby."

How will Karl react to this news?
And will they stay married?
Find out in A PROMISE FOR THE BABY
by Jennifer Lohmann,
available January 2014
from Harlequin® Superromance®.

REQUEST YOUR FREE BOOKS!
2 FREE NOVELS PLUS 2 FREE GIFTS!

◆ HARLEQUIN®

super romance®

More Story...More Romance

YES! Please send me 2 FREE Harlequin® Superromance® novels and my 2 FREE gifts (gifts are worth about $10). After receiving them, if I don't wish to receive any more books, I can return the shipping statement marked "cancel." If I don't cancel, I will receive 6 brand-new novels every month and be billed just $4.94 per book in the U.S. or $5.24 per book in Canada. That's a savings of at least 14% off the cover price! It's quite a bargain! Shipping and handling is just 50¢ per book in the U.S. and 75¢ per book in Canada.* I understand that accepting the 2 free books and gifts places me under no obligation to buy anything. I can always return a shipment and cancel at any time. Even if I never buy another book, the two free books and gifts are mine to keep forever.

135/336 HDN F46N

Name	(PLEASE PRINT)	
Address		Apt. #
City	State/Prov.	Zip/Postal Code

Signature (if under 18, a parent or guardian must sign)

Mail to the **Harlequin® Reader Service:**
IN U.S.A.: P.O. Box 1867, Buffalo, NY 14240-1867
IN CANADA: P.O. Box 609, Fort Erie, Ontario L2A 5X3

**Are you a current subscriber to Harlequin Superromance books
and want to receive the larger-print edition?
Call 1-800-873-8635 or visit www.ReaderService.com.**

* Terms and prices subject to change without notice. Prices do not include applicable taxes. Sales tax applicable in N.Y. Canadian residents will be charged applicable taxes. Offer not valid in Quebec. This offer is limited to one order per household. Not valid for current subscribers to Harlequin Superromance books. All orders subject to credit approval. Credit or debit balances in a customer's account(s) may be offset by any other outstanding balance owed by or to the customer. Please allow 4 to 6 weeks for delivery. Offer available while quantities last.

Your Privacy—The Harlequin® Reader Service is committed to protecting your privacy. Our Privacy Policy is available online at www.ReaderService.com or upon request from the Harlequin Reader Service.

We make a portion of our mailing list available to reputable third parties that offer products we believe may interest you. If you prefer that we not exchange your name with third parties, or if you wish to clarify or modify your communication preferences, please visit us at www.ReaderService.com/consumerschoice or write to us at Harlequin Reader Service Preference Service, P.O. Box 9062, Buffalo, NY 14269. Include your complete name and address.

This cowboy deserves
a second chance...

A Ranch for His Family
by Hope Navarre

Bull riding means everything to Neal Bryant. In his
quest for the championships, he's let everything else
go—including Robyn Morgan, the woman he loves.
Then he has a bull-riding accident that could turn his
rodeo dreams to Kansas dust. It's fitting—or maybe
it's fate—that she's the nurse at his bedside.

While recuperating on his family's ranch, Neal learns
how much he's missed. Robyn is widowed *and* has
a son Neal can't seem to resist...especially when he
learns *he's* the father. It's a dream he never allowed
himself to have. And now he needs to show Robyn
he's worth a second chance.

AVAILABLE JANUARY 2014 WHEREVER BOOKS AND EBOOKS ARE SOLD.

New from The Mysteries of Angel Butte series!

Everywhere She Goes
by Janice Kay Johnson

Standing between her...and danger

Returning to her hometown is Cait McAllister's chance to stand on her own. That means taking a break from men and relationships. Then she meets her new boss, the intriguing Noah Chandler. As the mayor, he's got bold plans for Angel Butte.

The most persuasive part of him, however, could be the way he looks out for Cait. Because when a threat from her past puts her in danger, Noah is there to protect her. And there's no way she can resist a man who has so much invested in keeping her safe.

AVAILABLE JANUARY 2014 WHEREVER BOOKS AND EBOOKS ARE SOLD.